# A DEVIL'S Own Luck

## ROWAN McALLISTER

Dreamspinner Press

Published by
Dreamspinner Press
4760 Preston Road
Suite 244-149
Frisco, TX 75034
http://www.dreamspinnerpress.com/

A Devil's Own Luck

Cover Art by Paul Richmond   http://www.paulrichmondstudio.com

ISBN: 978-1-61581-900-3

Printed in the United States of America
First Edition
June 2011

eBook edition available
eBook ISBN: 978-1-61581-901-0

To all the great people at Dreamspinner Press, my friends, and my new fans. Without all of your advice and encouragement from my first novel, this book would have never come to be. Thank you.

Chapter *One*

*London, October 27, 1820*

RAIN fell in a constant, heavy patter against the windows of his brother's study as William Carey stared irritably out at the street. Watching the various heavily bundled shapes scurry past, he mused that the weather would keep most of the idle indoors today, allowing their servants and tradesmen the freedom to go about their business unimpeded by those with nothing better to do than clog the streets and walks—those like himself. Watching them now, he could not help but wonder if the men and women of the working classes actually preferred the rain for just that reason. He would have to ask Stubbs the next time he saw him.

William chuckled to himself at the thought. He could almost see his manservant and oldest friend's reaction now. That grizzled face would deepen into an amused scowl, followed by a snort of derision aimed at "Sir high'n mighty," for it was not so many years ago that William himself had been plodding the streets of St. Ives Bay and scrambling through the muddy caves and shorelines of Cornwall and Devon, with Stubbs at his side, in worse weather than this. The only difference between him then and the people on the street before him now was that he had never been *forced* to scrape out that living. He had done it because he had chosen to, to amuse himself and because he had wanted the adventure… naïve fool with more bollocks than wit that he had been in his youth.

He knew better now. Looking back, he'd been damned lucky. His thoughtless quest for high adventure could just as easily have ended on the back of the three-legged mare or on a knife in the dark as standing comfortably in his brother's study with nothing better to do than watch the rain and good people of London at their toil.

He took another sip of his brother's brandy and turned from the window, glancing sourly about the room. He had been waiting for his brother for nigh on an hour now, and he was more than a little restless and annoyed. As his eyes lit on the bookshelves behind the desk, he toyed with the notion of taking down one of the handsomely bound volumes to help pass the time. Horace kept the most rare and prized of his collection—the ones meant to be owned but not read—in this room, and William was tempted on several counts to break his brother's unspoken prohibition and help himself. First and foremost among his incentives was that Horace had left him there, stewing, after summoning him so imperiously to his home. Second, there were quite a few rare volumes in the collection that William had yet to read. And last, but certainly not the least, for the look on his elder brother's face when he came upon William reading said book and lounging in his comfortable leather chair with a glass of Horace's best brandy in his hand.

A small, wicked smile spread over William's face as the image passed through his mind, only to fade away a moment later as he discarded the idea. He truly was not in the mood for reading, and the consequences of such a petty game would not be worth the rewards. If something should happen to the book, William would most assuredly never hear the end of it, and he would, more than likely, be forced to wait in the hall—or worse, in Eugenia's gaudily decorated parlor—on any future visits. He shivered in mock revulsion at the thought. Horace's wife did have the most appalling taste in decoration.

No, he had best leave the books alone and content himself with another drink. A self-satisfied grin curved his lips as he rolled the excellent vintage across his tongue. William preferred whiskey, but it wasn't a gentleman's drink, so Horace didn't keep any in his private stock. His older brother would already be put out that William had picked the lock on his hidden cabinet and purloined some of his finest brandy. A second affront would indeed be pushing things a bit far.

Sir Horace Carey, Baron Whitecastle, could be pompous and high-handed at times, but he was a good enough man all around and a much kinder head of the family than their father had been, that was for certain. He did not deserve more than a little prick to his pride for leaving his brother to cool his heels all afternoon.

As William sat down in his brother's chair and propped his boots on the edge of their father's old mahogany desk, he wondered again what could have prompted Horace to send for him so unexpectedly. They did not see one another often, despite the fact that they both lived in London for most of the year. They tended to travel in vastly different circles, and that was exactly how William preferred it. In fact, the only time they met anymore was for family gatherings, and even then, only the private family functions, the ones that did not involve any of Horace's Tory friends.

William was well aware that he was considered the black sheep of the family and that his reputation was a rather sore point for Horace. Charged with upholding the family honor after their father's death more than twelve years before, his brother was not at all pleased with the manner in which William chose to live his life... not that the fact bothered William overly much. At thirty-two years of age, he was well past his majority. He had his own fortune, completely independent of his family. His life was his own to live as he chose, and as long as he was not hurting anyone, he did not feel the need to answer to anyone for it. Needless to say, Horace rarely agreed with that sentiment.

The most amusing thing about his brother's disapproval was that the poor fellow did not even know the half of it. The *worst* Horace knew of him was that he was a bit of a gambler and a rake and may have had some less-than-upstanding business dealings and acquaintances in his youth. Though the London gossips had dubbed him everything from a buggerer of sheep to a murderous highwayman and pirate king, most of the stories were so outlandish as to be laughable, and few would openly admit to believing such fustian. Horace certainly would not.

If his brother had any idea of the truth amongst all the fantasy, any idea of the means by which William had turned the pittance of an inheritance their father had left him into the fortune he now possessed—or, for that matter, the fact that his bed-partners, though not *sheep*, were not always of the fairer sex either—William felt quite certain the man would succumb to a fit of apoplexy from which he might never recover. As William certainly did not want *that* to happen, lest he be forced to shoulder the burden of Whitecastle until his little nephew Robert was of age, he made every effort to ensure that his past as Gentleman Black, infamous free-tradesman of Cornwall, was far behind him. In fact, the only connection to his misspent youth that he had not left behind or buried was his man, Stubbs, and no amount of caution would ever make him give that man up.

William shifted in his brother's chair, and a twinge in his side reminded him that Stubbs was not the only connection he had left to that time. He lifted a hand to his ribs, instinctively covering the spot where a well-placed knife had nearly robbed him of his life. The scars on his body were a daily reminder of the folly of his youth and, unfortunately, a source of fascination for his lovers. The physical testaments to his idiocy were ever the topic of speculation among those he took to his bed, and as he would never divulge where he had acquired them, they only served to add to his reputation and mystique. There was only one person with whom he had ever shared all of his secrets, and that lady was long gone now.

William shook his head and stood. He was becoming maudlin, and that would not do. He impatiently crossed to the window again. He hated being left to sit idle like this. It made him dwell on things best left buried and pain that would likely never heal. He would give Horace until he finished the brandy in his glass and not a moment longer.

Interviews with his brother were never what one would call a pleasure. Having to wait for one only compounded insult upon injury. William had errands to run and a box for the opera. Arnold and King's *Up All Night* was a personal favorite, and he needed to get back to his own house soon if he was going to have time to dine and change before the curtain rose.

There was barely a swallow left in his glass when Horace's coach pulled up in front of the house. His brother pushed open the door himself and raced up the steps to the house, trailed by a flustered footman carrying an umbrella, and William turned from the window with a relieved sigh.

*At last.*

William threw back the last of his drink in one gulp and set the empty tumbler on the corner of the desk. When Horace entered, his brief nod and mumbled "William" were gruff and unapologetic, as always, but William was at least given a measure of satisfaction when his brother caught sight of the tumbler on his desk and frowned, glancing at the closed door to his *secret* cabinet. William only smiled placidly at his brother's sharp look and waited for his invitation to sit. He knew needling his brother like this was petty and childish, but it was a game he still enjoyed immensely, even after all these years.

When they were both seated, Horace set his elbows on the desk, steepled his fingers, and pursed his lips, but made no move to start their interview. As the silence stretched, William realized that something must be deeply troubling Horace for him to be so reluctant to begin. If William were a better man, he might have taken pity on his brother and opened the conversation himself, but he was not, and he was still a little miffed, so he simply leaned back, settled himself more comfortably in his chair, and studied his fingernails.

He did take the opportunity to examine his brother out of the corner of his eye, and what he saw did nothing to ease his mind. Horace had more silver in his hair than William remembered, and the lines on his face seemed to be etched more deeply into his forehead and around his mouth. William knew his own brown-black hair was littered with a few silver threads these days, but he liked to think they made him look more distinguished rather than simply older. He was not a vain man, but he knew well enough that his sharp good looks and devilish smile had gotten him more than his fair share in this world, and sharing those same features had not hurt Horace's political ambitions in the slightest either.

But as William looked across the desk at him now, in the gray afternoon light, Horace seemed old and tired more than distinguished, and William was given the impression that the world weighed quite heavily upon his shoulders. What with the Peterloo Massacre the year before and that awful conspiracy in February, it was no wonder the man looked tired. From what he had heard, William was not certain that political ambitions were at all beneficial to a man's health. Luckily, he had none of his own.

He had almost decided to concede defeat and open the conversation himself when Horace's steel-gray eyes met his and he finally spoke.

"I trust Giles kept you comfortable until I could arrive?" Horace's voice was tired and his tone formal, but it was the closest William would get to an apology and, recognizing it as such, he decided he would not dwell on his pique.

"Thank you, Horace. Yes, your man saw to it that I was comfortable while I *waited*." He could not help stressing that last word, just a little, to drive home the fact that he was not pleased.

"I am sure you have engagements this evening that you would like to prepare for, so I will be brief," Horace said, ignoring William's jibe and looking away to a point on the opposite wall. Clearing his throat, he said, "I would like to ask for your assistance in a certain matter. It is somewhat delicate, else I would have written rather than requiring we meet in person."

William raised his brows in surprise but remained silent. Horace never asked him for anything. It must be something "delicate" indeed if his brother was condescending to ask *his* aid. William watched patiently as Horace cleared his throat again and shifted uncomfortably in his chair before standing to pace the room.

Now William was doubly curious at his brother's level of unease. He turned in his seat, following the older man's progress as he paced to the windows, and waited for Horace to continue.

"Lydia has committed a bit of an indiscretion," Horace began, staring out at the street. His mouth twisted a little as he continued, "She has allowed the attentions of a most unsuitable young man, past the point of propriety, though thankfully nothing irreparable has happened."

William remained silent, absorbing the information. Lydia was Horace's eldest daughter, a pretty little thing, though a trifle simple in William's opinion. He was surprised more at the fact that she had been let out of someone's sight long enough to do such a thing more than that she had done it. Horace kept a close watch on all his children, lest they commit any blunder that might prove damaging to his reputation and political career. Lydia must have more wit than William gave her credit for if she had managed to give her watchdogs the slip.

"Eugenia and Lydia have retired to Whitecastle with the rest of the children for a bit of a holiday while I see to things here in London," Horace continued.

*Translation: I packed my daughter and my wife off to the country while I see to the damage.*

"Sounds as if you have things well in hand. What could you possibly need of me?" William asked, openly curious and relieved that it was not anything more serious than that. His brother really did take his reputation and honor a bit too seriously. It would be bad for his health if he continued to fret so over such trifles.

Horace grimaced and turned to face him as he said, "There is the small matter of some letters Lydia wrote the young man. Letters I would wish to see destroyed. I have attempted to contact him regarding the matter, without success, and I fear creating more of a scandal in retrieving them than if I had let the matter rest. *You*, however, have had more dealings with this sort of thing and might have better luck than I."

As compliments went, it was somewhat lacking, but William was amused despite himself. All those years of being the black sheep, of being lectured about propriety by their father and even, to a small extent, by Horace himself, and now that William had finally taken to the straight and narrow—well, as straight and narrow as he could get— his brother needed him to do some dirty work for him. It was most amusing. The only question now would be how much he would make the man squirm for it.

William sat back in his chair and stroked his chin while Horace stood rigidly by the windows. After only a few moments, William sighed quietly and decided he would not bother, not today. He had his own affairs to attend to, and he would only be prolonging the inevitable by keeping Horace in suspense. Though he was not close to any of his family, William had enough honor, of his own sort, that he would not let Lydia come to any harm. She was his niece, after all, and a sweet enough girl. He would get the letters for her sake, if not for Horace's, so there was no point in dragging this interview out any further.

"As you wish, brother. I will see what I can do about retrieving these letters for you, *without* a scandal. Give me the particulars, and I will look into the matter."

Horace's shoulders slumped as the tension left his body, and his face relaxed from the pained frown he had been sporting, though he did not smile. His brother never smiled anymore, and every time William saw him, he was grateful that Horace had inherited the title and not him. Having all that power and responsibility seemed to suck the gaiety out of life, and Horace seemed to become more like their father with every day he spent as Whitecastle. William shuddered at the thought, thanking Heaven that he had been spared such a fate and silently praying for Horace's continued good health.

"Thank you, William," Horace said, and William was sure *that* had cost him. "His name is Henry Bradshaw. They met on holiday in Bath, and he followed her back to town. He has no family or fortune of any note. The only connections he has are through a cousin, Edward Graves, fourth son of the Earl of Arundel. Graves is a member of your club, I believe, and I am told you can find him and Bradshaw there quite often of late."

William did not remember ever meeting Bradshaw, but if he were a member of Graves's circle, that would not surprise him. Edward Graves was one of the newest generation of young pups out to gamble away their inheritance before they even saw a penny of it, and William was long past that stage in his life. He still gambled to amuse himself, but he gambled to win, and he had learned long ago when it was best to walk away.

He *had* heard gossip that Graves might share some of his inclinations toward those of the same sex, gossip that Horace would not have been privy to, but Graves was a pompous little whelp, and though tall, fair-haired, and moderately handsome, he was not remotely attractive enough to entice William into seeing if a little *training* might improve him. William liked a challenge, but the rewards had to be worth the effort, and there was nothing that Graves had that William wanted.

The extent of his association with the man had thus far consisted of William's relieving him of his money at the gaming tables, and he had consequently found Graves to be a poor loser in addition to his other failings. William grimaced. His history with Graves might make retrieving the letters more difficult if Henry Bradshaw was close to his cousin.

William stood abruptly and straightened his coat. He needed to be on his way if he was going to accomplish everything he needed to this evening. "I will see what I can do, Horace. I will send word when I have news. Now, if you will excuse me, I have much to do before my engagement this evening."

"Of course. Good evening, brother," Horace said with a brusque nod.

William nodded in return, and made his way into the hall. When the footman brought his hat, gloves, cane, and greatcoat, he stepped out into the street and was relieved to find the rain had stopped. It would be easier to wave down a hack if he did not have to fuss with an umbrella. He was not in humor to wait for a servant to fetch a carriage for him. He had been cooped up in his brother's study for far too long, and he needed to stretch his legs a bit and be away from that house. The brisk, late autumn wind felt wonderful on his brandy-flushed cheeks, and the tension that invaded his body whenever he was forced to enter his father's house soon melted away.

William was able to find a carriage after only a few blocks, and as he sat comfortably in the coach as it wound its way through the damp, narrow streets, he decided he would need to alter his plans for the evening. He had originally planned to attend the opera and make the rounds between acts, in hopes of finding a willing companion with whom to spend the night. Cordelia, Hyacinth, and Mary, the "merry widows," as he called them, all loved the theater, and most nights he could find one or all of them in attendance and willing. He truly had not wanted to spend the night alone, this night of all nights, but now it appeared a trip to his club would be in order, and the widows would have to find companionship elsewhere.

When the carriage finally stopped as he directed, he looked out the small window and up at St. Olave's gray walls in the evening gloom. All thoughts of his plans for the night, his niece, and the merry widows faded to nothing as a familiar, bittersweet sadness filled his chest. He opened the door himself and stepped out onto the walk. He bid the driver wait and borrowed one of the lanterns hanging from the carriage, throwing the man a shilling to silence any protests.

The chill wind set his greatcoat flapping against his legs as he made his way along the outside of the church to the stone archway into the churchyard. He had a promise to fulfill, but it would not take long, and then he would be on his way home to a warm fire and a hearty dinner.

Smiling sadly up at the trio of grinning stone skulls above the old iron gate, William pushed inside with a screech of metal hinges and made his way into the quiet churchyard. The light was fading fast, and he had to hurry before they locked the gate for the night. Tower street ward was not a place he would choose to linger after dark in any case, though he had his cane and a few nasty surprises for any thief fool enough to think him easy prey.

In the weak light from the lantern, he managed to find the gravestone he was looking for quickly. He had been there often enough over the years that he could find his way with his eyes closed if it were necessary. In the back corner of the yard, a simple rectangular headstone, the name faded with age and barely discernible even in daylight, sat sheltered by a large tree. He knelt on the damp ground, heedless of the wet soaking through his coat and trousers, and pulled a small candle from his pocket. He lit the candle from the lantern and placed it in the ground at the base of the stone.

"Happy anniversary, my love," he whispered into the chill night air, and he closed his eyes.

Even now, six years after her death, he could still picture Cora's sweet and slightly wicked smile. The pain of her loss had lessened to a dull ache over the years, but he still missed her, most particularly on nights when he had not found a companion to while away the hours until dawn. During the day it was so much easier to keep himself occupied with one thing or another, though he was finding it harder and harder to keep himself from slipping into melancholy as his diversions failed, one by one, to hold his attention.

Cora had been his wife for such a short time, but they had packed a lot of loving into their four-year marriage. She had been a true partner to him in every sense of the word, his helpmeet and his savior at a time in his life when he could easily have let his recklessness destroy him.

They had met in St. Ives Bay, where he had been doing his damnedest to get himself killed. At the time, his recklessness with the excise men and coastguards had left even his partners believing him mad. Even Stubbs, loyal, stalwart Stubbs, had come close to walking away from him, fearing William would get himself and the rest of the band hanged. If he had not met Cora, William shuddered to think where he would be now.

She had been older than he and far wiser, the eldest daughter of a respected merchant family, beautiful and brilliant, with hair as black as coal, the heart of a rogue, and the face of an angel. She had taken him in hand and taught him discipline and control over his passions, taught him how to harness them and use them to create a future for himself instead of pissing his life away in a vain attempt to prove something to himself and the rest of the world. She had given him purpose and created the bridge he had needed to make the transition from rakehell and smuggler to upstanding gentleman of fortune... and to reconnect with his family.

Though she came from a proud and wealthy family, Horace had not approved of her at the start. He thought her far too old for him, but

11

once he had had an opportunity to know her and to see the transformation she had wrought within his younger brother, even *he* had succumbed to her charms. William had her to thank for everything he now possessed, and he was certain he would never meet a more fierce, determined, and unusual woman.

Smiling to himself at his memories, he blew a kiss at the candle and made his way out of the churchyard. He had promised her on her deathbed that he would light a candle for her every year on this day. She had not been a religious woman, far from it, but she had loved this little church with its odd, squat tower, its shadowed corners, and the gruesome trio of skulls welcoming you to the quiet yard. Hard to believe that in the bustle of Seething Lane one could find such a peaceful haven, but it was one of the reasons she had loved it so much. He grinned a little at the memory of how they had made use of some of those quiet corners and the bit of earth in front of the old gravestone where he had knelt, shielded by the tree's curtaining branches. It was those occasions that had made him come to love the place almost as much as she did.

His smile faded a little as he remembered the other promise he had made to her at the end, as the fever had slowly stripped away the strength he had so adored in her. It was the only promise he had ever failed to keep.

*"Promise me you will love again, William. Your heart is too wild to be left without purpose. Promise me you will find someone so I will not have to fear that you will be consumed by your own fire."*

He had promised her. How could he not? But he had not been able to keep his word. He *had* tried, over and over, but he had never found anyone who captured his heart the way she had, no one who had even come close. He knew she would not blame him. He could not help that he had not found anyone whom he could love. A man was lucky to find a love like that once in a lifetime. He played the odds at the gaming tables often enough to know that only a fool would bet on that kind of luck coming around again.

But she need not have worried about him burning up in his own fire. Since her death, he had been listless and filled with ennui more than overcome with raging passions. Perhaps his years with her had tamed him, or perhaps it was just that age had tempered him. He did not know. He had simply sunk into a life of indolence and dissipation without any real aim, and had very little to show for the past six years of his life.

William grimaced. He was getting maudlin again. It was time to be on his way. Shaking himself back into the present, he stepped back out onto the street and pulled his greatcoat a little tighter around him. He could not spend the night wallowing in the past. Cora would have been furious with him.

As he reached the carriage and handed back the lantern, William decided he needed to add another stop before he headed home to Mayfair, so he instructed the driver to take him to his house in Cecil Court, the secret house he kept for assignations that required more privacy than his other home could afford. It was only a little out of the way, and he wanted to talk to Stubbs and his wife, Maud, who kept house for him there, before the hour grew too late.

They might be able to aid him in his quest for the letters. Maud had been born and raised in the fetid stews of Jacob's Island. Before she and Stubbs met, she had spent many a year scraping out a living on her back in the rookeries, and though she had left that life behind when she married Stubbs, they both still did what they could for the poor souls who were not so lucky. With their connections in London's underbelly, his servants might be able to dig something up that William could use against Bradshaw or Graves, something to give him leverage in his negotiations. Lord and thief alike all found their way to the brothels of London, and any man's secrets could be had for the right price.

In all probability, he would not need to go that far with the young man, but he would rather have something to fall back on if Bradshaw proved difficult, and he would rather set the wheels in motion tonight than lose time later. If he was quick about it, he could stop at his rooms there, have a brief conversation, and still make it back to his Mayfair house in plenty of time to eat and get changed for the opera.

Chapter *Two*

LATER that night, William settled back in the seat of his carriage with a groan and adjusted himself in his trousers. The last few hours had been torture. All three of the merry widows had been in attendance at the opera, and all three had seemed bent on seducing him. Despite, or perhaps because of, the fact that early in the evening he had regretfully informed each of them that he had some family matters to attend to, they had whispered promises in his ears and ghosted fingers across his body at every possible opportunity.

He smiled in spite of his discomfort, remembering how they had seemed to be in competition to outdo one another in the boldness of their advances. If he had known that "playing the maid" would incite such frenzy, he would have tried it long ago. Though he normally liked to be the one directing the encounter, William was certainly not above sitting back and allowing himself to be on the receiving end once in a while, particularly if all three of them would be willing to play together, as they had hinted at when all of their other attempts had failed.

*But, no. Instead I am off to spend the evening with Robert Graves and his toady.*

William grimaced in distaste. What in God's name was he thinking, walking away from such a splendid opportunity?

*Horace had better be damned grateful when this is all over and done with.*

14

As he settled himself more comfortably in the seat, he mused sourly that at least thoughts of his brother and Graves were taking care of his most *pressing* problem, even if it brought him no pleasure. His pique only served to strengthen his resolve to settle the entire matter tonight if at all possible. The boy, Bradshaw, would give him the letters tonight or pay dearly, and that was all there was to it. Hell, if the lad was attractive enough, William might be willing to let him make it up to him personally... *after* he retrieved the letters.

When the carriage at last pulled up in front of his club, William let himself out and left word with the coachman to remain until he returned. As he walked through the doors and was divested of his belongings, he decided that the idea of wooing Bradshaw actually had some merit. If the rumors about Graves were true, it stood to reason that anyone in his circle might be of the same inclination, and William was not above using his skills in that arena if the man proved comely. Just because Bradshaw had seduced Lydia did not mean he would not be interested in a bit of fun, and William did not have to like him to bed him, after all. It would be far easier than blackmail, threats, or outright theft, not to mention a lot more pleasurable for *him*.

William smiled to himself at the thought. Perhaps the evening would not be a total loss, after all.

He took a moment to school his face into the bland and disinterested mien that all members of society perfected by the time they left their cradles before making a casual circuit of the rooms. The club was crowded, but it did not take him long to find Graves at the back of the second game room. He and his companions were making enough of a spectacle that William would have had to be blind and deaf not to spot them within moments of entering the room.

Relieved that his sacrifice had not been in vain and he would not have to come back another night, William signaled a passing footman and ordered himself a whiskey, then settled onto a low couch against the wall to study his quarry. He had chosen his position well, as it happened, for it gave him a clear view of the small circle of men but left him partially concealed by a fall of thick, gold velvet curtains... not that it was entirely necessary. The men were so absorbed in their own gaiety that William felt certain he could have stood in the middle of the room and gawped at them, and not one of them would have been the wiser.

There were four men in Graves's circle. If Bradshaw had accompanied his cousin, as Horace had indicated, he would be among them, and all William had to do now was determine which one he was. He was able to dismiss two of the men outright as being far too plain and too round to be Lydia's beau. Vain as she was, he could not imagine her showing any interest in either of them. That left only two others to choose from, so William concentrated his scrutiny on them.

The man standing opposite Graves was tall and lean, moderately attractive, with dark brown hair and a rather pathetic attempt at a moustache. His lips seemed to be set in a permanent sneer that William did not find at all appealing, but he supposed that would not necessarily be the case with Lydia, so he could not rule the man out. The other, the man standing closest to Graves, was an entirely different matter, and William found his interest more than mildly piqued with that one.

He was of average height, a few inches shorter than William's five feet, eleven inches. He had a handsome, heart-shaped face, large eyes, and bee-stung lips that bordered on being almost too full. He appeared to William to be in his early twenties, old enough to have lost some of the fullness of youth but still young enough to retain a certain softness in his complexion.

His interest fully caught now, William let his gaze roam higher and was captured by what had to be the most extraordinary head of hair he had ever seen. Though the short hairs clipped close to his nape were a plain, ordinary, dark brown, the silky waves covering his crown were a riot of browns and golds, fading to near white at the tips. The effect was quite striking and, coupled with the man's features, surprisingly attractive. For several moments William found himself almost wishing that the young man *were* Bradshaw, for seducing him would certainly not be a hardship.

The strength of his reaction surprised him a little. From a purely physical point of view, he had seen and bedded young men and women who were more beautiful. But there was something unusual and

16

captivating about this one, something that William could not quite put a name to just yet.

Fascinated and no little puzzled, William took another sip from his glass, giving his wits a moment to catch up to his loins. After watching the young man for several minutes more, William finally decided that it was not the beauty of the man's features that captivated him, but more their eloquence. The young man's every thought and feeling could be read on his face, if the observer were keen enough to understand what he saw. He was not speaking, laughing, or gesticulating wildly like his companions, but William could read nearly every thought that passed through his mind in the arch of his brows, the quirk of his full lips, or the narrowing of his eyes. Volumes were spoken in the few minutes he watched, even though the young man did not utter a single word, and the wit and passion he read there drew William in a manner that nothing else had in a very long time. William's heart sped up a little, and his breath quickened in reaction to the riot of emotions he could see just barely contained beneath the man's calm façade.

As he continued to watch, William noticed something else that added to his fascination. For all that he stood amongst them, the young man did not appear to be at all involved in their conversation. Graves appeared to be the only one paying him any mind at all. The others ignored him entirely, and though Graves seemed to make several overtures toward him, they were all met with short, clipped replies or angrily clenched fists and sullen silences. In fact, the more Graves edged toward the young man, the more the man moved away from the group. When William felt certain that the man was going to leave the room entirely, Graves shocked William by lifting a hand to the back of the young man's neck and squeezing, leaving it there for several long moments before sliding it around the man's throat, trailing his fingers lightly over his skin.

Startled at the proprietary nature of the caress, William looked about the room to see if anyone else had noticed the exchange. If Graves was always this indiscreet, it was no wonder there was so much gossip bandied about. From the look on the other young man's face, William was sure he would shake the hand off and continue out of the room, but to his shock, the lad froze where he was and made no other attempt to leave. He was pale and his anger was clearly stamped across his face, but he remained where he was, though his eyes darted warily about him.

The small circle continued their animated discussion, either unaware of or purposefully ignoring the exchange between the two men, and William settled himself back on the couch, only just realizing he had tensed and leaned forward in his seat. He continued to watch the group, hoping for some clues that would tell him how to proceed with his charge and who the handsome young man might be.

It was not long before William's patience was rewarded. Apparently Graves was either in his cups or out of his wits, for only a few minutes after his first indiscretion, he reached over and slid his hand down the back of the young man's coat and over his arse in clear view of the rest of the room. As William nearly dropped his drink in astonishment, the other man stiffened, fisted his hands at his sides, and marched out of the room, Graves right on his heels. William was on his feet to follow before he knew it. His mind reasoned that he could possibly gain some leverage over Graves if he followed them, but he was honest enough with himself to admit that was not what spurred him into action so quickly.

He left by the door at the opposite end of the room, so it would not be as obvious that he was following the other men. As he made his way toward the door at a sedate pace, he scanned the room to see if anyone else had noticed the exchange. No one seemed overly perturbed. In fact, they appeared merely relieved that the noise from the back of the room had lessened, leading William to hope that Graves's actions had gone largely unnoticed. A secret that was not a secret would be of little use to him.

William knew he risked losing them by showing *too* much caution, but his gambles usually paid off, and tonight luck still appeared to be on his side. As he calmly made his way out the front doors, waving off the servant with a brief "Only need a bit of fresh air" thrown over his shoulder, he spotted the two men disappearing around the corner.

He did not like walking the streets at night without his cane, but even unarmed, he could still give a thief an unpleasant surprise or two. His years on the coast, trading with all manner of foreign merchants and other smugglers, had taught him more than a little about defending himself—the dirty, back-alley kind of fighting that no real gentleman would ever stoop to.

As he turned the corner where he had last seen the two men, he thought for a moment his luck had run out, but then he heard heated whispers coming from a nearby alley and smiled. Creeping up on the opening to the alley, he hid himself in a darkened doorway to listen to their conversation. He was a little disappointed he would not be able to see them, but he was only willing to push his luck so far.

"Go back inside, Stephen."

"No! You're foxed and acting like a fool! Why am I here?" came the hissed reply.

"You are here because I wish it. That is all the reason you need."

"Not if you are going to continue to behave in that manner… in the middle of your club, for God's sake! Are you mad? What if someone saw?"

"No one saw a thing. And even if they did, they would not dare speak of it."

"Well, *I* am not the son of an earl. If charges are brought, your father will not be speaking for me! It is *I* who will be facing the gallows or at the least the pillory, not you." Even hushed and angry, the young man's voice stirred something in William. Stephen was quite the spitfire, and William found himself wondering how it would feel to have all of that passion directed at him.

When the young man spoke again, though, his voice was a little more controlled. "I will wait in the carriage until you are done here. I do not belong in that place as it is. They all know it."

"You will come back inside as I command. Remember our arrangement, Stephen. I will take it all back: the fine clothes, the house, the money, everything. Remember your place."

19

There was a frustrated hiss, and a few steps echoed on the pavement. When the young man spoke again, his tone was even more subdued and bitter. "I know my place well enough, but you should not have brought me here, not to your club, Graves. It just isn't *done*. Why must it be your club? Why can we not go back to one of your hells or even to that bloody Molly house again, where no one cares what you do?"

"They have grown tiresome, and I will do as I please. You would do well to remember that. I will hear no more about it. Back inside... *now!*"

It was quiet in the alley for several long moments before William heard footsteps coming closer and pushed himself further into the shadowed doorway. The two men made their way past him and back up the street, side by side, but no other words were exchanged. He could tell by the stiffness of the shorter man's shoulders, outlined in the lamplight, that he was not at all pleased, but he still followed Graves back to the club without further protest while William took a moment to absorb what he had heard.

He was not at all certain whether he was pleased or disappointed that the attractive young man was not Henry Bradshaw. On the one hand, it meant that he was not the young man who had attempted to seduce and despoil his niece, but on the other, it also meant that William had no real reason to pursue Stephen any further, most particularly now that he knew the man's relationship to Graves. Tempted as he might be to steal Graves's paramour, William needed to concentrate on getting the letters from Bradshaw, and angering the man's cousin and only connection in society probably would not get him what he wanted.

William was still a little shocked that Graves would have the audacity to invite his paramour to his club, and agreed with Stephen's assessment that the man might just be a little mad. Stephen definitely showed more wisdom and discretion than his keeper; that was certain. Shaking himself out of his preoccupation with the man, William made his way back to the club at a leisurely pace, stopping to order another drink and chat with a few casual acquaintances on his way back to the game room. By the time he returned, Graves's circle had dispersed and the men were scattered about the room, most sitting down for a run at the tables.

He spied Stephen in the back corner, drinking a glass of wine and staring at nothing, seemingly lost in his own thoughts. Despite the knowledge that he was merely Graves's kept man, William still found himself drawn to the young spitfire. Everything he had seen and heard spoke of a sharp wit and passionate nature, and William had to admit that that called to him, perhaps even reminded him a little of himself at that age. Stephen certainly had the speech and manners of someone much higher in station than one would normally find in the role of paramour. His clothes might not be as fine a cut as his companions', and William could detect a slight Northern accent in his speech from time to time, but the lad still had an air of education and refinement about him that was surprising.

William shook himself again and forced his eyes away from Stephen, scanning the room once more. He found Graves and the thin, sour-faced man he assumed must be Bradshaw seated at a table together near the middle of the room, and made his way toward them. As he approached the table, Alfred Wallis, a casual acquaintance, hailed him jovially and offered William his seat.

"Come, Carey! I am done for the night. Commerce has killed me, to be sure. My darling Emma will have my hide if I lose any more to my fine fellows here," he said, a pained grin splitting his round face.

"Thank you, Wallis. I will be delighted to take your place. My evening has just begun, so I still have plenty to lose to these fine gentlemen before I make my way to my bed," William answered with a bland smile for everyone at the table.

Just as William sat down, he caught an exchange of glances between Graves and his cousin, and a slight smile curved Graves's lips. The smile immediately put William on edge. There was something predatory about it that he recognized all too well, and after a few rounds of play, he realized why. The two men were working together, so subtly that only someone with his experience in these matters would even begin to guess what they were playing at.

They were skilled. William had to admit that Graves was cleverer than he had given him credit for. Either that or Bradshaw was the architect behind their little scheme. But William had spent years playing with men for whom cheating was a matter of course— expected, even—and these green boys were not clever enough to get the better of him for long. William smiled to himself. He would play booty to these fellows long enough for them to become careless, and that was when he would make his move. If all went well, he would have the letters in his hands before the break of day.

The play continued and became more intense, the bids and pots climbing higher and higher. They soon had a bit of an audience, as the other tables emptied and men gathered to watch. William noted with pleasure that Stephen was now among them, watching the game closely. Now that he was closer, William was finally able to see that Stephen's eyes were a lovely shade of amber, rimmed in dark brown— beautiful, even when they were radiating concern and exasperation, as they were now.

Stephen must have felt William's regard, for he looked up suddenly, and warm amber met William's steel-gray. William held his gaze for several moments with a lazy smile and a quirked eyebrow. When William did not look away, Stephen's jaw hardened and his eyes narrowed. William was not certain if the lad was attempting to look forbidding, but if he was, he was failing miserably. With lips so lush and full, the scowl was more sensual than forbidding, and the fire sparking in his eyes only made William want to take him somewhere private and watch that angry fire melt into the heat of desire… then desperate need… those plush lips softening even further, swollen with passion and kisses….

As William's eyes hooded at the thought, the young man's expression turned wary, his own eyes widening and quickly breaking away.

*Yes, little lamb. There is a wolf in the wood.*

After only a moment, however, he saw Stephen square his shoulders and raise his chin, meeting William's eyes again in angry defiance.

*The lamb has teeth,* he thought with pleasure, then sobered as he realized he should not be playing these games in the middle of his club. He had just named Graves a fool for his indiscretion, and now here he was, doing the same. Gritting his teeth, William returned his attention to the play. He did not have time for games of that sort just now, and if Graves had brought the lad as a distraction, William was not going to give him the satisfaction of knowing he had succeeded.

Graves and Bradshaw took turns at winning, occasionally allowing someone else to win a lesser pot to allay suspicions. William found it interesting that he was never among the fortunate. Perhaps Graves was still holding a grudge from their previous encounters.

The first time William won the round, it visibly unsettled Graves. Sweat appeared on his brow, and he cast several concerned glances at his partner. William decided to leave off and allow them to win for a while, hoping to convince them that his win had only been purest mischance. He needed them relaxed and overconfident.

Stephen continued to hover near the table, and William felt his gaze more than once, but he needed all of his attention for the game, so he could not spare the time to study the young man further. After only a few more rounds, Graves and Bradshaw appeared to relax again, and William decided it was time to put an end to the game.

"Well, gentlemen, I believe I am done in for the evening," he said with a loud sigh, hoping Graves would take the bait.

"Do not be shilly, Carey. You cannot leave now and sshpoil everyone's fun," Graves called out, slurring his words a little and making William smile.

He had noticed that both Graves and Bradshaw had continued to drink throughout the night, a fool move for men bent on fleecing their fellows, but something that definitely worked in William's favor. Thoroughly foxed and buoyed by their successes, they would be easy to manipulate into betting more than they could afford to lose, which was exactly what William needed.

"As you wish, gentlemen," William said, perhaps acquiescing a little too easily, but the two men were probably too much in their cups to notice at that point. "One more round, and then I truly must to be on my way. What say we raise the stakes a bit for this last one, to make things a little more interesting, hmmm?"

"What did you have in mind?" Bradshaw asked, his eyebrows drawing down in concern. It appeared that Bradshaw was not as foxed as his cousin, but William hoped Graves had enough influence to drag him along.

"Let us say we add another five thousand to what is on the table?" William replied, hiding his smile as he saw the man's eyes widen.

"We do not have lettersh for that large a sum with us, Carey. Do not be foolish," Graves scoffed.

"We are all gentlemen here, and we have plenty of witnesses. If we all swear we are good for it, that should be enough, I think," he responded with an amiable smile and a sweep of his hand around the room. "We can put it in the books, if you like."

Out of the corner of his eye, William saw Stephen flinch and clench his hands into fists, and a thought occurred to him: perhaps he could use the situation to gain more than just the letters… perhaps a little something for himself as well. While he had never actually desired a paid companion of his own, perhaps he could borrow Graves's for a while and satisfy his curiosity about the young man… among other things.

While he pondered the possibilities, he saw Graves and Bradshaw exchange several long glances. William was counting on Graves's pride not allowing him to back down in front of a room full of his fellows, even if his common sense decided to make an appearance. He knew the moment Graves decided to take him up on his bet. The decision was written all over him in the sloppy, cocksure grin that split his face.

"Done and done, Carey," Graves said, and Bradshaw reluctantly nodded his agreement.

The only other man left at the table with them was Frederick Worth, a man who had won and lost fortunes many times over at the club tables and could easily afford to do so again. William did not spare any concern for him when the man nodded and smiled, gesturing for them to continue.

Now all he had to do was win the game.

Luckily for him, the other two men were doing half his work for him. The code they were using to communicate with each other was easy to decipher. A Spanish merchant had taught William something similar years ago, and by telling each other their cards, they were telling him all he needed to know as well—at least, that was what he hoped. Though he was not betting any more than *he* could afford, he would rather not have to find another way to get the letters from Bradshaw.

The hum of conversation in the room had died entirely by the time the cards were dealt. Every man in the room seemed to be holding his breath, waiting on the outcome of their game. William knew there had been much larger sums won and lost at the club, but for tonight at least, they were the height of entertainment, and the result would be all over town by morning.

The buying and trading continued for some time without anyone knocking out, but soon enough, William had all he needed, and it became time to show their hands.

Worth, Graves, and Bradshaw each revealed their cards in turn, with Bradshaw holding the best hand of the three: the eight, nine, and ten of hearts. A smug smile played about the man's lips, twisting his pathetic mustache, as he waited for William to reveal his cards. William merely smiled blandly back at him and slowly placed the knave of hearts, knave of spades, and knave of clubs on the table, watching his opponents' eyes widen and their smiles fall a bit with each card revealed.

Graves stared at the cards in disbelief as his face flushed an angry red, while Bradshaw actually paled. If it were not for the fact that Bradshaw had seduced his niece, William might have actually felt sorry for him. The silence in the room stretched until Worth chuckled and slapped William on the shoulder jovially.

"Well, my good man, it appears as if you have done for us *all* tonight. Someday, Carey, you will have to tell me your secret, for I have never seen a better card player. No, I have not. You will have the note from my man tomorrow," Worth said as he stood and bowed to everyone at the table. "Until next time, gentlemen. I bid you good night."

As if that were the cue, the room erupted in conversation, and the crowd around the table dispersed. As he politely accepted the congratulations and compliments of his fellows, William scanned the room for Stephen, but the younger man had disappeared.

It took him longer than he would have liked, but eventually William managed to make his way out into the night, where he found Graves and Bradshaw arguing near the line of carriages. As he approached, both men fell silent, and William put on his blandest smile.

"Good evening, gentlemen. I wish to thank you for a most enjoyable game," he said.

A muscle in Graves's jaw jumped as he bowed politely in William's direction. "I will call on you tomorrow, Carey, if that is convenient?"

"Of course, my good man. I will welcome your visit," he replied.

Graves bowed again stiffly and turned to step into the carriage next to them, barking at the driver to take him home. He did not even spare a glance for his cousin. As the carriage pulled away, William caught a glimpse of white-blonde hair in the light from the streetlamp, but that was all. Surprised at the barb of disappointment he felt in his chest, he shook off his distraction and turned back to Bradshaw, who was nervously shifting from foot to foot.

When Bradshaw cleared his throat, William merely smiled pleasantly at him and raised an eyebrow.

"Umm, I beg your pardon, Mr. Carey, I do not know how to say this, but… I fear, at the present moment, I do not have the means to cover our wager." Bradshaw was looking down at his shoes now, and again, William might have felt pity for him if not for the fact that the man was a villain and a scoundrel.

26

"That is unfortunate, Mr. Bradshaw. I do not think the other members of the club will look fondly on your making wagers you cannot keep," he replied, allowing the man time to squirm in the silence that followed. It was late, however, and William wanted to get out of the cold and into his warm bed, so he did finally take pity on the man and come to the point.

Looking around to make sure there was no one near enough to overhear, he continued in a hushed tone. "Listen, Bradshaw. I have a proposition for you. I will forgive your debt and allow you to save face at the club, provided you do two things for me in return."

Relief was quickly followed by suspicion on Bradshaw's face. "I am listening, sir," he said just as quietly.

"Good. Then listen well, for I will not be repeating this offer. First, you and your cousin will never again commit a charade like you did tonight. Do not try to deny it. I know what you were doing, and I will know if you try it again." William gave Bradshaw his most deadly serious scowl and let his eyes turn cold and hard as he spoke. It was a look that he had perfected in his youth, and it had served him well for most of his life. Stubbs had once told him even *he* felt his blood chill when William used that look, though it had never been directed at him.

It seemed to have the desired effect on Bradshaw, for the man did not even try to deny what William was saying.

"Second," William continued, "you have something that I want. A certain set of letters from a young lady. Perhaps you know of what I speak?"

At Bradshaw's startled nod, William said, "Good. You will bring me those letters tomorrow, first thing. Every single one of them, mind you. I will know if any are missing. You will bring them to me, and you will forget you ever had them or even set eyes on the young lady. Am I understood?"

When Bradshaw nodded a little too quickly for William's liking, he speared the man with his eyes again, leaning in so they were nose to nose. "Do exactly as I bid, and tonight will be but an unpleasant memory. Cross me, and you will learn just how much truth there is in all that you may have heard of me."

Bradshaw swallowed visibly and nodded again as William stepped back and studied the man. Now that that smug sneer had been wiped from his face, William actually considered revising his earlier plans. Wide-eyed and chastened, he could almost see what Lydia might have found appealing in him, but the thought did not last long. A quick inventory of his body told him that even a chastened Bradshaw was not what he was in humor for. A certain fiery-eyed, sullen, and angry young man was far too much on his mind to waste time with this whelp, even if it meant a night spent alone.

William took another step back and turned to find the carriage he had hired for the night, throwing his final volley over his shoulder as he went. "Tomorrow morning, Bradshaw."

Chapter *Three*

THE next morning, Bradshaw called at the Mayfair house before William was even out of bed. His butler, Hume, brought him the packet as he sat down to breakfast. The note on top of the stack read: *As per our arrangement. Every one. You have my word. Mr. Henry Bradshaw.*

Sitting comfortably in his breakfast room, William smiled and ran his fingers over the pink satin ribbon binding the small stack. He was tempted to open them and read what his niece had had to say to the man, but decided against it. He was already more involved in the matter than he truly wished to be, and he was fairly certain he would lose his appetite at whatever drivel Lydia had spewed forth on the pages. The cloying scent emanating from the stack was vile enough, and currently he had more appetizing things to occupy his mind.

Graves should be arriving soon, and William fully intended to make the most of the situation. The man owed him five thousand pounds, money he knew Graves did not have. He would offer Graves the same chance to save face that he had offered his cousin. Only this time, the "something" Graves had that William wanted was Stephen, and "wanted" was putting it mildly after the dreams he had had the night before. It had been a long time since someone had aroused this level of feeling in him, and William was more than mildly interested in exploring the sensation to the fullest.

William smiled a little to himself in anticipation and sat back to enjoy his breakfast, but as first one hour and then another passed, his good humor began to sour. If Graves had decided to cut him and fail to keep their appointment, Stephen or no Stephen, William would make the man sorry for the affront. In fact, he had almost decided to give up the whole scheme entirely and force Graves to pay him every penny when he heard someone ring the bell. Hume entered shortly thereafter to give him Graves's card and ask if he was "at home." The peevish side of him considered telling him no, but in the end, he decided that that would not get him what he wanted, so he relented and had Hume show the man in.

Graves entered a few moments later, all smiles and charm, as if he had not kept William waiting all morning and did not have a care in the world. William recognized the bluster and bluff for what it was, so he decided not to allow himself to be distracted by it. This was *his* game. *He* had won. If Graves thought he could worm his way out of it, he was sadly mistaken.

"Good morning, Carey. I trust you slept well," Graves said as he took the seat William offered him.

"Good *afternoon*, Graves. Yes, I had a most restful night, thank you."

"Good, good. I am heartily glad to hear it." Graves cleared his throat and plastered on that cocksure grin that William disliked so much. "Listen, Carey, I have a proposition for you. As I know how much you enjoy a good bit of sport, I thought you might be interested in another wager, something to get your blood up, rather than another tiresome night at the tables."

William leaned back in his chair and steepled his fingers, favoring Graves with an indulgent, and patently false, smile of his own.

*What is the man playing at?*

William was not surprised that Graves had decided to play the aggressor in their encounter. It fit with everything William knew about the man. His father was an earl, after all, and even if he would most likely never see the title himself, it still gave him considerable weight in society. But why risk another wager? Why not just put William off with vague promises or even a veiled threat or two?

30

"I do not mean to be impertinent, Graves, but you are already in to me for a considerable sum. Why would you risk losing even more, and what could you possibly offer that would make it worth the risk for me?" William decided to do the unthinkable and actually be honest with the man.

"Oh, the money is of no consequence to men like us, Carey. Surely you know that. It is the thrill of the win. That is the real prize, is it not?" William knew *that* was a falsehood, but he was too curious to call the man on it. The conversation had not gone at all as he had planned, but that did not mean he could not still make the most of it.

"What did you have in mind?" he said, mirroring Graves's grin, though it pained him to do so.

"Well, I have heard it mentioned, on more than one occasion, that you have yourself a stallion that you are quite proud of. What say you to a little race between the two of us?"

"And what would be the prize of this race?"

"Double or quits."

William could not help that his eyes narrowed, just a bit, at that. Did Graves think him a fool? Where would a fourth son, still hanging from his father's purse strings, lay hands on that kind of sum?

He pondered those questions and more for a few moments before deciding how to use it to his advantage. "I like your thinking, Graves," he said, playing along, though the words almost stuck in his throat. "However, I have a slightly different prize in mind, I think."

He paused there, making it seem as if he were considering something he hadn't before. No need to make himself out to be too eager. Chances were, if he did not play along, he would never see a penny of the money or any part of Stephen. Graves was a worm and would probably find some way to wiggle free. Also, five thousand pounds was a fortune to throw away on a few nights of pleasure. If he won the race, he could have Stephen *and* have Graves indebted to him for a long time to come. It wasn't as if he had anything better to do with his time, and a horse race would certainly be diverting.

31

"As you say, for men like us, money indeed has little to do with these kinds of things." William paused again for dramatic effect and pretended to ponder the idea, then relaxed further in his chair and said, "I would be willing to wager against your current debt to me, plus, hmm... let us say, a week with your *companion* from last night. The young man who left with you in your carriage."

Graves's eyes widened and his mouth fell open, making him look for all the world like a trout, and William might have laughed if it were not for the fact that he was treading on some dangerous ground by revealing his interest in Stephen to a man like Graves. But as it was in both their interests that the nature of Stephen's service to Graves remain a secret, it was a risk William was willing to take.

Graves recovered himself quickly. William had to give him credit for that. His eyes narrowed in calculation within moments, and William only hoped the man did not decide to get greedy. If the whelp decided to push him, William would be forced to push back, and that *truly* would not get him what he wanted.

*Take the offer, boy. You'll not get a better one.*

"Four days with my companion. I am quite fond of him, after all," Graves shot back, surprising him.

William pursed his lips a moment. "Five," he countered.

Five days should be more than sufficient to satisfy his curiosity and his desire. If he ended up disliking the young man, it would be better for all concerned if their time together were shorter rather than longer.

"Done," Graves replied.

At this, William leaned forward in his chair. "Now, just to clarify. If you win, I will have your debt to me removed from the books by the following day. If I win, your companion stays with me, willing and eager, at a place of my choosing, for five full days and nights, and your debt stands. Are we agreed?"

"Agreed."

William had to work hard to contain his grin. Not only had he gotten Graves to agree to his terms, but Graves had also as much as admitted the man's connection to him, information he might be able to use at some later date. Now his prize was only a race away from being within his grasp, and Asmodeus, William's stallion, did *not* like to lose.

"So where is this little race to take place?" William said, keeping his tone disinterested so Graves would not sense his excitement.

"Highgate Village, at sunrise two days hence. That should give both of us time to prepare our mounts." Graves looked a little too pleased with himself, and William decided a precaution might be in order.

"May I suggest we bring in Arthur Billingsgate or Trenton Darrow from the club to judge the winner? I believe neither man has any connection to either of us that might color his judgment. We need not declare the stakes," William suggested, warming to the challenge.

"Done. I will send word to the club to inquire after either of those gentlemen," Graves said as he stood to leave.

"Excellent. Then, until then, I bid you good afternoon, Mr. Graves."

"Good afternoon, Mr. Carey."

Chapter *Four*

THE day of the race dawned dry and clear. There was a chill in the air, but William was certain the sun and the exercise would soon warm his blood. Asmodeus was restless, sensing the challenge to come, though to be honest the beast was rarely less than a handful. William kept him stabled outside the city for that very reason. That, and the fact that the rents were much lower and the beast had more room to run out there than in town. A cross and poorly exercised Asmodeus was not something William would wish on himself or any stable master.

As the small group gathered in preparation for the race, William looked about for Stephen, but the young man was nowhere to be seen. William felt a little prickle of unease at that, but dismissed it. Perhaps Stephen had been sent ahead and was waiting at the finish.

Graves sat his gray gelding impatiently as the servants and the judge readied the starting line. It was agreed that the two competitors would start south of the village, taking the road west, then north, circling the fields and finishing at the northern edge of the commons. Their servants and judge would pack up the carriages and take a leisurely stroll through the town, meeting them at the other side. They were out early enough that traffic on the road would be at a minimum, and a servant had already been sent ahead to make sure the road was clear.

William had to admit he was enjoying himself. It had been far too long since he had had a bit of excitement like this. Since Cora's death, he had immersed himself in hedonism of every conceivable nature, had engaged in plenty of games of skill and chance, but it had been a very long time since he had engaged in a wild and visceral challenge like this one... and with the addition of the promise of a handsome young man as reward, William was feeling more alive than he had in ages.

He felt his heart beat faster as they moved into position. Asmodeus was feeding off his excitement, and William was barely able to keep him in check as the beast swung his great black head around to nip at Graves's gelding. William was more than ready when the shot rang out, and Asmodeus took the lead immediately.

They careened down the narrow road, kicking up mud as they went, but though William held his stallion back to pace him for the race, Graves continued to stay more than a length behind him. Perhaps his mount was a sprinter and he wanted to catch William by surprise at the finish? If that were the case, William would have a surprise of his own, for Asmodeus had not reached anywhere near his full speed, nor was he even slightly winded. Big brute that he was, Asmodeus was surprisingly fast and had stamina few could match.

As they neared a sharp bend in the road, William slowed his mount, chancing a brief glance over his shoulder, and was bewildered by what he saw. Instead of continuing to follow him on the road, Graves had turned off on a track to the side that headed further west, *away* from the fields. Why on earth would the man take a longer route?

William felt another pang of unease and turned his attention back to the road ahead of him. He did not know what the man was about, but he would not win the race by looking over his shoulder. It took only a few moments more to make him eternally grateful he had made that decision, for just as he came round a bend in the road, he spotted a man leading a pony and cart, blocking the path in front of him. Cursing his luck, William thought fast and forced Asmodeus toward the low stone wall at the side of the road, urging him to leap the barrier and praying to God that the way was clear on the other side.

Asmodeus took the change in direction much more gracefully than William did and gathered his powerful legs beneath him, making the leap without even breaking stride. A more timid animal might have balked and reared, throwing him out of the saddle. Not for the first time, William gave thanks that Asmodeus was such a stout, aggressive beast. If William had not been so frightened for him, he would have been shouting with pride.

The field they were in was thankfully clear of hazards as far as he could see, so William chanced another look behind him to make sure the man and his cart had not been harmed. What he saw, in the brief glimpse he had before the man disappeared, was a young man struggling to right his wool cap over a riot of all-too-familiar gold and brown waves. William's temper nearly snapped.

Though Asmodeus kept galloping across the field, his ears were pinned back at the string of invectives that left William's mouth as he realized what had occurred. Graves, *the bloody bastard,* had planned this little interlude from the start and had nearly gotten William *and* his mount killed in the process... and Stephen had done the deed. William was of half a mind to turn Asmodeus about and thrash the man where he stood, but decided better of it. As Cora had said to him over and over, he might be a man of deep passions, but if he would only take pains to harness that fire, the world could be his for the taking. His victory would be made all the sweeter if he finished the race and claimed his prize. He could not touch Graves physically, and it was his word against Graves's if he wanted to bring charges.

*No. Win the race and claim your prize. They will both pay more dearly that way than any other.*

All this ran through his mind as Asmodeus made his way to the other end of the fallow field, and William kept a sharp eye out for any holes or uneven ground that might cause his stallion to injure himself. Ordinarily William would never have chanced a charge across an unknown field at such a pace, but in this instance, it actually worked in his favor. It cut nearly a quarter of a mile off his trip, and when he emerged at the other end, within sight of the finish, Graves was nowhere to be found.

Smiling in triumph, he eased Asmodeus back a little and allowed him to take the last leg of the race at a slower pace. As he neared the finish line, he spotted Graves on the horizon, returning to the road nearly half a mile behind him. William wished he could have seen the man's face at that moment, but he supposed he would just have to settle for his complete humiliation when he reached the finish line *long* after William.

He slowed Asmodeus to a trot within fifty yards of the finish and crossed it at little more than an amble. The stallion was breathing hard as William slid from the saddle, and he was grateful for the grooms that came up to tend to him. While they led the beast off to walk him down, William grinned at Arthur Billingsgate, their judge, and leaned back against one of the carriages to catch his breath. When Graves finally joined the party, Asmodeus let out a derisive snort before he was led away again, and William could not help but smile. He knew his contrary beast was disappointed with the race. From his stallion's point of view, he had been given no challenge at all. William would have to make it up to the big fellow sooner or later, but right now he had a blackguard to set down.

"Splendid race, Graves. I have to thank you for a most invigorating afternoon. I was afraid you had come to some sort of calamity there in the middle, when I lost sight of you. I had a bit of a surprise myself, but nothing we could not handle," William called out, smiling cheerfully at the other man, though any fool in possession of even half a brain could have seen the knife's edge in that smile.

Either Graves was not in possession of half a brain or he hoped to bluster his way out of the situation, for he simply retorted, "Thank you, Carey. It was indeed a fine race. You have bested me again, I fear. Let's not make it a habit, shall we?"

This was followed by a weak chuckle that William did not return. He simply raised his brows and waited silently with his arms crossed over his chest. The servants seemed to sense the tension in the air, for they all began busily packing and fussing over the horses and carriages, giving both men a wide berth. Arthur Billingsgate was the only one who approached them, and only for long enough to officially declare William the winner and receive assurances that the stakes would be seen to between the two of them.

Graves had little to say after that, and William was in no mood to exchange any further feigned pleasantries with the man. He simply said, "My man will arrive at your house tomorrow morning to collect my winnings. I trust all will be ready and waiting for him?"

Graves finally dropped the affable smile he had plastered across his face and scowled at William. "All will be in order, Carey. Five days. That is all."

"Of course. And we will still have to discuss the matter of your debt from the other night. I will give you some time on that score, however. At least until after I have collected today's winnings." William's smile was positively evil, he was sure of it, but he was not in the least sorry for it. The man deserved to be whipped for what he had done, and if one hair on Asmodeus's head had been injured as a result of his little scheme, William would have done it himself, fourth son of an earl or not.

Chapter *Five*

THE day he was to collect his prize, William woke at the ungodly hour of seven in the morning. He would have liked to blame his early rise on the strangeness of his surroundings, as he rarely slept when he stayed at his rooms in Cecil Court, but he was far too honest with himself for that. Despite his earlier anger, he was filled with an inexplicable nervous anticipation at the prospect of seeing Stephen again. It was exhilarating in a manner he had not felt in a long time.

The day promised to be cold and dreary. An icy drizzle pattered against the window as he crawled out of bed and moved to gaze down upon the street. He had decided to come to Cecil Court the night before to make sure he had everything he needed to fully enjoy the next five days. He rarely stayed there for more than a night, so the place had few of the amenities and luxuries he kept at his Mayfair house. Though Stubbs and Maud lived there and always made certain he did not go entirely without when he brought guests there, William had to admit he had never put much effort into seeing the house outfitted for company.

The large, four-poster bed with deep-red velvet curtains and counterpane was the only item of luxury he kept there, for it was the only item he used when he visited. But this time would be different. He would be spending five days and nights there, and though he would hopefully be spending much of his time in that bed, he still had several items delivered as a precaution, to make their stay a pleasant one. Who knew what Stephen would like or be in humor for?

And why did it matter so much to him that Stephen would be comfortable? The man was a paid companion and a cheat—why should he care? To this, William did not have an answer. He simply knew that he *did* care, at least enough to have several books, his chess set, his fiddle, and a number of other odds and ends packed up and sent to the house. As an added treat, he had also sent Stubbs and Maud out to the markets and the docks for the oils and exotic fare that could be bought, for the right price, from the crewmen returning from voyages to the East Indies.

William was still angry. The little shite was still going to have to make amends for nearly killing him on that road. William was fairly certain he had gained more than a few additional gray hairs as a result of the experience, but that did not mean he could not do a little wooing at the same time. He would not take the man to bed unwilling. He would never stoop to anything so barbaric. So a little romance would go a long way toward smoothing the way to his ultimate goal. William smiled a little as he envisioned Stephen spread out on his bed in surrender, then sighed and stepped away from the window to ring for Stubbs or Maud, whichever one chose to answer.

He allowed the atmosphere at Cecil Court to be much more informal than at his primary residence. Though Stubbs and his wife still considered themselves his servants and carried out any and all tasks without complaint, there was an unspoken understanding between them that there were some services they would not render. Dressing him was one of them. While he stayed there, William would have to fend for himself. Stubbs was no valet, and he had no qualms in informing his master of that.

Maud had not been with him nearly as many years as her husband, and therefore had more difficulty in behaving with such familiarity. She had only ever seen the *gentleman,* Mr. William Carey, so she viewed her position as his housekeeper with great pride and was far less comfortable with telling him to fend for himself.

True, she was a little rough around the edges, and even though she had worked hard to rid her speech of much of the cant she had grown up with, William doubted anyone of his acquaintance would have ever considered her for their household. But she had the biggest and warmest heart he had ever encountered, and he would not trade her for a hundred well-bred ladies.

"Good mornin', sir," Maud said as she entered his room, carrying a tray of coffee and biscuits.

"Good morning, Maud," he said, helping himself to a biscuit while she poured his coffee. "Will you have Stubbs prepare my bath?"

"Canna', sir. 'E's gone to pick up yer guest like ye asked for las' night. But I got water boilin' in the kitchen. If ye like, I'll go an' fetch it for ye. E'en picked up summa tha' special oil ye fancy at the docks to pour in't... and more for *later*," she replied, rubbing her hands in her apron and winking slyly at him.

William could not help but grin back at her. Standing there in her starched apron, her graying brown hair pulled into a prim chignon at her neck, few would guess she had been a painted nymph of the pavement for much of her youth.

Nothing shocked Maud. The fact that her husband was bringing her master a young man to play with did not discompose her in the slightest. There were even things that Stubbs blushed and turned away from that Maud did not bat an eyelash at. It was one of the things William loved best about her. He could be himself here, in the privacy of this house, without fear of censure, and both Maud and Stubbs would take his secrets to their graves.

"Thank you, Maud. That would be wonderful," he replied with another indulgent smile as he relaxed into his favorite chair and sipped at his coffee.

She left him to himself and went about readying his bath while William sat quietly and pondered how best to begin his interlude with Stephen. This was a new experience for him, borrowing someone else's plaything, and he had no idea what to expect. He had paid for pleasure a time or two in his life, mostly after Cora's death, when he had needed it to be completely impersonal and solely on his own terms, but he had not needed to bother with any of that in years. He had never had the need or desire to keep a companion of his own. His lovers had all come to him eagerly, whether the initial seduction had been their idea or his. The situation he found himself in at present was nothing like what he was used to, and he was not quite sure what to make of it. Nor what Stephen would make of it, for that matter.

As he bathed and dressed himself for the day, he continued to puzzle over it. Had he been a different sort of man, he felt sure doubt and regret might have crept into his thoughts sometime during the hours he waited for Stubbs to return, but William was not prone to such things as a rule. He knew he wanted Stephen in his bed, and he was fairly certain that would happen with little effort on his part. What he did not know was what else he wanted from the man, and therein lay his confusion. He worried over it for some time until he began to pace the room in agitation.

A sudden vision of Cora sitting across from him at dinner and shaking her head popped into mind and pulled him up short.

*Oh, my love, you are so like one of those horrid blunderbusses your men were always so fond of,* Cora's laughing voice teased him from his memories. *If one is not careful to load and aim you properly, you are more like to blow up in one's face than ever to hit the target.*

William smiled at the memory and shook his head. Perhaps because he had not been *aimed properly* in so long he was making more out of his curiosity than the situation warranted. Stephen was a cheat and a paramour. The only thing William should be agonizing over was how to gain the most pleasure from his body before sending him back to Graves. Anything else was merely the result of a strange restlessness on his part and should be put from his mind.

William nodded firmly at his reflection in the full-length looking glass standing in the corner of his bedchamber. He would not question his motivations any further. He would simply sit back and enjoy his reward, and when the five days were ended, he would send his prize back to his keeper, and there would be an end to it.

He descended the stairs to his study in much calmer spirits and settled into his chair by the fire to read while he awaited Stubbs's return. As the hours passed, however, his spirits took another turn, and not for the better. By four in the afternoon, he had moved from merely cross to incensed and then on to deeply concerned for Stubbs's welfare, as Maud fretted about her husband being gone for so long without word.

When at last he heard the front door open and close, he leapt from his chair and made his way to the hall, almost beating Maud to her husband. Though the man made comforting noises to his wife as he held her in his arms, he scowled something fierce at William over her shoulder, and William decided the best course would be to remain silent until the man had seen to his wife.

"Now don't go workin' yeself inta fine fettle, m'love. I baa'n't harmed none. Go into kitchen, and I'll awnly be a moment. I have a few words for Master. Go on now," Stubbs murmured to her as he set her away from him and gave her a pat on her arse. Though Stubbs had lost some of the speech of his home after living in London for nearly a decade, William was always reminded of the coasts when the man spoke.

Maud gave her husband a mildly affronted look over the pat on her rump, but was much too occupied with wiping her eyes on her apron for him to pay it any mind. She moved quietly past William on her way to the kitchen and disappeared before Stubbs opened his mouth again.

"Tha's some peach ye wagert on, sir. I tell ye tha'. Sure ye canna turn 'im in for aught else?" Stubbs said with a sour twist to his lips and a jerk of his head toward the parlor doors.

"Long carriage-ride, old fellow?" William said with a sympathetic smile.

Stubbs snorted. "His lairdship kep' m' waitin' in the kitchen fer hours, and as fer that 'un...." He jerked his thumb in the direction of the front parlor, where William assumed his guest waited. "Ye'll see soon enough, sir." Stubbs snorted once more, bent and lifted a small wooden trunk onto his shoulders, and then headed up the stairs without another word.

Pursing his lips in concern and annoyance, William continued on to the parlor and his guest. He took a moment just outside the room to look himself over in the gilt mirror hanging in the hall, and fussed a little with his cravat. As he'd tied it himself, it did not even approach the perfection his valet could have achieved, but it would have to do.

William rolled his shoulders under his dark blue wool coat and tugged a little at his silver and blue silk waistcoat. He had been told the colors flattered his gray eyes and dark hair, and he hoped that Stephen would agree, though now he was not certain that he cared. It appeared that Graves was still playing games, and William was beginning to believe he might regret ever entering into that wager.

He shrugged his shoulders again and gave himself a wry smile in the mirror. There was no help for it now, and a man liked to look his best when beginning a seduction. He stared at himself in the mirror for a few moments more until his eyes slid to the portrait reflected from the wall behind him. Cora's eyes laughed at him from that portrait, and he could not help but smile back, some of the tension leaking out of him. He had hung the painting there so that she could laugh at him anytime he spent too long in front of that mirror, whether out of vanity or melancholy. The artist had captured that hint of wickedness hidden just behind her green eyes, making that particular portrait of her perfect for its current location.

Some of William's past guests had been uneasy with her smiling down on them as they entered the house, but William did not particularly mind. They had not known Cora as he did. He was certain, if she had lived, that she would have joined in on any number of the nights he had indulged in at that house, saucy wench that she was. It was not as if he kept it hanging in his bedchamber, for God's sake. The portrait was just a reminder to laugh at himself, not a shrine. He smiled again and shook his head.

*Time to greet my guest.*

As William entered the room, he spotted Stephen by the windows, staring out at the rain, and he was surprised to find he could not read the expression on the young man's face. At the sound of his entrance, Stephen turned, and a somewhat sullen pout quickly replaced the unreadable look.

William put on his most charming smile and gave a slight bow in Stephen's direction.

"Good afternoon and welcome to my home. We have not been introduced. I am Mr. William Carey. You may call me William."

He paused a moment, waiting for Stephen to reciprocate, and after a few moments and a rather disdainful look at his surroundings, the young man bowed slightly toward him and said, "Good afternoon, Mr. Carey. I am Mr. Stephen... Smith."

William raised a brow at the slight pause before the surname but chose to ignore it. The man's real name was of little consequence, really.

"Well, Mr. *Smith*, would you care for some refreshment while we get to know one another?"

"No, thank you," Stephen replied, and he turned back to the window.

*Well, this is a rather inauspicious beginning.*

William chose to ring for Maud anyway and settled himself in one of the two chairs surrounding his small chess table. Silence reigned in the room until Maud entered with a knock and an actual curtsey before saying, "Yes, sir?"

William was touched by Maud's efforts and smiled warmly at her. "Will you bring some tea and a light tray for us, please?"

"Certainly, sir." Maud bobbed another awkward curtsey and left, closing the door behind her.

"You have an... *interesting* home here, Mr. Carey," Stephen commented from his place by the window, and William could hear the disdain dripping from his words. The man's shoulders were tense beneath his brown wool coat, and his arms were crossed over his chest.

Deciding not to react to the young man's tone, William continued to watch him and simply said, "It serves its purpose."

"Indeed," Stephen sniped back at him. "I would have expected something different from a man of your... *distinction*."

William laughed at that, and Stephen's jaw tightened. "Well, I could hardly invite you to the family seat, Mr. Smith, now could I?" he said.

"I was not aware that I was here by *invitation*, sir," Stephen said quietly, and William felt a twinge of guilt at that. Perhaps the young man was truly unhappy at being passed off to another man. Perhaps he had feelings for Graves. Having never kept a paramour of his own, William had no idea the level of attachment one might develop in such a situation.

"If you do not wish to be here, Mr. Smith, you are more than welcome to leave at any time," William said soberly. "Stubbs will take you back to your home, and Graves and I can come to some other understanding regarding his debts to me."

Stephen's gaze jerked away from the window and met his. "No! That will not be necessary, sir," he said in a rush as he moved to stand by the other chair, gripping the back tightly in his hands.

William was a little puzzled by the strength of his reaction, but decided to let the matter drop for the time being. He would play this out a little longer before he tried to make any decisions as to how best to proceed.

"Well then, please sit down, Mr. Smith, and we shall spend a little time getting to know one another."

Stephen sat in the chair opposite his, giving William a much closer view than he had had up until that point. Maud had lit the lamps and the fire in the room to help chase away some of the gloom, and William found the way the lamplight glinted off of Stephen's hair and the gold in his eyes to be quite enchanting. He could not help a lazy smile from crossing his lips, half laughing at himself for being such a romantic sod and half at the blush that crept over Stephen's cheeks under his regard.

As William continued to study him in silence, Stephen's eyes became wary, and he licked his lips nervously. William's eyes dropped immediately to Stephen's mouth with the act, and his gaze heated. He purposefully let his eyes slide to Stephen's lap, then drew it slowly back up to meet the younger man's eyes again, allowing his smile to turn just a little wicked in the process, while Stephen squirmed under his scrutiny.

He was on the verge of deciding that they really did not need to *talk* to get to know one another better when Maud entered with a brief knock, carrying the requested tray. William sighed and leaned back in his seat. He had not realized he had leaned forward.

Maud did her best to serve the tea, but she had not had much practice with the tiny, delicate china service. She rarely had to perform such services for him with company, as he usually served his guests himself in the bedchamber. By the time she had finished, she had clacked the cups together enough that William feared they would crack and overfilled them to where the tea puddled in the saucers. William felt terrible for putting her through such an ordeal, as he realized he had never seen the good woman so flustered before. He should have taken over and allowed her to get on with her other duties.

"Perhaps we should have asked for tankards of ale instead. I am sure she would have known better what to do with those," Stephen said snidely just as Maud was leaving the room.

"And perhaps you should remember your own place before you cast judgment on others while you are a guest in my house," William replied with an equal amount of bite when he saw the embarrassed and angry flush on Maud's cheeks as she closed the door.

Stephen's eyes flashed fire and his lips twisted, but he did not say anything else, which William was thankful for. The lad could say what he wanted about the house, but William would not tolerate him insulting his servants. A certain amount of pride and conceit could be dealt with, but William would not allow anyone to treat his friends with contempt.

"Do you play chess, Mr. Smith? Shall we play a game while we enjoy our tea?" he asked as he tried to cool his temper.

He was letting the lad fluster him, and he did not know why. He was nearly as upset at himself as he was at Stephen. The boy had been ill-mannered from the moment he'd stepped into the house, but it was not anything William had not dealt with before from any number of people. Yet, for some inexplicable reason, coming from this young man, it angered him more than with anyone else.

"Certainly, sir," Stephen replied through clenched teeth.

They played in silence for a long time, sipping at their tea. William decided to allow things to settle between them before broaching any other subjects, and Stephen seemed content to maintain the silence.

Despite his general disapproval of Stephen's behavior, William had to admit the man played very well. They played for several hours, and William only barely pulled the victory after Stephen checked him twice. It reminded William why he had been interested in the young man in the first place, watching his thoughts play across his face as that keen wit worked against him. Stephen's mind was lively and quick, and William found himself truly enjoying the challenge the man gave him. If William had not had nearly a decade more experience at the game, he was fairly certain the lad would have beaten him.

"You are an excellent player, Mr. Smith. Who taught you to play so well?" William asked with a genuinely pleased smile.

Stephen's face, which up until that point had been alight with interest and passion for the game, closed off completely at the question, and William was instantly sorry he had asked. "I learned, here and there," he said quietly, without meeting William's eyes.

*More prickles than a hedgehog,* he thought with a purely internal sigh.

"Well, they obviously taught you well, whoever they were," he replied instead. "Ah. I believe I smell Maud's marvelous cooking, which means we have an hour or so before dinner. Perhaps you would like a short time to rest and wash before then?"

"Yes, that would be very kind of you. Thank you," Stephen said, eyeing him warily.

"Excellent. I have some letters to write, so I will have Maud or Stubbs show you to your room, then call you when dinner is served," he said as he rang the bell.

48

When Stubbs entered, ignoring Stephen and doing his best not to scowl, William could not help an amused smile. It seemed his man had not let go of his earlier pique. Either that or Maud had told him what Stephen had said about her. Either way, when William instructed him to take Stephen to the room where his trunk had been placed, all he received in return was a grunt as the man turned around and left the room, not even looking to see if Stephen followed.

When they were both gone and he was alone, William sighed loudly and covered his face with his hands. This was not going well at all. He was not sure just what he had expected, but whatever it was, *this* was not it. Watching the young man for the past few hours, he had felt like kissing him and throttling him by turns, and he still was not quite sure which impulse would win out.

He did not have any letters to write. He had left all that nonsense in Mayfair. He simply needed a little time away from Stephen so he could think. The rational part of him said he should cut his losses and send the young man back to Graves. It was obvious that he did not wish to be there, so perhaps it would be better for all concerned if William simply sent him on his way and went out to find some more congenial company.

William let the idea settle for a few moments as he made his way to his study and poured himself a tumbler of whiskey. Settling back in his chair, he swirled the drink around in the glass, the flashes of lamplight through the amber liquid reminding him of Stephen's eyes.

He snorted at himself in disgust.

*Besotted, romantic fool.*

Perhaps after a bit of a rest and some time alone, Stephen's humor might improve? Perhaps if they got to know one another better?

At least whatever Maud was making smelled delicious. He could wait another couple of hours and see if a fine meal and good wine might smooth out some of his guest's sharper edges. As it was, William had to admit that he had not really made much of an effort at seducing the young man yet. He had been thrown off balance by Stephen's late arrival and his bad manners to such a degree that he had not even tried to woo the man.

Did one need to woo one's paid companion?

William supposed it could not hurt. And if, after a little wooing and fine food, the lad was still acting churlish and unpleasant, then William would send him on his way and give up on the whole mad scheme, whether Mr. *Smith* protested or not.

Decision made, William sipped at his whiskey, picked up the *Times*, and settled in to pass the next hour in peace before beginning his campaign to seduce his prickly paramour.

Chapter *Six*

STUBBS came for him an hour later to inform him that dinner was ready. The older man was no longer scowling—well, any more than usual—so William did not bother to question him further. He simply set his paper aside and stood to follow, ordering Stubbs to fetch his guest as he continued on to the dining room.

The house was quite small, so the dining room was not much to look at. Like all the other rooms in the house, it was cramped, with bare, sanded-wood floors and grayish-white walls. A small oval table, hardly large enough for two, sat in the center of the room, with not much room to either side for Maud or Stubbs to serve them. Looking at it with fresh eyes, William supposed he should have put a little more effort into seeing the place decorated. Though he rarely spent much time there, perhaps Stubbs and Maud would have appreciated some pleasant touches here and there.

He shook his head. Stephen, by his mere presence, was causing him to question things he had not concerned himself with for years. Without even entering the room and nary a word spoken, the younger man had managed to make William ashamed of his dining room. William made a promise to himself then that he would not allow the younger man to make him lose his composure again. He was going to charm the spines right off that little hedgehog if he had to pull out every weapon in his arsenal to do it.

At least there was a fire in the grate, and Maud had chosen candles rather than lamps. The softer light made the room seem warm and cozy rather than small and shabby. The crisp white table linens and delicately painted china were a nice touch as well.

William moved to the far chair when he heard footsteps in the hall. As Stephen entered, edging warily around Stubbs, William noted that the younger man had changed for dinner. Though not in black, he looked quite handsome in a dark green wool coat and russet waistcoat. William smiled in appreciation and kept the smile in place despite the audible sniff of displeasure he heard from Stephen as the young man gazed about the room.

"Good evening, Mr. Smith. I trust your room was satisfactory and you had a pleasant rest?"

"Thank you, sir. The room is… satisfactory and the bed… *clean*," Stephen answered stiffly.

William sighed and motioned for Stephen to sit while taking the other seat himself.

"I am glad to hear it," William replied, with only a hint of sarcasm coloring his words.

Maud entered a moment later, followed by Stubbs, both carrying trays laden with covered dishes that soon took up every empty space on the small table. Stubbs moved to the door while Maud filled their plates. William could barely hold back a laugh as he noted the manner in which each of them was served. While steamed mushrooms and boiled, seasoned potatoes were spooned gently onto his plate, Stephen's food was roughly dropped into a jumbled heap onto his. The potatoes made a resounding *splat*, followed by the *slap* of a large slice of ham and a tumble of beans and mushrooms.

Indeed, William *would* have laughed at the scene if Stephen's face were not getting more and more pinched and Maud's eyes more and more challenging. The temperature in the room seemed to be increasing by the minute. Stubbs waited in the doorway, tension radiating off of him as if he were just waiting for Stephen to say one word against his wife, and William decided this needed to end before there was all-out warfare.

"Thank you, Maud, Stubbs. I believe that will be all for the evening. You have worked wonders with this meal, Maud. I am sure we could not possibly ask any more of you tonight."

"Thank you, sir." Maud met his gaze and smiled a little sheepishly. She plunked the wine carafe in front of Stephen and took the empty tray with her as she made her way to the door, a slight flounce in her walk. Stubbs simply grunted and closed the door behind them.

William sighed and picked up his fork to start his meal but stopped when he realized Stephen sat with his head bowed, his eyes shut and his lips moving. When Stephen raised his eyes and found William staring at him, he blushed and set to work on his food.

"I beg your pardon, Mr. Smith. I should have offered a blessing," William said, though in truth he never bothered with such things before his own meals. He had no idea the young man was religious.

Stephen fidgeted in his seat a little, looking uncomfortable. "You need not find religion for my sake, sir. Though if I were you, and I spent much time with *them*," he said, gesturing toward the door with his hand, "I might take it up."

"I am not sure I understand your meaning," William replied, the warning clear in his voice.

Stephen's eyes narrowed a little, but he showed no other signs that he understood William's tone. "Well, to be completely honest, sir, with that man in the house I should be afraid to go to sleep at night for fear I would wake to find my throat cut. You really do have the most interesting taste in servants, Mr. Carey," he continued with a laugh and a sour twist of those full lips.

Reminding himself of his resolution to make one last attempt to tame this shrew rather than cast him out on his arse, William took a calming sip of his wine and said, "They suit me quite well, actually."

Stephen finished chewing a bit of ham before he answered with another haughty laugh, "From what I have heard of your reputation, sir, I suppose that is to be expected."

William sat back in his seat a little further and smiled. Jibes at his reputation had little effect on him. He found them rather amusing for the most part.

"And what is it that you have heard, Mr. Smith?" he asked, letting his amusement suffuse the question.

Stephen's jaw tightened, and he took several long moments to eat before he answered.

"I have heard any number of tales told of your exploits, Mr. Carey. Some say you were a privateer during the war, sinking dozens of ships and killing hundreds of men. Others, that you were a thief, a highwayman, and a smuggler. That now you are merely a bounder and a cad, a rake and a cheat."

"You of all people should know better than to cast stones, Mr. Smith, most particularly on that score," William replied, no longer attempting to mask his anger. He had had just about enough, and Stephen's poorly chosen reminder of his and Graves's treachery pushed William into at last making a decision regarding his impertinent guest.

Stephen stared at him for a moment in shock, then paled and looked away. "I do not know what you mean, sir."

"Do you not? Well, perhaps the next time you choose to take a walk in the country with your pony and cart, you will keep a better grip on your cap, hmmm?" William replied acerbically.

Stephen's eyes met his then and held for several long moments before dropping away again. At least William read guilt and shame in that look. The young man was not a total loss if he could feel shame for what he had done, even if it was not enough to make William change his mind about sending him on his way.

"If you knew, then why did you not say anything? Why not bring charges?" Stephen asked quietly as he pushed away from the table and stood, hands clenched nervously at his sides.

"It would not have gotten me what I wanted," William replied simply, holding Stephen's wary gaze until understanding lit his eyes. "But I think now that I have made an error and that I should indeed return you to Graves." William pushed his chair back and stood. "I will summon Stubbs and have him fetch your trunk and escort you home."

"No. Wait," Stephen said, quickly moving across the room and stopping only inches away from him.

As William waited, puzzled and nearly out of patience, Stephen stepped closer, hesitated a brief moment, then raised his hands to William's face. The younger man roughly cupped his chin and searched his face for several long moments before dropping his hands to William's shoulders and shoving him backward, until his back connected with the wall. Before William could overcome his surprise, Stephen pressed their bodies tightly together, buried his hands in William's hair, and began kissing along his jaw—nibbling, licking, and biting at the line of skin just above his cravat—and grinding their bodies together.

William was too shocked to do anything but lay docile under Stephen's onslaught. From the moment the younger man had walked into his house, William had been out of sorts in one manner or another, and his inability to adapt to this sudden change in his guest's behavior was but one more example of that. For all of his life, William had been a man who could react quickly and decisively to any new situation, yet here he was, swooning like a maid while Stephen did marvelous and savage things to his neck and ear with his lush lips, sharp teeth, and agile tongue.

While William continued to lay passive under his attentions, Stephen's hands tightened in his hair, and he pressed their bodies even closer together, pinning William to the wall. William found himself completely surrounded by Stephen's strength, his heat, and his scent—a blend of crisp earth, cloves, and clean sweat that sent William's heart to pounding and all of his blood racing to his cock. The scent was musky and male and nothing like the cloying sweetness of the perfumes that so many in London chose to bathe in, and William found himself suddenly light-headed with need.

Under the spell of that scent and the feel of that hot mouth and firm body pressed against his, it took William less than a breath to decide that whatever this was, whatever Stephen and Graves might have done or might still do, he did not need to make sense of it at the present moment. He might be a fool for bringing this young man into his home, but he was not fool enough to turn away an opportunity such as this.

With a growl, William shoved Stephen back enough to remove his cravat and allow the younger man better access to his throat. When Stephen moved close again, William buried his hands in the mass of golden-brown waves he had been itching to lay his hands on for days and yanked the man against him. Stephen groaned in response to his rough treatment and tightened his own grip in William's hair again, renewing the ferocity of his attentions to William's neck and jaw.

Not to be outdone, William let go of Stephen's hair, yanked his coat back, and bit into the thick muscle joining his neck to his shoulder. He then licked and sucked through the soft linen of Stephen's shirt to soothe the hurt, while sliding his hands down Stephen's back and drawing the coat completely off. Stephen released his grip on William's hair only long enough to be freed from his coat and to yank William's own coat off before slamming their bodies together again and moving his attentions to the other side of William's neck.

Now free of the annoying hindrance of Stephen's coat, William let his hands roam roughly over the smoothly muscled planes of his back and down to the firm, high mounds of his arse. William squeezed hard, filling both hands with that glorious flesh, momentarily entranced by its perfection. If he had known that such a treasure as this was concealed beneath the tails of Stephen's coat, William would not have wasted any time at all in taking the younger man to his bedchamber... and would probably have saved himself a great deal of aggravation in the process.

Stephen gasped and moaned against his neck as William used his hold to grind their groins together again, while sliding his fingers as far into the crease of Stephen's arse as the fabric of his trousers would allow. William then leaned back, pulling away from Stephen's assault on his neck and slanting his lips toward the other man's, intent on capturing another treasure he had been denied too long. But before he could lay claim to that bounty, Stephen suddenly jerked his face to the side.

"No," he panted. "No kissing. I do not care for kissing."

"No?" William asked, disbelieving and disappointed.

When Stephen shook his head, William cupped his chin and ran his thumbs over those full lips, letting out a growl of frustration. Stephen remained pressed tightly against him, but William could see the younger man's eyes turning angry and wary. William closed his eyes and took a breath to calm himself. He desperately wanted to kiss those lips, but he would not force the issue, not if it meant a stop to what they were doing. His body was crying out for more, and he had no intention of denying it, so instead of pressing the matter, he merely nodded and moved to kiss along Stephen's neck and ear, returning his hands to Stephen's tempting arse.

He continued to play with that glorious piece of flesh, alternating between rough grasping and teasing his fingers along the crease until the other man moaned and pulled away sharply, his cheeks flushed and his amber eyes dark with passion.

Before William could read anything more in his expression, Stephen slid to his knees and tore at the placket of William's trousers. Head bent, that glorious fall of golden-brown waves shielding his face from view, Stephen pushed his hand roughly inside and drew William's aching cock free of its confinement. Such rough play was not normally William's preference, but he supposed he could be persuaded to it as long as Stephen continued to touch him. He gripped the warm silk of Stephen's hair tightly in his fist and pulled it away from his face so that he would not miss a moment of what was to come.

Stephen glanced briefly up into his eyes, but wasted no time in gripping William's cock tightly around the base and dragging his hand up the shaft, drawing his foreskin high up over his sensitive crown, then pushing it down again, collecting the moisture that escaped the tip in his palm.

The rough, callused skin was another sensation William was unaccustomed to from the ladies and gentlemen of his more recent acquaintance, but he only had a moment to ponder the novelty before that gloriously rough palm made another sweep of his sensitive head and his thoughts scattered on a moan. Good God, Stephen certainly knew how to use his hands. William leaned back against the wall and spread his legs farther apart to give the man more room, and Stephen took advantage of the move by settling his hand at the base of William's shaft and leaning forward until William's swollen crown touched those beautiful lips.

William held his breath in anticipation as Stephen's tongue darted out and swirled around his crown. The beautiful young man at his feet teased inside his foreskin and tongued the ridge and the slit until William's breath was forced from his lungs on a desperate moan and his knees began to shake. Stephen obviously knew how to use his mouth as well, and William was quite certain that he would be reduced to begging if the man did not take him inside soon.

Thankfully Stephen saved him that humiliation by teasing him only a few moments more before opening his mouth and drawing William's cock deep inside. William watched avidly as Stephen's swollen, pink lips slid down his shaft until they met his hand, engulfing him in wet heat. Stephen held him in the tight confines of his throat only a moment before hollowing his cheeks and drawing hard on William's shaft, pulling back until only William's crown remained inside.

"God!" William choked and trembled, never taking his eyes from Stephen's face. The man's amber eyes, though darkened with lust, twinkled up at him, and William felt certain Stephen would have been smiling if his mouth were not otherwise engaged.

William had yet to see Stephen smile, and might have considered it worth a pause in what they were doing if the man was not lavishing such wonderful attention on his prick and scattering his few remaining wits. He did feel an inexplicably tender emotion bloom within his chest at the sight of the young man taking such obvious pleasure in pleasuring him, and he could not help cradling the man's face and running the backs of his fingers tenderly down the lad's cheek, even as his body tightened painfully in response to what was being done to it.

Some of that tender feeling must have shown on his face, for Stephen's brows suddenly drew down, and he closed his eyes and suddenly lunged forward, stuffing William's cock far back in his throat, twisting his mouth and sucking hard as he drew back up the shaft. He repeated the move several times more, setting a fast rhythm guaranteed to push William over the edge in a matter of minutes if he did not force the younger man to slow down. In the flood of glorious sensation, William did not even notice that Stephen's other hand had reached into his trousers until he felt a warm, rough palm cradling his bollocks and rolling them in his palm.

"Good God! Enough!" William ordered between panting breaths, pulling hard on Stephen's hair when the younger man did not cease immediately.

Stephen finally let loose then and fell back on his haunches, staring angrily into William's eyes. The sight of Stephen, on his knees, his lips swollen and wet, his eyes flashing fire and his head tilted at an awkward angle by William's fist in his hair, was almost enough to force William to spill right then, without even touching his cock. He had to take several deep breaths to calm himself, and only then did he loosen his hold on the younger man's hair, rubbing his hand gently along Stephen's scalp to soothe any hurt that he might have caused. After a few soft caresses, William slid his hand further down and cupped Stephen's chin, running his thumb tenderly over those beautiful, moist lips.

"If I am going to last long enough to see to both of us, we will need to slow down," William said with a rueful smile. "Shall we retire to my bedchamber?"

Anger was replaced by confusion in Stephen's eyes, but before William could question it, the younger man gave a single sharp nod of his head, stood quickly, and headed for the door.

William hurriedly set himself to rights, blew out the candles on the table, scattering wax in his haste, and rushed after Stephen. Maud would likely scold him later over the mess, but at the moment, William did not care.

He followed close behind Stephen as the man quickly climbed the steps to the upper floor, which gave him an excellent view of two of Stephen's finer features, flexing beneath the wool of his trousers. William was still a bit puzzled by Stephen's behavior, but he would not allow that to distract him from more important matters. A man had needs, after all.

When he reached the landing, Stephen paused, waiting for William to precede him into his bedchamber. William barely had time to thank Maud silently for seeing to the fire and leaving a table lamp burning before Stephen's body slammed into his, turning him and pinning his back to the wall. As he was becoming somewhat accustomed to this kind of treatment, William quickly suppressed his initial instinct to fight and kept himself still while Stephen attacked the buttons of his waistcoat. But when Stephen grabbed his wrists hard and slammed them back against the wall after William had merely reached down to help him, William decided that he had had about enough.

William had never been much of a one for pain during coupling. He understood that there were many who liked that sort of thing, but he did not happen to be one of them. Therefore, he had no interest in sitting back and allowing Stephen to knock him about. If this was the sort of play that Stephen preferred, then he would strive to give the younger man what he wanted, but it would be on William's terms.

"Do you like it rough, Stephen? Do you want me to take you hard? Is that what you want?" he asked, his voice sounding husky even to his own ears as he used the younger man's given name for the first time.

Something flickered in Stephen's lovely eyes, but it was gone before William could put a name to it. Too soon it was replaced by that challenging, almost angry look that William was becoming quite familiar with.

"Yes. Take me. Fuck me. Now," he panted.

William smiled his most predatory smile and wrenched his wrists from Stephen's grasp, grabbing the younger man's shoulders and swinging him hard, into the wall, face-first.

"Your wish...." he said as he lunged in and latched onto Stephen's neck, biting and sucking, forcing his knee up, high and hard, between Stephen's thighs.

Stephen moaned and writhed against him, pulling at his hold, but William held him pinned, squeezing his wrists in a painful grip. He let up only long enough to strip off Stephen's waistcoat, falls, and shirt, popping off buttons and tearing linen in his haste. He then slammed the younger man back against the wall and held him in place with the weight of his body, grinding his erection against Stephen's arse. Stephen hissed and grappled with him, but William knew far more about this kind of wrestling than Stephen possibly could, so the young man could not manage to free himself.

William held him there for several moments until Stephen's shoulders relaxed and he stopped fighting William's hold. He then stepped back, releasing Stephen from the wall, but when the younger man swung around and grabbed for him, William stepped to the side, grabbed his arm, hooked his leg around Stephen's, and used the younger man's own momentum to send him tumbling face-first onto the bed.

William quickly dropped on top of him, pinning him to the mattress. He shoved his hand beneath Stephen's writhing body, tearing at the placket to his trousers, and then climbed off the bed and jerked them down the younger man's lean legs, stopping only when they caught on his boots. William immediately climbed back on top of his fiery lover, straddling him and sitting on the backs of his naked thighs. He took a brief moment to simply absorb the beautiful sight before him and to luxuriate in the feel of the smooth, taut globes of Stephen's arse, now bared to his hands. Part of him would have much preferred to take his time and get to know every glorious inch of Stephen's body, but he let those wistful imaginings go and contented himself with giving Stephen what he wanted. It was not as if he was morally opposed to a good, hard fuck, after all; it just would not have been his first choice.

By now Stephen had propped himself up on his elbows, making it easy for William to grab a fistful of his hair and drag the younger man up onto his knees, forcing him to arch his back against William's chest. Keeping one hand tight in his hair, William slid his other around to the front of his lover's body, down the taut, lightly furred plains of his chest and belly to grip his cock. William was quite pleased to find it to be nearly as long and thick as his own, hard, flushed, and pulsing in his grip. He gave it a good, hard tug and then another, eliciting a moan from the man in his arms. Stephen did not struggle, though he was still breathing heavily and held himself stiff in William's embrace.

"Do you like that, Stephen?" he whispered against the other man's ear before nipping at his earlobe.

"Yes!"

"More?"

"Yes!" His cry turned into a hiss as William let go of his hair and moved his other hand down to cup and roll his bollocks roughly, tugging at them.

"You want me to fuck you? Ride you hard until you are begging me for release?" With those words, William ground his aching cock against Stephen's bare arse and gave Stephen's parts another hard tug.

Stephen pushed back against him and shuddered. "God, yes!" he gasped.

William did not need to be told twice. He quickly released his hold on Stephen's bollocks, grabbed him by the back of the neck, and shoved his head back down to the mattress. Stephen stayed in position, exposed for William's pleasure, while William finished removing his own waistcoat, falls, and shirt. William climbed back behind his lover then and grasped his buttocks, hard enough to bruise. He spread Stephen wide and spat into the divide, trailing his fingers through the wet and teasing Stephen's opening with them. The flushed rosebud quivered under his questing fingers, but he took no time to admire it. He simply wet his fingers a little more and pushed the first inside. Stephen moaned into the mattress, and William could not help echoing him as the younger man's channel gripped his finger tightly. William broke into a sweat as every pulse of Stephen's body around his finger sent an answering throb of need to his cock.

He spat again on Stephen's opening and used the added wet to work a second finger quickly inside. He twisted and thrust those fingers in and out, pulling more grunts and moans from the man beneath him, all of which combined to make William light-headed with need. He had to rest his sweating brow against the top of Stephen's arse as he worked to stretch and loosen his hole, glad for the first time that night that Stephen wanted it to be rough, for it meant he did not have to take the care he normally would with a partner. As soon as Stephen began thrusting back and writhing on his fingers, William withdrew them, tore open the placket of his own trousers, and positioned himself at Stephen's opening.

He spat once more in his palm and quickly slicked his cock with it, the spit mingling with the fluid already leaking from his crown.

"Tell me once more that this is what you want," William demanded, his voice hoarse. He needed to hear Stephen say it. He could not see Stephen's face, buried in the mattress as it was, so he needed to hear the passion and desire in his voice.

"Yes! Fuck me, damn you!" Stephen's hissed reply changed to a sharp cry as William pushed inside.

He was not gentle. He did not ease in. As soon as Stephen's opening relaxed enough to allow it, William thrust forward, burying himself to the hilt.

"Dear God," William grunted. He had to clench his teeth hard to keep from climaxing as a wave of intense pleasure crashed over him.

Stephen cried out again and bowed backwards off the bed, raising himself up on his hands as far as he could go. William lunged forward, pushing Stephen's shoulders back down against the mattress before gripping his hips and pounding into the younger man's body. As he thrust over and over into that glorious haven, he tried to concentrate on anything other than the slick heat squeezing his cock, the pungent, musky smell of their bodies, or the loud slap of their flesh coming together. He knew he could not last long at this frantic pace. His blood pounded in his ears, and his heart was fit to burst from his chest, it thudded so violently against his ribs. He could not remember the last time a lover had worked him into such a state. It was wonderful and terrifying all at once.

*A man could die from pleasure such as this, though it would not be a bad way to go.*

Before he was past caring, William reached around to claim Stephen's cock and was surprised to find him only half-hard. The discovery caused his rhythm to falter and forced him to slow, tamping down on his raging need for release. "Stephen…?"

The younger man did not answer. He simply lifted up on one arm as his other hand joined William's around his cock, pumping hard. In only a few breaths Stephen was fully hard, growling and bucking against him, forcing himself back onto William's cock and clenching his channel so tightly that William forgot why he had stopped. Stephen was a savage creature beneath him, fucking their joined hands and fucking himself on William's cock. All William could do was try his best to hold on and not fall from the precipice before his bed partner.

At last, when William thought he could not wait a moment longer, Stephen went stiff beneath him, thrust sharply into their hands, and cried out, the slick evidence of his release coating their joined hands. Barely a breath after, William let himself go on a howl as Stephen's arse clenched around him. He collapsed on top of the other man, sending them both sprawling onto the mattress, and tried desperately to catch his breath. Stephen lay still, panting beneath him.

As soon as William gathered his wits, he rolled off of the younger man and croaked, "Forgive me. I did not mean to crush you."

His cock slid free of Stephen's body as he moved, and Stephen let out a quiet moan but still did not move. Now that they had stopped their exertions, the chill in the room was quickly turning the sweat and other fluids on William's body to ice, forcing him to action much sooner than he would have liked. He sighed and swung his legs over the side of the bed, pulled his trousers up from where they'd tangled in his boot-tops, and partially buttoned them. He then stumbled to his washstand, grabbed a flannel from the pile Maud had left, and made his unsteady way back to Stephen's prone body. He sat on the bed and reached around to tend to Stephen, but the young man quickly sat up and snatched the flannel from his hand.

"I can see to that... thank you," Stephen said, without meeting William's eyes. Even in the dim light of the lamp, William could see the flush that spread across his cheeks.

"Of course. If that is your wish," he replied, then stood to go put more coal on the fire.

By the time he had finished and turned around again, Stephen already had his trousers up and his shirt back on and was headed toward the door.

"Stephen?" he said sharply, stopping the man's retreat. William walked to where he stood, stopping just behind him. He was close enough to feel the warmth of Stephen's skin and smell that intoxicating scent of his, but he did not touch. The young man's rigid stance and wary eyes made William cautious.

"Where are you going?"

"To my room."

"Why?"

"I'm very tired and need to rest."

"You can rest here. There will be no fire in your room. You would be much warmer here with me."

To that there was no reply, only a stiffening of the younger man's shoulders. William sighed and brought his hand up to rub his aching temples. He was too tired to argue with Stephen again that night, so he simply said, "You may go. *Tonight*."

Stephen continued his journey toward the door, but before he could close it behind him, William called his name again. The young man turned and looked at him through the crack in the door, his amber eyes still wary.

"I prefer not to sleep alone. The nights are getting colder now, and we will both be much more comfortable in my bed. I will give you your privacy tonight, if you insist upon it, but tomorrow night and thereafter, I will expect you to sleep here, with me. Am I understood?"

Stephen's jaw tightened, but he said nothing, merely gave a curt nod and closed the door behind him, leaving William frustrated, perplexed, and alone.

Chapter *Seven*

THE next morning dawned sunny and bright, in stark contrast to William's mood. He had lain awake for a long time after Stephen left, trying to solve the puzzle that was Mr. *Smith*, and he had had very little success at the endeavor. He had finally given in to exhaustion hours later, but though the angle of the sun told him he had slept half the morning away, he did not feel at all restored. He continued to lie abed, staring blankly at the walls, until Maud knocked at his door sometime later.

"Sir, I 'ave yer tray."

*Lord bless that woman.*

"Come in, Maud," he called back, sitting up.

She opened the door and walked in, bringing with her the aforementioned tray and the blessed scents of hot coffee and buttered scones. She left briefly, only to return from the hall with a steaming iron kettle that she placed on the coals to keep warm.

"I do believe I love you, Maud. I am quite certain, if Stubbs had not found you first, I would have swept you up in a heartbeat," William teased as Maud retrieved the tray and set it on his bed.

Maud merely raised her eyebrows and smirked, her gaze sweeping the room and taking in the clothes scattered about the floor and the rumpled bed linens.

"Oh, wouldya, now?" she laughed, propping her hands on her ample hips.

"Most certainly, my dear," William replied with his best cocksure grin before helping himself to one of her delicious scones, the butter dripping all over his fingers.

She tsked and handed him his napkin before pouring his coffee and flouncing to the door.

"Ye'r jus' flatterin' an old bawd so's she keeps ye spoilt and loungin' in bed when ye' oughtta be tendin' to tha' hellion ye brought to this 'ouse. Go on now and finish yer brekkers a'fore I 'ave to fetch yer *fine gentleman* a nope on the custard." Maud waggled her finger at him with that last and closed the door firmly behind her.

William sighed, some of the good humor he had gained with teasing Maud souring again. He wondered what Stephen must have said to the woman *now* that put her in such high dudgeon. Maud must be truly out of patience with the man for her to go so far as to chastise her master and threaten his guest with bodily harm. Stephen certainly was not going to make his stay easy on any of them.

As William sipped his coffee and felt its blessed warmth suffuse his limbs, a plan began to form in the back of his mind. He was not quite ready to give up on the lad entirely. Things between them had not gone at all as he had planned, and though they had both seemed to enjoy their first taste of one another, there had still been something missing, something just a little queer about the whole affair that did not sit well with him at all. He simply could not leave things as they were. It was not in his nature to give up without a fight.

By the time he had emptied his first cup and poured his second, William had finally decided his best course would be to do something that would get them out and about, something less intimate than being trapped indoors, trading quips and insults, all afternoon. Perhaps if he gave Stephen a day of gaiety and lighthearted merriment, the young man might drop his guard. William knew there had to be more to the man than the haughty and angry spitfire he had been presented with thus far. There was a vulnerability and depth of emotion flickering behind his eyes at times, just out of reach. William was certain of it.

68

His instincts had never played him false before. He had to trust in that and assume he simply had yet to discover how to reach the man.

Of course, he could be deluding himself. His cock could very well be overriding his better judgment without him even being aware of it. This would not be the first time that had occurred—although his cock had rarely played him false either, so it hardly mattered, really. William smiled against the rim of his cup and gave a purely internal shrug. He would not know for certain until he tried, so that was what he would do.

He set aside his cup and left the warmth of his bed with renewed resolve. Donning his slippers, he lifted the kettle from the coals and splashed its contents into the basin on his washstand, then stripped off his shirt and wet a flannel to wash. After a good wash and a shave, he carefully selected his clothing, donning a pair of gray suede trousers, a robin's-egg-blue paisley silk waistcoat, and his dark blue wool coat.

He then pulled on his boots and took a moment to admire himself in the mirror. His hair was still a little damp from the quick wash. It framed his face in gentle near-black waves, and even though he had not slept well, his eyes looked clear and his complexion healthy. The bright blue of his waistcoat made his eyes look more blue than gray, and William was quite pleased with the effect. It softened the hardness of his eyes a little, and anything that made him seem softer and more approachable could only help with his mercurial companion. By the time he had finished assessing himself, the sun was high in the sky, and William knew he needed to go find Stephen if they were going to have any time to enjoy the day.

He made his way quickly down the stairs, past the empty parlor, and stopped just inside the doorway to his study. Stephen sat in a chair by the window, staring out at the street, the book in his lap seemingly forgotten. The sunlight coming through the glass set his hair alight, creating a halo above his head. William caught his breath at the beauty of the sight, until his mind reminded him of the irony of that metaphor and he had to chuckle.

Stephen's head whipped around at the sound, and the illusion was completely shattered by the angry turn of his countenance. "Something amuses you, sir?"

"No. My apologies. I was simply struck by a passing fancy, nothing to concern you," William replied with his most self-deprecating smile. It seemed to work, for he could see Stephen's shoulders relax a little beneath the light brown wool of his coat. He was pleased to note that Stephen had chosen fawn-colored suede trousers and his sturdy boots for the day, so he would not need to change for what William had planned for them.

Stephen must have noticed the pleasure in William's continued regard, for his cheeks began to flush, and he shifted restlessly in his chair.

*Tread carefully, old man. Light and gay,* that *is your aim for today, remember?*

William cleared his throat and stepped further into the room. Leaning casually against the mantel, he said, "I thought we might take a ride through the park today, if you were up for a bit of exercise?"

Whatever Stephen had been expecting him to say, it clearly was not that, for the young man looked very confused. "You wish to take me riding in the park with you?" Stephen asked, a hint of his disbelief coloring his tone.

"Yes. If you think it would be something you might enjoy. If not, we could certainly do something else, I suppose."

"No, no. I would like that very much." Stephen stood suddenly and moved a step toward him in his earnestness, his excitement at the prospect quite plain.

And there it was, that brief flicker of vulnerability and hope that William had been looking for. It was gone in an instant as Stephen settled back on his heels and his face returned to its habitual frown, but William had seen it just the same. He could not help smiling his first genuinely happy smile since Stephen's arrival.

"Excellent. If you are so disposed, we may leave as soon as Stubbs can fetch our things," William said, his tone matching his newly lightened mood.

Stephen still looked unsettled by William's behavior, but he only said, "I am ready."

William rang for Stubbs and informed him of their plans. The older man's craggy face showed bemusement, but he knew his master well enough to know there was method to his madness, so he said nothing, merely fetched their coats, gloves, and hats and opened the door for them.

There was a stand only a few blocks from the house, so William never bothered to send Stubbs for a carriage. In a few short minutes, they were on their way. Stephen remained silent for the entirety of their journey, though William could feel the younger man's curious eyes on him often.

It took nearly half an hour to wend their way over to Mayfair, much to William's irritation. It seemed everyone in London was taking advantage of the weather that afternoon, making the streets nearly impassable. When they finally stopped, William looked up at the white stone facing of his brother's townhouse and smiled in relief. He paid the jarvey, then set out for the end of the block with an obviously bewildered Stephen on his heels. The younger man sent him several sharp looks as they made their way to the mews behind the houses, but William simply ignored them and continued walking.

When he reached his brother's stables, William drew himself up to his full height, squared his shoulders, and plastered on his most haughty and authoritative smile before calling out, "Peel! Where are you, man?"

In mere moments, a harried older man with wispy white hair and a thick mustache came bustling into the alley. "Mr. Carey, sir. Forgive me, sir, but I had not been told to expect you," Peel said. The stable master's words were polite, but his bushy white eyebrows were drawn low over his eyes, and his overall demeanor screamed his disapproval at William's sudden appearance.

William merely smiled condescendingly at the old man, playing the spoiled and dissolute younger brother to a tee. The man had never liked him, even when William was a child, and had never found it necessary to conceal that fact from a younger son, though he never would have dared make his dislike so obvious in front of William's father. William liked toying with Peel almost as much as he did with Horace, for that very reason.

"Truly, Peel? My apologies, but I felt certain my brother would have mentioned it to you. My young friend here and I are desirous of a ride in the park, and as I know my brother's beasts are ever in need of exercise, I offered my services and that of my friend in that capacity. I know Sir Carey would never wish for his brother to be seen on the back of a *hired* nag, so I thought it would be most advantageous for all concerned if we took the two grays off your hands for the afternoon," William said with a jaunty smile and a negligent wave of his hand toward two of the horses in their stalls.

Peel's lips pinched together until they were white, but the man dared not contradict him. Horace would be at his club, as he was this time every Tuesday, so word could not be sent to the house to question William's claim. Peel would not risk insulting his master's family by refusing to give him what he required, so the man truly had no choice in the matter. When William cast a glance over his shoulder at Stephen and caught the man frowning at him in disapproval, he did feel a small twinge of guilt for putting the servant in such a position, but it faded quickly under the stable master's all-too-familiar scowl. There would be no harm done. They would return the horses well exercised and long before Horace might have need of them.

Stephen shifted nervously behind him, but William simply ignored him this time and waited for the servant to respond.

"Of course, Mr. Carey, sir, as you say, sir," Peel gritted out before calling his grooms to saddle their mounts.

"Thank you, Peel. We will return before four." A short time later, William mounted his gray and set the beast walking to the head of the alley. Stephen mounted his horse at the same time, casting a concerned and apologetic look toward Peel, and followed William out of the mews.

"You lied to that poor man," Stephen accused after they had cleared the alley.

"Only a little," he replied with a shrug of his shoulders.

"You should be ashamed of yourself. He could lose his position when his master discovers his mistake."

"Your concern for Peel is most admirable, Mr. Smith, but it is not necessary. Peel will suffer no more than a little aggravation and embarrassment. My brother may be many things, but a harsh master he is not. He is kind to his servants. Peel has had his position for decades. The man is in no danger of losing it. The only one who will feel the brunt of Horace's displeasure will be me. I assure you."

"I hope for his sake you are correct," Stephen harrumphed, then fell silent again.

William was not entirely certain what devil had possessed to him to borrow his brother's horses instead of hiring his own. The idea had come upon him in the carriage as they had approached Mayfair, and, ever a man to listen to his instincts, he had decided to indulge the whim. His mood was in need of lightening if he were to have any success at doing the same with Stephen's, and niggling at his brother was always a sure means of bringing a smile to his face. William *did* smile then, and shrugged off the mild unease that had crept upon him under Stephen's censure. What was done was done. There would be no point in dwelling on it. Particularly not now, when he was headed for a lovely ride in the park. The sun was shining and the air crisp with the bite of autumn. He had gleaming, quality horseflesh beneath his seat and a handsome companion at his side. A man could not ask for much more than that.

They rode in silence for the rest of the short journey to Hyde Park and, once there, entered the stream of carriages and riders taking advantage of the sunshine to see and be seen by society. The track was not crowded, as many had already retired to the country, so William was happy to find they would not be jostled about and could have a pleasant and peaceful ride together.

He kept to the slower track and watched Stephen watch the people around him. Unease crept up on him again, as Stephen did not appear to be enjoying himself in the slightest. In fact, his young companion's back and shoulders were becoming stiffer by the moment, and he kept anxiously adjusting his cravat and brushing at nonexistent dirt on his coat sleeves. A sudden, unpleasant thought occurred to William as he was reminded of Stephen's words from the alley that first night at the club: *"I do not belong.... They all know it."*

William frowned. Stephen was obviously discomfited, and that was the opposite of his aim for the afternoon. He wanted Stephen relaxed and jolly, not fretting over his appearance and his situation. There was no reason for it that William could see. Though his clothes were not cut to perfection, perhaps, they were of fine quality. Graves had not stinted in seeing him fitted out. Nothing in his appearance bespoke anything but a gentlemen. William decided a certain amount of levity was in order... and perhaps a little lesson in the supposed superiority of London society.

He dropped his horse back a little so he and Stephen could ride abreast and cleared his throat to get the younger man's attention.

At Stephen's curious glance, he asked, "Do you see that lovely lady in pink satin with the white fur muff and mantle?"

Stephen looked confused but followed his gaze to a landau not far from them, containing two young ladies of about Stephen's age, giggling and fluttering their eyelashes at a pair of men who were laughing and bowing dramatically over the backs of their horses.

When Stephen nodded, he continued, "That is the newest Lady Hollingwood and her sister Miss Forsythe. The Earl of Hollingwood is a crusty old badger nigh on thirty years his young wife's senior, but with enough of a fortune, it is supposed, to make him handsome enough in the lady's eyes. Do you see the young man in livery driving their carriage? The one whose handsome face is pulled into a most frightful scowl at present?" William watched as Stephen turned his attention to the man driving the landau and nodded.

"That would be the new Lady Hollingwood's lover, and from the look on his face, he does not approve of her paying such attentions to those fine young gentlemen. Though perhaps his jealousy is more for Miss Forsythe than the lady, as I have heard he has a certain affinity for both sisters."

Stephen turned shocked eyes toward him, but William simply smiled blandly and sought out his next target. As it happened, his next quarry came to *him* in the form of a sour-faced elderly woman in black crepe, directing her driver to push through the slower moving traffic and forcing William and Stephen, and anyone else in her path, to the side so that she might pass.

"The Dowager Lady Illingworth," William nodded to the old woman, who merely frowned disapprovingly at him and turned her head away. At Stephen's questioning look, William smiled. "She married the Earl of Illingworth some thirty years ago and garnered a certain celebrity as a great patroness of the arts... of one artist in particular, I believe, a young painter with the most shocking tangle of ginger hair. I cannot remember the name just now, but it is of little matter. The poor lady lost her husband unexpectedly in a *hunting accident* a mere five years into their marriage. The incident was made even more tragic by the fact that the lady was carrying their first child at the time. Her husband's passing thankfully did not appear to tax her health too greatly, however, for she was blessed with a healthy baby boy and heir to the title three months after his passing. A beautiful babe by all accounts... with the most glorious mane of ginger hair."

William grinned as Stephen's lips quirked, signaling that he had understood William's meaning. Buoyed by that small success, William continued with his tales for their entire circuit of the park. Most of the gossip he related was quite old, but as Stephen gave no indication that he had heard any of it before and appeared to be enjoying the telling of it, William was more than happy to continue.

Though he pretended to keep his attention on the people around them, William watched his companion frequently out of the corner of his eye and caught the young man smiling more than once. He even startled a laugh out of Stephen during his description of the queer habits of Lord Wardell, whose stately home overlooked the park. The poor fellow was housebound with poor health, but missed his childhood pony so much that he paid a man to come to his home once a week, wear the creature's saddle and bridle, and prance about the lord's study, whinnying and eating apples from his hand.

Stephen's laugh was choked off almost immediately, but not before William could see the transformation it wrought in his face. In that moment, William thought he had never seen anyone more beautiful. A smiling and laughing Stephen was a glorious sight to behold, and William only wished he knew the secret to keeping him that way. When it disappeared, William merely sighed quietly and searched among the crowd for another means of bringing it back again.

All too soon, the sun began its descent toward the horizon, and William realized they needed to begin their journey home. As they headed toward his brother's house, Stephen's demeanor unfortunately changed again. His shoulders stiffened and his face tightened, forcing another resigned sigh out of William. The day had been so lovely, he hated to see it end, but despite his companion's mercurial humor, William did feel a sense of accomplishment at cracking Stephen's shell, even for a little while—though the feeling was short-lived once they entered his brother's stables and were greeted by Peel, sporting a smug smile and a note from William's brother.

*I would be most obliged if you would favor me with a few moments of your time before you return home this afternoon.*

*Sir Horace Carey, Baron Whitecastle.*

William sighed. "I fear we will have to delay our return whilst I speak with my brother," he said to Stephen when they were out of earshot of Peel and the other servants. "I am summoned."

Stephen twisted his lips and rolled his eyes, giving William a look that positively shouted, "I told you so."

William merely grinned sheepishly, making a last, valiant effort to keep the mood light, and led the way to the front of his brother's house. Giles let them in and led them into Eugenia's parlor instead of directly to his brother's study, much to William's displeasure. But as

William was not alone and Horace and Stephen had yet to be introduced, he supposed that Giles could hardly have done anything else. Still, being forced to wait within the confines of Eugenia's bright-pink and mustard-yellow travesty of a parlor was a punishment all its own, and put him in a sour temper before he had even spoken to his brother.

Giles returned after only a few minutes to lead William away. Horace did not deign to leave his study and allow himself to be introduced to Stephen, and William decided that it was probably for the best. Stephen did not deserve to be subjected to Horace in a temper, and William certainly did not want to suffer the mortification of being dressed down in front of his volatile companion. He might say something to his brother that he would come to regret.

"I will be only a moment," William said to Stephen. "I am sure Giles will return to see that you receive some refreshment while you wait."

Stephen was looking more tense and ill at ease by the moment, and William hoped his brother's tirade would be a brief one.

"Certainly. I will await your return," Stephen said formally, no hint as to his temper evident in his tone.

William frowned in concern but followed Giles back to his brother's study. He found Horace sitting stiffly behind his desk, a severe frown upon his face and storm clouds in his gray eyes. Again William was struck by his older brother's resemblance to their father, and the similarity did nothing for his own temper. Seated behind that bloody old desk, scowling down his nose at William, it was almost as if the past twenty years had never happened and Horace the elder was about to deliver one of his infamous speeches to his youngest son. Horace did not even have the decency to rise on William's entrance, and William could feel a small tick start in his jaw. His good humor and high spirits were fading nearly as fast as Stephen's, and he was in no mood to play games with his brother now.

Giles left at a nod from Horace, closing the door behind him, and they were left to stare at one another in silence while the butler's footsteps echoed down the hall and faded to nothing. Would that that silence had continued, for what replaced it was even less congenial. Over the next quarter of an hour, William's spirits plummeted and his temper frayed as he was subjected to a harsh and biting catalogue of his moral depravities, selfishness, and complete lack of concern for his family's reputation. The worst part of it all was that Horace's tirade had nothing to do with his actions of that afternoon—had little to do with him at all, in fact.

Apparently, just that afternoon, Horace had been made aware of some gossip, from an unknown source, that linked William with the fifteen-year-old daughter of one of Horace's political allies. William could not remember the chit's name, and he stopped even trying when it became evident that Horace would not stop for breath long enough to allow William to refute the charges made against him.

By the time that quarter of an hour had passed, William was livid and no longer listening to a single word his brother said. The injustice of his accusations and the complete lack of respect with which they were delivered cut him deeper than he had thought possible. Never in the entirety of his life had William been a man to show interest in girls barely out from behind their mother's skirts, not even when he was a boy himself. Horace *knew* that. The girl was Lydia's age, for God's sake. What on earth would lead his brother to believe he would turn defiler now? And when had Horace forgotten that William was a man himself now and, if not perhaps worthy of his admiration and approbation, at least worthy of courtesy and good manners?

When Horace finally paused for air and before he could get started again, William stood abruptly and slammed his fist down on their father's desk. "Enough!" he barked.

At the loud crack upon the desk and sharp command, Horace visibly started. He had begun pacing the room in agitation halfway through his tirade, and had ended up across the room from William, silhouetted against the window.

"When you are in humor to speak to me with more respect and allow me the opportunity to defend myself, you may send me another invitation to your home. I will then decide if I am inclined to *accept* your invitation. Until then, this interview is over!"

"William!" Horace barked at him as he turned and made his way to the door.

William did not bother to respond. He simply made a curt bow in his brother's general direction and left the room, closing the door sharply behind him. He made his way back to the parlor, all the while trying to rein in his temper and mask his discomposure. He must not have been particularly successful, for the moment he entered the parlor to retrieve Stephen, the younger man looked up from the tray of tea and sandwiches before him and narrowed his eyes. The reaction ignited William's temper again as he realized what little ground he had managed to gain with Stephen had indeed been lost, and he was very near to not giving a damn.

He collected Stephen, found a carriage, and saw them back to Cecil Court with nary a word spoken between them. When Stubbs opened the door for them, Stephen brushed past the man and headed for the stairs without a backward glance. Stubbs then turned back to William, his eyes full of questions, but William merely shook his head. "Not now, Stubbs. It has been a long day for all of us."

"Is there aught I can fetch ye?" Stubbs asked as he closed the door.

"No, thank you, Stubbs. All that I require lies within the confines of the decanter in my study, and I do not require your assistance with that," William replied with a humorless smile.

Stubbs merely shrugged in his usual taciturn manner and turned to make his way back to the kitchen. Emotional upheaval and to-do were not his purview. The man was loyal, solid, and dependable, but he had no interest in the passions of those with more sensitive natures. It took a great deal to push Stubbs into a fit of temper or to force him to involve himself in such "nonsense," as he would call it.

That night, William was grateful for that. He was in no humor to discuss his present state, and the older man would not know what to do with him even if he were. The thought of gruff, grizzled Stubbs attempting to hold his hand and listen compassionately while he spilled out his woes made William smile, and some of the tension and anger left his body.

"Stubbs?" William called after the man's retreating back. "Will you tell Maud not to put herself to too much trouble over dinner? I am not particularly hungry and can fend for myself. And will you ask her to check in on my guest?"

At Stubbs's scowl, William sighed and rubbed his temples. "I know, Stubbs. I know. Just ask her, as a favor to me... please? We skipped luncheon in favor of a ride in the park, and though I believe he was given a little refreshment at my brother's, I should think he is quite famished by now."

Stubbs's scowl softened a little, and he gave William a single nod before continuing on to the back of the house.

William trudged on to his study, suddenly feeling drained and hollow. The day had certainly not ended as he had wished, and he did not have the energy to deal with anything more that night. The disagreement with his brother had touched a nerve he did not know he possessed, and he was still smarting from it. He poured his first whiskey and downed it in a single swallow. The burn helped some, so he poured himself another.

He was working on his third when all hell broke loose.

The quiet of the evening was rent by a sudden crash from the upper floor, followed by muffled shouting. William was out of his chair and up the stairs in a flash, tearing down the hall toward the sounds. The sight that met him when he opened the door was of shattered china and various consumables scattered about the floor. Maud stood with her face flushed and her hands on her hips, an empty tray dangling from one of them, next to an enraged Stephen, who was spewing insults at her in only his shirt and trousers, now wet and stained with wine and other unnamed things.

Before William could say a word, Maud threw up her hands, tray and all, and stormed past him, disappearing down the hall, her eyes brimming with tears.

"Get out, you bloody cow! Keep yourself belowstairs, where you belong!" Stephen shouted at her retreating back.

"That is enough!" William shouted at him in turn. "I will not have you insulting my servants nor my friends in my house again!"

Stephen turned to him then, his eyes wide with outrage. "So it is all well and good for your *friends* to try to cave in my head and pour my dinner down the front of me, but *I* am not allowed to speak ill of them?" Stephen yelled at him.

"I am certain Maud did not willfully attempt to injure you, Stephen," William bit out between clenched teeth. "And as you still appear quite hale and hearty, there was therefore no harm done. I will replace your clothes."

William could feel that he was a hairsbreadth from losing his temper now, so he tried to take a moment to calm himself, but a loud thumping on the stairs heralded Stubbs's impending arrival, and he cursed and rushed into the hall to intercept the man. His friend's face was contorted with rage, and he had murder in his eyes. William grabbed him by the shoulders and forced the man to look him in the eyes.

"I will handle him, Stubbs. Please," William pleaded.

Stubbs's nostrils flared and his jaw twitched, but he made no further move to enter Stephen's room. Locking his fierce gaze with William's, Stubbs gritted out, "Ye'll see t' back of 'im now or I'm bown't fall out wit' lad most unpleasant-like. I'ma gonna brick 'is 'ead."

William gave him his most solemn look and said, "You have my word that I will see to it that he does not upset your wife or anyone else in this house again."

Stubbs grunted and wrenched himself out of William's grasp, stomping back down the stairs to his wife.

William gritted his teeth and walked back to Stephen's bedchamber, slamming the door behind him.

"What is the matter with you!?" William yelled at Stephen.

"What is the matter with *me*? I was minding my own business, sitting quietly by the window, when that... *woman* attacked me without provocation!" Stephen spat back at him.

"That aside, your behavior has been abominable since the moment you entered my house. You have been rude, spiteful, and disrespectful to myself and my servants without cause."

"If that was how you felt, then why did you even bother with the outing this afternoon? If I am so far beneath you that I do not even deserve an introduction to your brother when I am standing in the man's house, why did you even take me there in the first place?"

William reeled at the venom in Stephen's words. The injustice of his charge reopened the wound Horace had created only hours before. "My relationship with my family is none of your concern! I had not intended for us to enter the man's house at all!"

"Now we come to it! The truth at last! I am nothing but a lowly farmer, beneath the notice of men such as you except when you want to fuck! Don't deny it! I see it in your eyes! I hear it in your voice! You bring me to this filthy place with only your cutthroat servant and his harridan of a wife, dirty little secret that I am, and then you parade me about the park telling tales, no doubt believing me such an ignorant buffoon and country cousin that I would believe your every word! You made me party to your deceit with that poor stable master, playing him for a fool as well! You shame and humble those around you for your own amusement! I suppose you have had quite the laugh at my expense. You're no better than Graves! It is no wonder you keep such creatures about you, for who would stay with you otherwise? Why did you bring me here? And who is that woman in the hall!?" Stephen continued, without pausing for breath.

William stared at Stephen, his mouth agape in shock, for a solid minute as he attempted to understand the questions and everything else the lad had been shouting at him. Stephen had changed the direction of their conversation so quickly and so erratically that William was having a difficult time making any sense of his words.

*Farmer?*

*Woman in the hall?* William looked back, trying to see if someone was indeed behind him, but the door was still shut, and they were still the only two people in the room.

*Is he mad?*

"What woman?" he asked, completely flummoxed.

Stephen rolled his eyes and said, as if to a child, "The woman in the painting, in your front hall."

William would have been relieved that at least the man was not seeing people who were not there if it weren't for the bile dripping from his tone.

"My wife," he gritted out through clenched teeth, trying and failing to keep hold of his temper.

Stephen's eyes widened for a moment, then narrowed dangerously. "And does your *wife* know what you do here?"

"Perhaps," William threw back at him.

He was in no mood to correct Stephen's assumptions. The subject of his wife was not up for discussion, most particularly as William was only a few sharp words away from strangling the young man.

"*Perhaps* I should find her and tell her then!" Stephen shot back at him.

"Be my guest. I am sure she would love to hear every wicked detail." William did not know what possessed him to say it, but he was in too much of a temper for regrets at that moment.

Stephen gave him a disgusted look and spat back at him, "I should have known. It would take a whore and a slattern to marry *you*! Did you pull her out of the gutter with the other one? I hope, at the very least, you bathed her first!"

William's temper snapped then, and his vision went red. He walked calmly toward Stephen and stopped only a few inches in front of him.

In a deathly quiet voice he barely recognized as his own, William said, "Again, you of all people should not have brought that up. Perhaps you need a reminder of what *you* are. As you obviously need something better to do with your mouth, I will provide the means of occupying it for you. Get on your knees!"

When Stephen only stared angrily at him, William narrowed his eyes and dropped his voice lower, allowing it and his eyes to ice over, "Get on your knees or get out of my house. Those are your choices."

Stephen's eyes did change then, radiating hurt and disbelief for only a moment before they went dead, and William felt a strange twist in his gut, past the haze of his rage. Stephen took a sharp breath, closed his eyes, and slowly slid to his knees, reaching for the placket of William's trousers as sanity returned to William and the red cloud cleared from his eyes. The sick feeling in the pit of his stomach grew stronger, and bile rose in his throat. Disgusted with himself, William knocked Stephen's hands away, turned on his heel, and stalked out of the room, slamming the door behind him. He rushed down the stairs, past Stubbs and Maud, who stood holding one another on the landing, grabbed his cane from the stand, and let himself out into the night without a word spoken.

He walked blindly in the dark for several blocks before the cold finally made itself known through the fog of his regrets and self-flagellation. He had left without his greatcoat, his gloves, and his hat, and the clear autumn night was chill, with no clouds to keep the day's heat. William wrapped his arms tightly about his chest to ward off the ever-present breeze from the Thames and looked about him. Shaking his head, he could not help a pained grimace at his own folly. At least he had remembered his cane.

# Chapter Eight

WALKING alone through St. Giles at night was not the wisest course William could have taken. He had not made the choice consciously, but the consequences of his impulsive action were becoming all the more apparent the farther he walked down the street. Despite the cloudless skies, the moon was but a sliver above him, and the street was quite dark. There were a few streetlamps, but not enough to keep the darkness at bay, and he began to sense shadows moving within the shadows behind him. A part of him welcomed what those shadows might hold: the opportunity for a good fight. After the day he had had and the shameful manner in which he had behaved, William was aching for someone deserving to vent some of his frustrations on.

Instinct for self-preservation, however, cautioned him to take care and move to someplace more public. As a savage anticipation chased away the fog of self-recrimination, William's pulse quickened and his wits sharpened. He surveyed the neighborhood, looking for the best spot to confront his unseen followers, and spotted a streetlamp on a corner not far away. He made his way there quickly, stopping just before the circle of light so he would not be blinded, and turned to wait for his pursuers.

The place was not ideal, but it was the best he could find at that moment. There, at least, he could not be trapped in an alley, and at the crossing of two streets, he would be visible to passersby. The watchmen, though largely ineffective, could still be counted on to discourage some would-be thieves, and though William was itching for a fight, he wasn't a fool. He had no inkling of the number or nature of the men following him, and if he could discourage even one of them by keeping them out in the open, it would improve his odds greatly.

Before the shadows around him could react to the change in his behavior, William decided he had better take control of the situation, hoping to keep his pursuers off-balance.

"Good evening, gentlemen," he called amiably into the darkness. "How may I be of assistance to you this fine evening?"

The shadows were silent but for the faint shifting of cloth and the scrape of boots over stone. Then, from a little way off to his right, a gruff voice said, "Rag o'er yer blunt an' yer bobs."

The other men in the shadows, seemingly encouraged by their companion's bravado, moved closer, and William was finally able to gauge their number—much to his dismay. Four large men in rough, soiled clothes moved slowly out of the darkness. Two of the men bore cudgels, while a third carried a rope. As the fourth man, presumably the one who had spoken, moved closer, William caught the distinctive glimmer of steel in the lamplight, and he grimaced.

*Four armed men? To rob one?*

"I fear, gentlemen, I will be unable to satisfy your request. As you see, I have left my home without even my coat this evening, let alone my purse and the baubles to which you refer," William called back at them, changing his right hand's grip on the handle of his cane and placing his left on the shaft.

"We'll take tha' pocket watch an' pretty stick, then," the same man replied.

William was fairly certain, even were he to give in to these demands, he would not remain unscathed. Something struck him as odd that these men should be lying in wait so near his house and yet had followed him so far.

Hardening his tone and drawing the sword concealed within his cane, he said, "Again, I fear I cannot oblige you."

When the men hesitated for a moment, shifting nervously and looking to one another, William struck, lunging for the man on the right, the apparent leader. If he could take that man down quickly, it might scatter the others and keep them from presenting a united front.

The leader was quick on his feet, though, and dodged to the side as William came for him, receiving only a slash across the arm instead of the belly wound William had sought.

The man swore, clutching his bleeding arm, and screamed at his companions, "Don' jus' stan' there, blast ye! Mill 'is canister!"

William quickly backed away, trying to increase the distance between them. He could not allow any of the men to close with him if he was to survive this. This was not a fencing match between gentlemen. There were no rules of engagement. His only advantages were the reach of his weapon and his speed and agility. He had to keep moving and hope that they were discovered or that he managed to subdue his opponents before his strength gave out.

He swiped his blade in a wide arc at the three men who had rushed in front of their wounded companion. They each leapt back, out of range, one of them stumbling into their leader and giving William an opening to dart to the left, back toward the streetlamp. If he could keep it behind him, he could use their night blindness to his advantage.

The two men still standing followed him, while the third struggled to free himself from his fellow. In the light from the lamp, William could see the men more clearly now, though their rough, squinting faces struck no chord of recognition. The man on his left struck first, swinging his cudgel hard at William's arm in an attempt to jar the light sword from his hand, while his companion closed on the right, spinning the rope he held in a wide arc at his side. William twisted his wrist and shoulders, allowing most of the force of the first man's blow to slide off his blade ineffectually, and stepped between the two men to avoid the rope that flew through the air where he had been standing only a moment before. At the sound of metal hitting stone, William realized the rope had something metal attached to the end of it that had missed his head by only a few inches. Gritting his teeth, William continued his movement, spinning around behind the first man, slamming the metal-tipped wood of his cane into the man's side and sending him to his knees, crying out in pain.

William danced back out of range of the other man, who was gathering his rope for another throw, keeping the man's wounded companion between them. Glancing to the side, he noticed the other two men had recovered and were now making their way toward him. William made for them, knowing the man with the rope could not get a clean shot if his companions were in the way. The other two must have realized the same, for they backed away from him and split up, attempting to block his retreat. William hissed in frustration and darted back toward the lamp. The man with the rope squinted in the light and started to spin his weapon at his side again, preparing for another throw.

William bent his knees in an almost-crouch, holding both the cane and the sword before him and preparing to leap out of the way. The move would put him in reach of one or both of the others, but he would just have to hope his luck would hold and he could catch them by surprise with the move.

The man with the rope grinned evilly at him and began to swing the weapon faster and faster, the metal hook at the end making a queer hum as it spun through the air. William was crouched and ready, but the strike never came. A moment before it appeared the man would release the weapon, the rope went lax and the hook dropped suddenly to the ground, followed a moment later by the man who carried it. Without pausing to count his good fortune, William turned and lunged at one of the other two men standing behind him. He was rewarded with a grunt and the feel of flesh cleaving beneath his blade. He danced back out of range as the last man standing, the man with the knife, lunged at his unprotected side. William pivoted and slammed his cane into the man's overextended shoulder, sending him tumbling into the darkness. When he caught sight of a shadow behind him, he quickly spun around again, raising his weapons and preparing to strike.

Relief flooded him when Stubbs's craggy, grinning face greeted him, and Stubbs raised a cudgel of his own in salute. William did not pause in his amazement but immediately swung to face the darkness about him, his back to Stubbs, ready for more, but there was no one to fight. His attackers were already limping off, back from wherever they had come, the injured being held up between their fellows.

William seriously considered going after them. His blood was up, and now that he had Stubbs with him, they could make short work of the villains. He even took a few steps in their direction before his shoulder twinged and he realized that he was too old and had too much wit to go haring off after a band of thieves in the dark. Now that the heat of battle was over, the chill night air burned its way through his chest with each panting breath he took, and his limbs announced quite firmly that they were not as limber as they used to be. Smiling ruefully at himself, William turned back, walked the few steps to Stubbs, and clapped the man on the shoulder.

"Thank you, Stubbs. You are the best of men, always there for me when I need you!"

"Aye," was Stubbs's simple reply, though the man had quite a self-satisfied grin on his face. He stepped away from William then and moved into the shadows, coming back a moment later with William's greatcoat and hat. "Maud feared ye might catch chill."

William smiled in gratitude and took his things, donning them while Stubbs cleaned his sword on a scrap of cloth and returned it to its sheath. William took his cane back from the man and echoed his self-satisfied grin, then drew his arm around his servant's shoulders. "What say we go to the Angel, and I will buy us a pint to celebrate the fact that, even after all these years, our clubs are still stout and our swords have not lost their edge?"

Stubbs snorted at the double meaning in those words and nodded his head. They turned and headed up the street in the opposite direction from the way they had come. They would take a different path back to Cecil Court... just in case.

They stayed at the Angel Pub for more than an hour in companionable silence. Stubbs drank heartily and listened with rapt attention to a couple of serving girls singing songs to a loudly appreciative audience, while William sat lost in his thoughts. Now that the excitement of the evening had faded, all he was left with was self-recrimination for the appalling manner in which he had behaved and his failure to achieve what he had wanted with Stephen.

Yes, in William's defense, Stephen had said some terrible things and made Maud cry, but William should never have lost his temper. He was *better* than that, but he had behaved like the spoiled little boy with the evil temper that he thought he had left behind long ago. The boy who had run away to Cornwall and taken to a life of smuggling simply to spite his dead father and anyone else who ever failed to believe in him.

William grimaced into his empty tankard. He had completely lost his temper for the first time in years, and as if that were not bad enough, he had allowed a man nearly ten years his junior to get the better of him and push him to it. A young man who seemed bent on pushing him from the moment he had entered his house.

As realization dawned on him, William suddenly straightened in his chair and set his empty tankard on the table.

That was it. From the moment Stephen had entered his house, the man had moved from insult to insult: first William's home, then his servants, then to William himself, and finally, to his wife. The lad had deliberately baited him from the beginning, and he had been too preoccupied with wooing and strategizing to even see the ploy for what it was. But why? What could he possibly gain?

William puzzled over it for a long time, but he could not come up with any satisfactory answers. Now that he knew it was a ploy, much of his anger at Stephen seeped away, leaving only regret and a new resolve in its wake. He would get the truth out of Stephen if it were the last thing he did, and he would do it with honey instead of vinegar. He had an apology to make. Whether or not the man deserved it remained to be seen, but William needed to give it for his own pride and honor. He had never treated a lover so shamefully in his life, and he needed to make things right between them.

He looked up to find Stubbs watching him closely, a puzzled and concerned look on his face. William smiled and asked, "Are we ready to retire for the night?"

At Stubbs's wary "Aye," William rose and led the way out of the Angel and back to the house. He allowed Stubbs to relieve him of his coat and hat, then continued on to the back of the house while his man closed, locked, and bolted the door. William walked past his study and on to the kitchens with a purpose. He would need Maud's help in preparing the scene for his apology.

When he opened the door, William found Maud scrubbing away at a large copper pot, muttering to herself.

"...'igh n'mighty 'e is... fancies 'isself a real swell, 'e does... naught but a Margerie an' a filthy backgammoner...."

William raised his eyebrows at the venom in the sweet woman's tirade, and Stubbs coughed loudly behind him to catch his wife's attention. The poor woman jumped guiltily and flushed scarlet when she saw who stood in the doorway.

"Beggin' yer pardon, sir, I...."

"Peace, Maud." William raised his hand to stop her flood of apologies. "You and your husband have every right to be angry at our young Mr. Smith, and I will not begrudge you that. The young man was appallingly rude to you, Maud, and he *will* apologize, just not tonight. Tonight I do not wish to quarrel anymore with anyone. I wish peace in my house. Can you give me that?"

"A'course, sir, anythin'," Maud said, nodding her head vigorously, the flush of embarrassment still staining her cheeks.

"Good. Thank you both. Now, I will assume that our guest has not left yet?" Maud twisted her lips and nodded. "Well then, I have a few requests for the evening, and after that, you may both do as you please, for I will not be needing you further. First, I would like a hot bath to be prepared."

"Oh, yessir. I put t' kettle on for ye, thinkin' ye might catch chill. Seein' as 'ow ye left wit'out yer coat," she said, a hint of motherly disapproval working its way past her chagrin.

William smiled. "Thank you, Maud. That was very considerate of you. You and your husband both take excellent care of me. Are the items you bought for me at the docks in my bedchamber?"

"Aye, sir," Stubbs answered.

"Excellent. Well then, all that I require of you is a light tray of food and drink to be brought to my bedchamber, the bath prepared, and the fire stirred up. I have not eaten since this morning, and I am beginning to feel it," William said as he snatched an apple from the table in front of him.

"We'll see t'it, sir," Maud replied.

William smiled at her again and nodded to Stubbs. "Thank you both. Do not worry. All will be set to rights come morning, I assure you."

*One way or another.*

William bit into the apple and headed off to his study, but paused in the doorway and turned back with a wicked smile. "And Maud?"

At her puzzled look, he grinned. "In all fairness, Mr. Smith is not the only backgammoner in this house. I am quite fond of the game myself."

As Maud gaped at him and flushed an even darker shade of crimson, Stubbs made a sound halfway between a choke and a snort, and William laughed and walked off to his study. He would give Stubbs and Maud a chance to see to his wishes, and himself a chance to eat, before going up to see Stephen. The whiskey and the ale were making him a bit giddy, and he needed to settle himself before he attempted anything with Stephen.

By the time he had finished his apple, his servants had climbed the stairs three times, and William decided it was time to set his plan into action. Taking a deep breath, he took the lamp from his study and slowly climbed the stairs, making his way to Stephen's bedchamber. He knocked on the door and waited. There was no answer, so he knocked again. When he still heard nothing, he turned the knob and let himself in.

The room was dark, and the fire had died out in the grate. In the light from his lamp, he saw that the food and broken china from earlier had been gathered into a small pile on the floor, and a stained rag next to it gave testimony to its usage as a mop for the wine. At first glance, William thought perhaps Maud was mistaken and Stephen had left, for there was no sign of him, but a slight movement out of the corner of his eye called William's attention to the seat near the window, and there he found his guest. William walked over to where Stephen perched, still dressed only in his stained shirt, trousers, and stocking feet.

"You are still here," William said gently to the bowed head below him.

"Yes," Stephen replied in an almost-whisper.

William dropped to one knee in front of the man and cupped his chin in one hand, stroking his thumb across that full lower lip.

"What am I to do with you?" William sighed as sad and wary amber eyes met his. He smiled sadly back at Stephen, and the wariness in the young man's eyes turned to confusion as he searched William's face.

William took a deep breath and plunged on. "There is much we should speak of and much that should be said, but I do not believe we should do so tonight. We cannot seem to speak to one another without sparring and quarreling, so I will only ask you this: do you wish to go home, Stephen? I will see you get there safely and release Graves from his debts to me if that is what you wish."

William waited, holding his breath, for Stephen to answer. Despite all that had happened between them, or perhaps because of it, William hoped the answer would be no. His plan for the rest of the night would mean nothing if Stephen only wished to return to Graves. William well knew he could have given up on the man several times in the last day and night, but something in him would not allow it. Something in him needed more from Stephen. The idea of letting him leave twisted something painful inside him. There was no rationalizing it. It simply *was*.

Stephen's eyes widened in surprise at William's last words, but he still remained silent. When he did not answer, William feared the worst, but he had to ask anyway, to hear it from Stephen's lips. "Do you, Stephen? Do you wish to go home?"

William was surprised by a short bark of bitter laughter from the younger man. "Would that I *could* go home," Stephen muttered. Then he gravely raised his eyes to meet William's and said, "However, to answer the question as you intended it, no, I do not wish for you to send me back to Mr. Graves's house, not yet."

William was puzzled by Stephen's queer response but stopped himself from asking about it. Tonight was not for lengthy conversation. They were both too raw for that, and that road only seemed to lead them into discord. He would continue with his plan and hope understanding and answers would follow.

"Very well. If that is your answer and you truly wish to stay, then I would ask a boon of you for tonight. There has been much unpleasantness exchanged between us in so short a time, and I am partly to blame for it. This evening I behaved shamefully toward you, a fact I am not proud of."

Stephen frowned in concern and shook his head vigorously. "No, I—" he began earnestly, but William placed his fingers over the man's lips, silencing him.

"Please do not argue with me, not tonight. That is the boon I would ask of you. No words. Not until tomorrow. You may tell me all you wish. You may praise me or castigate me. You may damn me or beg my forgiveness, whatever you wish, just not tonight. Tonight is my apology to you for the shameful manner in which I behaved. Will you allow me that?"

Stephen's lips trembled beneath his fingers, and his eyes shone a little bright in the lamplight, reassuring William that he had taken the right course. *This* was the Stephen he wished to know—filled with great passions, yes, but a deep well of tender feelings as well, feelings he kept hidden behind anger and vitriol but that were there just the same.

Stephen took a deep breath through his nose, searched William's face once more and nodded hesitantly. William smiled in relief, a truly open and happy smile that had Stephen's eyes widening and fixating on William's mouth. As the young man continued to stare at his mouth, William's smile turned to a grin, and Stephen flushed and suddenly looked away.

"One more matter before we begin my apology... regarding my wife," William felt compelled to say. When Stephen's eyes returned to his, William continued. "My wife is dead and has been for many years. You have no need to fear a vengeful harridan swooping down upon us, I assure you."

William stood without waiting for Stephen's reaction and offered the young man his hand, smiling gently down at him. Stephen still looked a little wary, but he slid his hand into William's just the same and allowed himself to be pulled to his feet. When Stephen would have let go, William tightened his grip and began leading him out of the room. He could hear Stephen's breath quicken as he led the younger man down the hall to his bedchamber, and his own pulse quickened in response.

William was pleased and grateful to find that Maud and Stubbs had prepared everything as he had requested and more when he entered the room. The coals were piled high in the grate, with a large iron kettle steaming above them. A copper bathing tub sat steaming in front of it, and a tray of cold meats, breads, cheese, and autumn fruits sat on the small table by the window. The lamps had been turned low, candles lit and set about the room, and a small brazier near the window sent plumes of perfumed smoke from the East Indies into the air. Those last details must have been Maud's doing, and he silently thanked the woman for her thoughtfulness. She knew what a sensualist he was, and despite her feelings for his guest, she had endeavored above and beyond his orders to give him this. He would have to remember to thank her come morning.

William led Stephen to the center of the room and left him for a moment to close and lock the door. He ordinarily would not have bothered, but he was certain Stephen would be more comfortable knowing the door was locked. Turning back to face his guest, he watched Stephen sniff the air and gaze nervously about the room. William wasted no time in returning to his side. He did not want the bath water to get cold before he had even begun his seduction, and he did not want to give his quarry any chance to change his mind.

Stephen's eyes returned to his, full of questions and a little trepidation, but William merely shook his head. "No words, Stephen. Please, just let me pamper you for a little while. I know this is supposed to be my apology to you, but it would mean a great deal to me if you would allow me to do this."

When the younger man sighed and nodded, William undid the fastenings of Stephen's soiled shirt and helped him pull it over his head. The shirt was ruined with wine and other stains, so William merely threw it into a corner of the room and began undoing the buttons on Stephen's trousers. He knelt then to help Stephen off with them and removed the young man's stockings as well, leaving him completely bare to William's hungry gaze. Their first night together had been rather rushed, and William had not been given much chance to savor Stephen's beauty. He hoped very much to correct that gross injustice this evening.

Kneeling in front of his lover, William let his gaze roam over the younger man's body. Golden-brown hairs lightly dusted Stephen's lean, muscled calves and thighs, sparkling a little in the flickering candlelight. A darker, thicker patch nestled between his legs, surrounding the base of a fair-sized, dusky cock that was rapidly swelling under William's regard. A line of hair ran up the flat expanse of his belly, meeting the dusting of hair across his chest, and William could not resist running his fingers along that path, feeling the soft hairs tickle his skin. He followed the trail up to Stephen's copper nipples, already drawn taut and dark, swirling his fingers through the hair surrounding them and grazing his palms over the pebbled nubs.

Still on his knees and only a hairsbreadth from Stephen's cock, William smiled, hooded his eyes in lambent appreciation, and tipped his head back to meet those expressive amber eyes. Stephen watched him avidly, his tongue darting out several times to wet his sinfully full lips, begging with actions what he could not with words. William knew exactly what the man wanted, but he was not going to be rushed. He would take things slower this time—even if it killed him.

He ignored Stephen's silent plea and climbed to his feet, dropping his hands down to run the backs of his thumbs up Stephen's inner thighs as he stood, enjoying the man's sharp intake of breath and the twitching of his cock. William's own trousers were feeling a bit uncomfortable at present, but he was certainly old enough and experienced enough to know that pleasure only increased by delaying gratification. He could wait and find a measure of pleasure in prolonging his own sweet torment as well as his lover's.

He smiled at Stephen's slightly disappointed look and cupped his chin, leaning in to kiss him tenderly on the cheek and then just underneath his jaw. William still desperately wanted to take Stephen's mouth, to kiss him with all the tenderness and passion he was feeling, but the young man had said he did not care for it, so William would have to content himself with kissing him everywhere else.

Smiling, William drew back and led his lover to the bathing tub. Stephen obediently sank into the water with a sigh and wrapped his arms around his bent knees, looking up expectantly for William to give him some direction. William was relieved that Stephen appeared willing to let him lead for a while, and even if it was only as an act of contrition, William could make use of that.

When Stephen was settled, William removed his own coat, waistcoat, and cravat, retrieved the thick cloth Maud had left on the mantel, and pulled the heavy kettle from the coals, pouring the hot water into the end of the bath to warm it up again. He then went to his wardrobe and withdrew the glass vial and jar Stubbs had purchased for him, setting the jar on the night table by the bed and taking the other back to the bath.

Under Stephen's puzzled gaze, he rolled his shirtsleeves up and uncorked the small vial, pouring some of the liquid into the bath. Almost instantly the smells of sharp earth, sweet spices, and musk filled the air, and William drank it in with sensual delight.

Patchouli.

William had fallen in love with the scent the first time he had smelled its heady fragrance, and had made sure the men on the docks knew he would pay handsomely for it and any other exotic oils and spices they might "find" lying around after the Company had unloaded its cargo. He could find such things at more reputable markets, but he had always been a proponent of free trade. Even if he did not engage in it himself anymore, he could still support those who did.

William drew a small stool next to the tub and watched with pleasure as Stephen's eyes closed and his body relaxed against the linens draped behind him. Well pleased with himself, William picked up the sea sponge and small jar of soap next to the tub and began washing Stephen's body with it. Stephen's eyes, now darkened to a deep, toffee color, opened and watched him for a time before sliding closed again as he surrendered to William's ministrations.

For a long time, William simply played, running the soft sponge over the planes of Stephen's body and learning the feel of every muscle and bone as it shifted beneath the smooth marble of his skin. He avoided the most obvious places, only making a cursory pass of Stephen's pleasure centers in favor of teasing other areas and learning what else his young companion might like. Stephen's ribs and nipples were very sensitive, as were his underarms and his belly, just under the bones of his hips. The younger man squirmed and moaned whenever William passed over those places and was excessively responsive to even the lightest touch, making William wonder at his apparent preference for such rough play their first night together, but he put such questions to the back of his mind for that night and simply concentrated on doing what seemed to give them both the most pleasure.

When he felt the water cool again, he rose and retrieved the ewer from the washstand, dipped it in the tub, and nudged Stephen's shoulder to get him to lean forward. He then used some of the soap to wash Stephen's glorious mane, scratching his nails through the swirls of short, dark hair at Stephen's nape and drawing the longer, golden waves through his fingers until all traces of wine and food were gone and Stephen was groaning and trembling under his hands. William then quickly filled the pitcher again and rinsed the younger man's hair. The bath was barely tepid now, and he did not want Stephen to catch a chill.

After grabbing a large flannel from his washstand, William drew Stephen to his feet and helped him from the tub, wrapping him in the cloth and slowly, sensually rubbing him dry. He moved behind Stephen then and began drying the younger man's hair, smoothing the flannel over his head and squeezing the bright multi-colored waves within its folds. When he looked up to find Stephen watching them both in the large looking glass in the corner, William found he could not look away. They made a beautifully erotic picture, framed in the glass as they were, Stephen bare but for the flannel and William clothed in only his shirt and trousers. He dropped the flannel and ran his hands down Stephen's body, watching their progress across skin turned golden in the candlelight. Stephen watched as well, leaning back against William's chest and arching into William's caress like a cat.

Stephen's cock, which had fallen a little during his bath, filled anew under William's gaze, jutting out prominently before him, and William was suddenly overcome with the need to feel that flesh pulsing in his hands. Stephen was so warm in his arms and smelled of clean soap, patchouli, and that unique blend of cloves and musk that was all his own, and William could not help but reach down and wrap his hand around that beautiful instrument between his legs. He wrapped his other arm around Stephen's chest and pressed their bodies together, grinding his aching cock against the perfection of Stephen's arse, closing his eyes and burying his face in the damp, sweet-smelling hair at his nape.

Stephen moaned and pumped his hips, grinding his arse back against William and pushing up into his fist. William opened his eyes again to find Stephen still watching the two of them in the glass, his mouth open and wet and his eyes needy. William had to turn away and take deep breaths against Stephen's neck as he tried to compose himself again. He did not want fast and frenzied, he had to remind himself—at least, not tonight. When he let go of Stephen's cock and gripped his hips to stop his movement, Stephen's frustrated and confused eyes met his in the glass, and William let out a breathless chuckle.

"Not yet. Give me just a little longer," he whispered against Stephen's ear before giving it a tender kiss.

Stephen shivered in his arms and visibly struggled with himself before unexpectedly giving William a wry smile that quirked his lips and crinkled his eyes in a most delightful manner. The younger man took a deep breath of his own and let it out with a shaky sigh, while

William struggled with the strange constriction in his chest at the sight of that smile.

Stephen stepped away from him then and strode toward the bed, giving William the much-needed distraction of that gorgeous arse sauntering away from him. With a wicked grin of his own, William followed, turning the young man around, sliding his hands down to cup and knead that glorious arse while he nibbled and bit along Stephen's neck. Before he could become carried away, however, he stepped back again and ordered a flushed and panting Stephen to lie down on the bed.

While Stephen did as he was told, William made use of his bootjack, stripped off his trousers, stockings, and shirt, and added more coal to the fire. Stephen watched from the bed in obvious appreciation, stroking himself languidly. William growled low in his throat at the sight and stalked back to the bed, batting Stephen's hands away from himself and replacing them with his own. He stroked and teased his lover's cock with his hands while he settled himself between Stephen's thighs, forcing the younger man to spread his legs wide and bend them at the knee. Stephen's lips parted on a gasp that turned into a soft moan as William's thumb toyed with his crown, rasping across his slit and smoothing the pearly fluid he found over the flushed head and into the folds of his foreskin.

"God, please. Please, Will—ungh!" His plea was cut short when William leaned in and drew Stephen's crown into his mouth, lavishing attention on it with his tongue and lips, sucking hard, then teasing and flicking his tongue across it.

William drew back. "Say it again."

"*Please.*"

"No, not that. My name, say it again," William demanded.

"William."

"Will, just Will," he corrected as he lowered his mouth back to the prize.

"*Will!*" Stephen all but shouted as William dove back on his organ and took him to the back of his throat, burying his nose in the coarse thatch at the base and reveling in the fullness, the scent of arousal, and the tremors of the body convulsing beneath him.

William loved this, sometimes more than finding his own release. He loved bringing his partners aching and trembling to the edge of the precipice, their cries of pleasure in his ears, their trembling bodies beneath his, the taste of their sweat and impending release on his tongue. It was purest heaven to him.

Hearing Stephen's continued entreaties, William decided he would give him what he asked. The man was still young and would recover quickly, so William could continue with all that he had planned after easing the poor man's need.

He set up a steady rhythm, drawing hard upon Stephen's shaft, hollowing his cheeks with the effort and swirling his tongue before plunging back down again. He circled the base with his fist, gripping it tightly, and pumped in concert with his mouth. Stephen continued to pant and writhe beneath him, thrusting hard against the restraining hand on his cock and fisting his hands in William's hair.

It was not long before Stephen's cries changed in pitch and his movements lost all rhythm, heralding his release. William dove down hard, swallowing around the crown lodged deep within his throat, and Stephen screamed, his body locking up and his spend pulsing into William's welcoming throat. William cradled Stephen's cock in his mouth, milking every last drop from the younger man and only letting up when Stephen moaned in protest. William let the spent cock slide from his mouth, aware of how sensitive it could be after such a hard release.

He kissed his way up Stephen's heaving chest, straddling his waist. Glazed eyes followed his progress, and Stephen's hands reached for William's cock. William was hard and aching, but he intercepted those hands and brought them to his lips, kissing each tenderly and rubbing his beard-roughened cheeks against the knuckles.

"Not yet," he said simply, and he rolled off Stephen. "Turn over and lie on your stomach."

Stephen gave him a slightly puzzled and sleepy look that was quite adorable, most particularly as his hair was in disarray about his head and his face was still flushed. When William merely motioned impatiently with his hands, Stephen rolled over on his stomach and looked at William over his shoulder, raising his eyebrows and quirking a smile.

William smiled in return, and his mouth started to water at the sight of Stephen's arse rising so temptingly from the mattress. He took a deep breath and told his cock to be patient, then straddled the backs of Stephen's thighs and reached for the jar he had placed on the night table. The white salve was a little hard in the container, and William had to hold it in his palms until the oil warmed enough to be spread. The faint, sweet smell of coconut filled the room as William spread the oil across Stephen's shoulders and back.

"William, you do not have to—" Stephen began, but William cut him off.

"Hush. Not tonight, remember? Now lie back and let me do what pleases me. If I do anything you do not care for, you may tell me. Otherwise, please do me the honor of allowing me to apologize properly."

Stephen held his gaze for a few more moments, obviously torn, then gave him that half-smile again and laid his head upon the pillow, drawing his hands up underneath it and relaxing his shoulders. William went to work at once, rubbing the exotic oil into Stephen's skin and enjoying the smooth glide of his hands across the muscles of his back. He kneaded and rubbed Stephen's flesh until the younger man lay in a puddle on the mattress; then he grinned evilly and moved lower, taking the taut globes of Stephen's arse in each hand and squeezing and kneading them, drawing them apart and pressing them back together, teasing until Stephen was no longer lying lax beneath him but pushing back into his hands, seeking more.

With a chuckle from low in his throat, William slid back, nudging Stephen's thighs further apart with his own. He moved his hands to Stephen's hips then, encouraging the younger man to raise them higher, and Stephen was quick to oblige him. William sat back on his heels as

Stephen rose up on his elbows and drew his knees up under his body. The new position gave William an excellent view of Stephen's entrance and his dangling bollocks and cock, already half-hard again. William dove forward then, grasping Stephen's buttocks again, pulling them wide and dragging the flat of his tongue over the puckered opening, wetting it liberally and teasing it the tiniest bit with the tip of his tongue.

A choked sound came from the head of the bed, and William looked up to find shocked amber eyes staring at him over Stephen's shoulder. William merely raised an eyebrow and waited, but when Stephen did nothing but stare at him with his mouth agape, he grinned and slowly lowered his head back to the cleft of Stephen's arse.

He set to work with fervor then, licking and teasing at Stephen's hole, kissing the flushed rosebud and sucking at it until it bloomed enough to let him push his tongue inside. He ravished Stephen's opening then, plunging his tongue into that tender flesh and swirling it around, doing all to that nether place that he craved to do to Stephen's mouth until the younger man was gasping out incoherent pleas and shaking and William could not hold out another moment. His cock was so hard it was set to pound stakes, and he feared any further delay might provide an unsatisfactory conclusion for both of them.

William drew himself up on his knees and gathered more oil from the jar. He warmed it in his palms and gingerly smoothed it over his aching organ, taking care to provide as little stimulation as possible. He then placed his dripping crown at Stephen's opening and slowly pressed inside, moaning in relief as the slick, hot channel wrapped around him in welcome.

"God, yes," Stephen breathed out beneath him, and William would have seconded that declaration if he had been able to speak.

He stroked into Stephen's willing body slowly and sensually, wanting to feel every nuance of his lover's response and prolong their pleasure as much as possible. He changed the angle of his thrusts by slow degrees, trying *not* to think about how wonderful it felt, until Stephen reared up on a cry, informing William that he had found what he was searching for. At that, William set to work stroking over that spot as best he could until his own need took over and he began pounding into Stephen's willing body without thought or reason. In the throes of passion, William was able to maintain enough consideration to reach for Stephen's cock, but found that the younger man had already beaten him to it and was furiously pumping himself in time with William's thrusts.

That was all it took for William to let go completely and thrust over and over with abandon until the pounding in his ears and the beast coiled in his loins roared forth, setting stars to dancing in front of his eyes. He flooded Stephen's body with his seed but continued pumping until he felt Stephen stiffen beneath him and his channel contract around William's cock, squeezing every last drop from him. They collapsed in a pile of sweating limbs and panting breaths until William's head cleared enough for him to roll off of the younger man.

On shaking legs, William retrieved the damp flannel from Stephen's bath, blew out the candles, and banked the coals before returning to the bed. Though there were still plenty of coals in the fire, the air felt quite cold on his sweat-dampened body, and he was shivering by the time he made it back to the bed. He leaned over Stephen with the flannel and paused, but this time the younger man made no objection, so William gently wiped his body, and then coaxed him to climb beneath the counterpane. Stephen gave him a sleepy smile and curled into a ball on his side, and William gave himself a cursory wash, climbed in, and curled around him, basking in his lover's warmth and fragrant skin. They were both asleep within minutes. It had indeed been a very long day.

*Chapter* Nine

WILLIAM woke to the dim gray of predawn with a smile on his face and a gnawing ache in his belly. He had forgotten to eat last night. He smiled, thinking of all that had distracted him, and decided that food could wait a little longer. He rolled over and reached for Stephen, so that he might enjoy the warmth and smoothness of the younger man's body for a little while, but his hands found naught but empty linens. Frowning, William sat up and wiped the cobwebs from his eyes, searching about him in the faint light. It took only a moment to spot Stephen's shadowed form, sitting naked on the edge of the bed, his elbows on his knees and his head in his hands.

"Stephen?" he asked in concern.

When there was no response, he reached for the younger man's shoulder and found it icy to the touch. Stephen trembled a little beneath his palm, and William sighed in consternation.

"Come along, Stephen. You will catch your death out here. Come back to bed," William coaxed, gripping Stephen's shoulders firmly and pulling him back onto the bed.

Stephen did not fight him; he simply allowed himself to be drawn down to the mattress and then curled into a ball, away from William. William drew the counterpane back over them and curled himself around Stephen's chilled body, chafing his limbs and trying to give the younger man as much warmth as he could. Stephen was shivering violently in his arms after only a few minutes, so William held him even tighter, cradling him against his chest until the shaking had abated.

When Stephen lay warm and quiet in his arms again and all William could hear was the quiet patter of rain on the windows instead of the chattering of his lover's teeth, he kissed the back of Stephen's neck gently and asked, "Will you tell me what is the matter?"

He felt Stephen's chest expand within the circle of his arms as the younger man drew in a deep breath and let it out on a sigh. "Can you forgive me? " Stephen whispered.

"What are you asking forgiveness *for*?" William replied. He had hoped to postpone their inevitable conversation until he had had some coffee and a little breakfast, but if Stephen was in humor to apologize, William had best take advantage of it.

Stephen rolled onto his back, took another deep breath, and lifted sad eyes to his. William propped himself onto his elbow and met Stephen's gaze kindly.

"For everything. For all that I have said… about your wife, your servants, yourself. I know what I said was cruel. I know it was untrue."

"Then why did you speak so?" William brushed Stephen's rumpled hair out of his eyes and smoothed his hand tenderly across his cheek.

"To make you angry. It was so much easier to hate you when you were angry with me." Stephen sighed, and a pained smile played about his lips. "I did not wish to admire you."

"And do you, Stephen? Do you admire me?" William held his breath, waiting on Stephen's reply. He did not know why the answer was so important to him. He was not quite ready to give substance and definition to all that he felt for this passionate and vexing young man, but he could not deny that he cared what the man thought of him.

"Yes. Yes, I do admire you, very much," Stephen said with a quiet, breathy laugh.

William grinned, more than willing to show how pleased he was with the answer. He pulled Stephen close and gave him a loud, smacking kiss on the forehead before pulling away and smiling happily into his eyes.

"Excellent! I am very glad to hear it. I admire you very much as well," he said, laughing. It had been a long time since such a simple declaration had held the power to make him giddy, but he would not question the feeling, only devise schemes to make sure it continued.

"I cannot think why," Stephen responded with a laugh of his own, and William could tell by the tightness in that laugh that it was only partly in jest.

William sobered then and cupped both his hands around Stephen's jaw, gazing deeply into his eyes. "I can. You have wit and passion and fire... though I prefer it when it is not aimed quite so sharply at me," he answered with a little laugh. "You have beauty, strength, and honor—" William's catalogue was cut short when Stephen winced suddenly and looked away from him.

"How can you speak of honor after what I have done?" he asked in a pained whisper.

William pulled his face back again and stared deeply into his eyes, "You have honor, Stephen. It may have fallen away a time or two, but I have seen glimpses of it in the past two days. Who was it chastised me so for lying to my brother's stable master? You feel remorse for what you did the day of the race, do you not?"

"I should not have done it. I did not think he could take anything more from me, but that day he did, and I *let* him. I gave over what little pride and honor I had left and nearly got you killed because of it. If anything had happened to you, I do not think I could have ever forgiven myself." Stephen's eyes were anguished now, begging William's forgiveness. "I should not have done it... consequences be damned!" he continued fiercely.

"What consequences?" William could not help but ask.

Stephen looked away from him again and shook his head. "I cannot tell you. I am sorry, but I cannot. I can only ask for you to forgive me in that as well." Stephen turned back to him then, searching his face. "Can you? Can you forgive me?"

107

William decided not to press for answers just yet. He was dying of curiosity, but he could be patient. The rewards for his patience thus far had more than made up for his pains, so he could wait a little longer and hope his luck held true.

"If you will forgive me for last night, then I will most happily forgive you. No more will be said about it," he said, holding Stephen's gaze so the man could see his sincerity.

He was very glad that he did when Stephen's face broke into a radiant smile and the younger man grabbed his face between his hands and kissed him hard on the mouth.

"Thank you," Stephen said when he pulled away, and William could not help the giddy smile that split his face.

"I thought you did not care for kissing," William teased, raising his eyebrows and smirking at the younger man.

Stephen looked up at him through his eyelashes and flushed.

"I lied. I suppose it depends greatly on whom I am kissing," he said in an embarrassed tone.

"Does this mean I have your permission?" William asked as casually as he could manage around the sudden racing of his heart.

Stephen sobered a little and looked deeply into William's eyes again. "Yes," he whispered.

"Thank God."

William did not waste another moment. He swooped down and claimed Stephen's lips, gripping his jaw in both hands and plunging his tongue into Stephen's willing mouth. He penetrated deep into the recesses, and then pulled back, savoring the taste of him, the heat of his mouth, and the silk of his tongue. He sucked on Stephen's delectable lips, mapping every inch of them and glutting himself on their softness. He kissed and sucked and licked until they both had to break away, gasping for air.

"I have desperately wanted to do that from the first moment I saw you," William admitted breathlessly, resting his forehead against Stephen's.

"I, too," Stephen whispered, "though I could not admit it, even to myself. I... I was angry and ashamed that I was to be your prize, but part of me was not at all unhappy that you won."

William leaned in and took his mouth again, gently this time, tenderly nibbling at his lips and languidly probing just inside. They lay like that for a long time, wrapped around one another, sharing the warmth of each other's bodies, simply kissing and stroking without urgency, and again William felt something deep within his chest tighten.

He pulled back then and simply looked at Stephen's flushed face and kiss-swollen lips, smiling happily until the younger man looked away uncomfortably. William sighed and decided he had pushed far enough for one morning. He rolled out of bed and moved quickly about the room, unlocking the door, stirring up the fire, and adding more coals to it. When Stephen began to rise from the bed, William said, "Don't."

Stephen stopped his progress and turned a puzzled frown toward him.

"I think we deserve a day in bed, don't you?"

"Stay in bed all day? When neither of us is ill?" Stephen asked, his tone bordering on scandalized.

William grinned and leered at Stephen. "Most particularly as neither of us is ill. Have you never spent a day in bed before, just for the pleasure of it?"

"Well... *no*," Stephen replied, as if the very thought were unheard of.

"Well then, I shall have to give you a lesson in how to do it properly." William grabbed two shirts from his wardrobe, throwing one to Stephen and pulling the other over his head. He lifted the tray of food that Maud had left the night before and hurried back to the bed.

After setting the tray on his night table, William dove back under the covers and curled his chilled body around Stephen's, stuffing his cold hands into the younger man's underarms, making him yelp and squirm.

"Lesson number one," he said, laughing as he tried to hold onto a bucking Stephen. "Whosoever is allowed to remain warm and comfortable in bed whilst the other must see to practical matters pays a forfeit to his partner on his return to bed."

Stephen was laughing as well now, though he still fought William's icy grip on him. The sound of Stephen's laughter had an even stronger effect on William today than it had the day before, and William could not help grinning madly, almost like a child again.

Soon enough, William's hands were warm, and Stephen stopped fighting him, though he turned an affronted frown on him when William finally let him go. William only grinned unashamedly back. He grabbed the tray then and set it on the bed, poured wine for the two of them, and settled back against the pillows.

"Wine? For breakfast?" Stephen asked doubtfully.

"Unless you would like me to ring for Maud and order her to bring us something more suitable?" William replied casually, sipping from his glass.

"I do not believe that would be wise. At least not until I have had a chance to make an apology to the woman," Stephen said.

William smiled, pleased that Stephen intended to apologize to his servants without William having to ask. He sipped his wine happily and watched his young lover bow his head for a moment before partaking of his own wine. When Stephen opened his eyes and saw William watching him, he flushed a little and set to nibbling at the meats and breads on the tray.

"You may say your blessing aloud if you wish. I should like to hear it."

Stephen met his gaze and smiled slightly. "It is nothing. I am not a particularly religious man. I simply know how easily the comforts and necessities of this world can be taken away, so I try to remember to be grateful when they are given to me."

William raised his eyebrows, hoping Stephen would say more, but the man shook his head and went back to his meal. William sighed quietly and reminded himself once more to be patient. He helped himself to some of the food and drink until his glass was empty and some of the gnawing hunger he had woken with was assuaged. Then he picked up an apple and began slicing it into wedges with a small knife. When he was finished, he rolled onto his side and offered a slice to Stephen but snatched it away again and shook his head when Stephen reached for it with his fingers.

Smiling at his lover's confusion, William leaned in and stole a kiss, then said, "Lesson number two: breakfast in bed. Open."

Stephen opened his mouth obediently, and William popped the slice inside, giving the younger man time enough to swallow before leaning in to claim his mouth for another kiss. Tart apple and Stephen made a delectable combination, so William repeated the process a few more times before moving on to the cheese and some more wine. They took turns after that as Stephen warmed to the game, and soon they forgot all about the food and drink and were kissing one another deeply and passionately.

William set the tray back on the night table and climbed on top of Stephen, pushing his shirt up and molding their bodies together. Stephen's cock pressed hard into his belly as William ground his own erection into the meat of Stephen's thigh. Soon they were both panting and moaning, arms and legs wrapped firmly around one another, each wrestling with the other while trying to gain as much contact as possible. When the need for release became too much for him to bear and Stephen's needy moans told him his lover was just as far gone as he, William leaned back, pulled his shirt over his head, and panted, "Give me your hand."

Stephen met his gaze. His eyes were nearly black with need, but he did as he was told without a word. William shifted, straddling his lover's hips so that their cocks came together, then wrapped both their hands around them. There would be no slow crescendo this time. They both pumped frantically at their joined cocks and thrust forcefully with their hips. William could not take his eyes away from Stephen's face as the younger man stared, enraptured, at the sight of their purple and swollen cock-heads, oozing pearly fluid, disappearing and reappearing through their clasped fists.

"Oh God!" Stephen moaned as he pumped his hand and his hips more frantically.

William grunted and increased his own efforts, trying to keep pace. Stephen was so close now; William could hear it in the whimpers and moans the other man no longer made any effort to stifle. William was on the edge of the precipice himself, but he did not want to miss a single second of Stephen's pleasure. He wanted to see every expression that crossed the younger man's face, every drop of sweat that fell from his brow, and every shiver of his body as he gave himself up to the moment and to William.

"Will!" Stephen cried out as he threw his head back into the pillows and his body went rigid on the bed.

William kept pumping their hands, stroking Stephen through his release, then pulled back a little and pumped his own cock alone, shooting streams of his seed over Stephen's stomach and chest, the sight pushing him to a smaller secondary eruption that splashed over Stephen's cock and mingled with Stephen's seed on his belly. William dropped his hands to the mattress, propping himself up on his arms and gasping for air above Stephen, simply gazing at his spend splashed over that lovely body. It was beautiful and wicked, and it touched something quite savage within him.

As Stephen continued to lie, gasping for breath, William began smoothing his hand through their combined offerings, smearing the cream into Stephen's skin, coating his stomach and cock with it, and moving lower to rub it across his sac and down to his opening. He looked up to find Stephen watching him with that fire in his eyes that William had come to crave, and he doubled his efforts, gathering more of their seed and pressing it into Stephen's hole over and over, pumping his fingers into his lover's body.

Stephen's cock began to fill again, and William had to smile. *Ah, the resilience of youth.*

He leaned in and licked some of the fluid from Stephen's belly, lapping at him like a cat with cream, his eyes and his smile turning possessive and feral. William could only imagine what he must have looked like just then, for Stephen's eyes grew wide, and he could not seem to look away.

William growled low in his throat and was just about to climb back up and take Stephen's mouth again when there was a quiet knock at the door.

"Sir? I 'ave yer tray."

It was Maud, ever-caring and faithful Maud.

William swore under his breath, but chuckled in resignation as Stephen scrambled underneath him to pull his shirt down and the linens up. William grabbed the shirt he had discarded and rolled off of his young lover, calling out, "Come in, Maud."

The woman came bustling in, bobbed him a slight curtsy, and carried the tray of coffee and breakfast pastries and puddings to the small table by the window. Without another word, she went to the fire to stir the coals as usual, studiously ignoring the young man in William's bed. Stephen watched her warily, but said nothing. When William turned to him, raising his eyebrows and giving a wave of his hand in Maud's direction, Stephen flushed and shook his head. William frowned, his eyebrows drawing down in displeasure, but Stephen threw him a pleading look and gestured toward his clothing—or lack thereof.

William could not help but roll his eyes. Stephen was being silly. Maud would not care one whit what he was wearing when he made his apology, just that he made the damned thing.

"Maud," William called out over Stephen's outraged gasp, "I believe Mr. Smith here has something he wishes to say to you."

Stephen's eyes threw daggers at him, but William merely smiled calmly at him, gesturing for him to proceed.

When Maud rose up from her position by the fire and turned haughty eyes in Stephen's direction, the young man cleared his throat nervously and said, "I wish to offer you my sincerest apologies, madam, for any offense I may have given you. I have no excuse for my behavior and so can offer none. It is my dearest hope that you can find it in your heart to forgive me for what I have said to you and the manner in which I have behaved. You have my word that I will treat you with the respect you are due from this moment forward."

Maud raised her brows at his speech and glanced briefly at William before turning her attention back to Stephen. She weighed him with her eyes for several long moments before shaking her head and smiling. "Well now, I s'pose I can do tha for ye," she began. Then she wagged her finger at him and said, "Keep a civil tongue in yer 'ead an' keep '*im* 'appy an' allus forgiven."

"Thank you, madam," Stephen said quietly, and William could see his shoulders relax a little.

"Do ye need aught else, sirs?" she asked as she turned smiling eyes to William. William smiled back at her, knowing she told only the truth and wondering at her ability to forgive and forget so easily, especially when one thought of the cruel and unforgiving world she had come from.

"Mr. Smith and I intend to spend the day up here, Maud, so it will not be necessary to bother with fires anywhere else. I would like for you to bring up the books I left on the table in my study, if you would. Beyond that, we shall see to ourselves, thank you."

Maud removed the tray from the night before and placed the breakfast tray in its place before bobbing another curtsy and making her way out of the room. When the door had closed, William turned proud and smiling eyes back to Stephen, only to receive a pillow full in the face.

"How could you?" Stephen hissed at him, drawing his arm back for another swing.

William pulled the pillow away before Stephen could strike and lunged for the younger man, wrestling him back to the bed and pinning him there under his body.

"Why are you angry?"

"I was not clothed! How could you make me face her and give my apology when I was not properly prepared? When I was not decent? After we just... it was humiliating!" Stephen said, staring up at him angrily.

William sighed and let go of Stephen's arms to cup his face gently, remembering the words his lover had shouted the night before: *You shame and humble those around you for your own amusement!* Perhaps there was some truth to them after all.

"Forgive me. I should have allowed you to do it in your own time. I *am* sorry. I simply wanted to get the unpleasant business over and done so that we could enjoy the day together. Maud does not care if you are properly dressed or not, I assure you."

"I *do* care," Stephen grumbled, not quite ready to let go of his pique.

William stroked his fingers down Stephen's cheek and looked deeply into his eyes, giving Stephen his most contrite face. "Forgive me?"

Stephen's lip quirked despite his efforts to the contrary, and William's smile turned into a grin. "You forgive me," he said with surety.

"Perhaps," Stephen replied.

William leaned in for another kiss and only pulled away again when Maud knocked and brought in the books he had requested. He thanked her and set them on the bed as the good woman collected their soiled clothing from the floor and left the room. He then played proper host and poured coffee for both of them. They sipped in silence for a time; then William pulled the books out and showed them to Stephen.

"What shall we read today? You choose."

Stephen gave him another puzzled look. "You truly intend to spend the entire day abed?"

"Certainly. Have you never done it? Not even once?"

"Certainly not. Not unless I was ill, and I am rarely ever ill."

"Not with Graves?"

Stephen flinched then, and his lips twisted. "I do not wish to speak of Graves. But to answer your question, no."

"Farmers are very industrious and hardy folk, I believe, not indolent and prone to vapors, as we are here in town," William said flippantly. He was fishing now, but he could not seem to stop himself. Surely the man would not feel the need to hide every little detail about himself.

Stephen gave him a startled and wary look but did not comment, and William had to struggle to hide his disappointment. It seemed he would have to wait a little longer before Stephen would feel comfortable confiding in him.

"Well then," he continued, as if Stephen's reaction were of no consequence, "we simply must continue on with your education in the fine art of sloth so that you may develop a finer appreciation for it."

At Stephen's snort, William simply smiled and nudged the small stack of books closer. "Choose."

"Will you at least allow me to wash and find another shirt?" Stephen asked, drawing the offending garment away from himself with a disgusted grimace, and William remembered what they had been doing before Maud had interrupted them. He grinned and leaned in for another kiss while he helped Stephen remove the sticky article.

"Certainly," he said as he again climbed out of bed and rummaged through his wardrobe for another shirt. He rinsed the damp flannel from the night before in the cold water of the bathing tub and threw it to Stephen. "It is very cold," he warned.

Stephen caught the cloth but simply held it in his hand, staring at William and blushing a little.

"Would you like me to do it? As I did last night?" William asked.

Stephen blushed harder and shook his head. As he drew the counterpane up to his chin and appeared to wash himself beneath its concealment, William became quite puzzled by his sudden shyness.

"Why so modest? We have just spent the last two days getting to know one another very well. I hardly think you need be shy now."

"It is different in the daylight. I am not used to being so cavalier about such things. Forgive me if I do not share your feelings in these matters." Stephen's tone had sharpened a little toward the end, and William could tell he had offended the man's sensibilities.

*Slow down. You have only just gotten your hedgehog to lower his spines. Do not throw away the ground you have gained.*

In an effort to lighten the mood again, William chuckled and bounded back into bed, shoving his cold bare feet under Stephen's arse, startling another yelp out of him. "There is nothing to forgive, my sweet. I find it quite endearing, actually." Stephen gave him another wounded look, but could not hold it as he, too, burst into laughter.

"You are incorrigible."

William grinned, kissed Stephen tenderly on the lips, and smoothed his hands through the younger man's hair. "Yes, I am."

Stephen searched his eyes for a time, seeming as if he wanted to say more, but William was disappointed again when the younger man simply looked away and gathered the books into his lap. William propped himself back on his elbow and watched Stephen's face as he perused the titles. The tenth book of Milton's *Paradise Lost* was given a nod, as was Daniel Defoe's *Captain Singleton*, but Stephen's face flushed scarlet at the tattered little copy of *Fanny Hill*, the pretty little translation of *Heriodes*, and the newer volume titled *Don Juan* from Lord Byron.

Under William's amused gaze, Stephen lifted *Paradise Lost* and held it in his hand for a time, then set it down again and picked up Lord Byron's scandalous work and met William's eyes with a rueful smile.

"Excellent choice." William took the book from him and plumped his pillows before settling back on them and lifting his arm in open invitation for Stephen to cuddle against him. Stephen hesitated for a moment before moving into his embrace, settling his head against William's shoulder as William began to read aloud.

They passed several hours in that manner, with the rhythmic patter of the rain on the roof and the occasional clatter of a cart in the street below the only reminders that a world existed outside of *Don Juan* and their comfortable little nest. William would have liked to keep them there, just as they were, forever, but his throat eventually became dry and his voice hoarse from reading for so long. When he stopped and put the book aside to have a drink of his cold coffee, Stephen drew away from him and sat up in the bed facing him, a grave and mournful look upon his face.

"Is something wrong?"

Stephen seemed to be struggling with something, but William had no idea what it could be. They had already made their apologies and forgiven one another, and nothing else had changed since the morning, at least not that William was aware of. He waited in silence, completely at a loss, while Stephen seemed to gather his thoughts—or his courage.

"I never believed it could be like this... between two men," he whispered, meeting William's eyes again and seeming just as confused as William felt.

"I do not understand. Be like what exactly?"

Stephen took another deep breath, obviously struggling to find the words. "That... that men could be tender and gentle with one another without one of them having to play the woman. I have seen and heard of many men who have formed lasting bonds, where they treated one another with respect and caring as *friends*... but as *lovers*? I...." Stephen stopped and shook his head.

William longed to gather Stephen back into his arms, to offer what comfort he could, but his instincts told him to wait, to let the man work through whatever conflicts he was experiencing. William did not truly understand what Stephen meant or what had him so upset. One should *always* treat a lover with tenderness unless one's lover asked one to do otherwise. Man or woman, it should not matter.

Trying to make some sense of Stephen's turmoil, he said, "We all need caring and tenderness sometimes. That does not make us womanish, Stephen, merely human. 'Tis not only a woman's province to show tenderness among friends *and* lovers."

"You cannot possibly understand. This all seems so simple for you. You desire both women and men. You are the ram, not the ewe. But *I*, I have never desired a woman in that way, *never*. I cannot even perform with a woman as a man should. I have only ever desired men... desired for them to... to be inside of me, to...." At that, he flushed scarlet and dropped his eyes to his lap. "How can I want such things and *not* be womanish? How can I expect my lover to treat me as an equal, or at least as a *man*? In school we were just boys playing about, we did not... but after, with Graves...."

Stephen shook his head, and his mouth twisted bitterly. "I have been to the molly houses. I have seen the boys there dressed in women's clothes and painted faces. I have been to the private parties, the *orgies*. It is all so tawdry and sordid. I never wanted any of that, but what I *do* want...." Stephen buried his face in his hands, and William felt his heart twist. This subject was obviously one that had been tormenting him for a long time.

"Is that what Graves told you? That loving could not be tender or respectful without you playing the woman? That men could not be men and still treat each other with tenderness and physical affection?" Was this what had inspired Stephen's roughness their first night together? William clamped down on his anger. It would do neither of them any good right now.

"Stephen, look at me. Please, look at me." William waited until Stephen met his gaze. There were no tears, but the anguish was visible just the same in the clenching of his jaw and the angry cast to his eyes.

"You *are* a man, and a good one, from what I have seen. There is nothing womanish about you, nor would I wish you to be so. You take pleasure in another man's body because it feels good—more than good.

It certainly does not make you less a man or less worthy of respect. There are many women I have known who would not consider some of what we have done together to be within their realm at all." He could not help but chuckle a little as he said that, thinking that some of his lady companions would have been scandalized had he suggested such a thing—though not *all*, most assuredly not all. He sobered again and leaned forward earnestly. "You are correct that I do not know what it is like to desire only men. I have experienced both, and I can tell you, for a certainty, that bedding a man and bedding a woman are not at all the same, though I think both should always be treated with kindness and respect. I hope you do not feel that I have treated you like a woman or that I have demeaned you."

William hoped he was saying the right things. He had little experience with such fears and insecurities. By the time he had realized his own feelings for other men, he had already separated himself from the rest of polite society by indulging in nearly every other sin proscribed in the Bible. One more had made little difference at that point. He knew who he was, and he was the same man with female bed partners as he was with men. He had many flaws, but he always tried to treat his lovers well.

"You have not," Stephen answered, easing his fears. "I did not mean you. I…. Last night and today have been wonderful. I never believed that it could be so comfortable, so natural. I am sorry. I should not burden you with such things." Stephen shook his head again, and William *did* gather him into his arms then. He pulled the younger man close and buried his face in the soft, fragrant waves of Stephen's hair.

"I *do* understand what it is like to want something that the world tells you you should not," William whispered against the top of Stephen's head. "I do know that much. And, if you have not realized it yet, I *do* wish for you to burden me with such things. I do wish to know you, to know *of* you, to hear your thoughts and desires. If you would only share them with me."

Stephen sighed, the moist heat of his breath caressing William's neck through the open collar of his shirt. "I would like that very much.

But I cannot. I have a duty to more than myself. I have a family to protect and provide for."

"You're married?" William felt a sudden twist in his gut and drew back to search Stephen's face.

"No. Nothing like that," Stephen was quick to reassure him, placing a hand to William's cheek and shaking his head emphatically. "I did not lie. I told you I cannot perform with a woman. I would not subject a woman to that kind of lie. I speak only of my mother and my sister, but... I cannot say more. Please, please don't ask."

William sighed in relief and frustration. Patience was truly not in his nature, and he was quite proud of himself for showing a remarkable amount of it in the last two days—at least remarkable for *him*—but it was wearing thin. "Surely you have heard at least some of the tales about me, Stephen. I would hardly be one to cast stones. Whatever your secrets are, whatever you may have done, they can hardly compare with what you have heard of me."

"It isn't that. You have born witness to the worst that I have ever done. I simply cannot afford to have certain things revealed to my family. What is between Graves and I... there is a history there I cannot speak of and debts that I must repay. That is all I can say. Please do not ruin what time we have left by asking more of me, for I cannot give it."

William could tell by the set of his jaw that forcing the issue would only end in contention between them, so he bit his tongue and simply nodded. When Stephen merely continued to look at him dubiously, William gritted his teeth and said, "You have my word. I will not broach the subject further while you are under my roof."

Stephen raised his eyebrows a little at William's choice of words but nodded and smiled cautiously back at him. Rewarded with that smile, William allowed his frustration to melt away and pulled Stephen back into his arms, easing them both back onto the pillows.

William knew now, from what little Stephen *had* said, that his early assumptions as to Stephen's position with Graves were in error. He did not know what hold Graves had on the young man, but Stephen was obviously not with the man because he wanted to be spoiled and taken care of. William would simply have to continue to be patient and hope his virtue was rewarded.

"Shall we continue with our reading, then, or would you like for me to ring for tea and sandwiches?" William asked as he cuddled Stephen in his arms and let his questions rest for the present.

Mirroring William's light tone, Stephen replied, "Sandwiches would be lovely, thank you. And as I know your voice could use a rest, I will read for a while, if you like."

"That would be lovely," William replied, "but I believe I have something I must take care of first."

At Stephen's adorably puzzled look, William grinned and dove beneath the covers, pushing himself between Stephen's legs and taking his flaccid cock in his mouth in one quick movement.

Stephen let out a startled grunt that quickly turned into a moan as William applied suction to the rapidly filling flesh within his mouth. William luxuriated in the sensation of Stephen's cock filling with blood, the soft skin becoming rigid and taut above his tongue and pressing into his throat and cheeks. Stephen's hands found their way into his hair, stroking and petting in an aimless fashion, as if he had lost the ability to control and direct their course. William would have grinned at that, but his mouth was more agreeably engaged. Stephen may have denied him one avenue by which to win him, but that did not mean that there were not others he could explore. The more time he spent with the younger man, the more certain he became that he could not allow their acquaintance to end after only five days. For the first time in years, he felt alive and driven toward something other than the next conquest or the next empty diversion, and his instincts all screamed for him to cling to the source of that fire with every weapon in his arsenal.

He continued to lavish attention on Stephen's cock, sucking and teasing by turns and immersing himself in the sheer hedonistic pleasure to be had from swirling the silken flesh and salty flavors over his lips and tongue until Stephen cried out, "Stop!" and pulled hard on his hair.

Surprised, William pulled back enough to look at Stephen's face from beneath the counterpane and frowned in confusion.

"Please. I do not wish to spend until you are inside me again," he gasped, then blushed as he seemed to realize what he had said.

William grinned and slid up Stephen's body, taking his mouth and sharing the flavors of Stephen's pleasure with him. The younger man moaned in his mouth and deepened the kiss, sucking on William's tongue and causing William's cock to twitch and tighten painfully between their bellies.

"As you wish," he panted when they broke apart. William quickly drew his shirt over his head and reached for the jar of coconut oil on the night table on Stephen's side of the bed.

He dipped his fingers inside and gathered some of the hardened salve as Stephen lifted his knees to pull William into the cradle of his thighs. William quickly pressed the white cream to Stephen's opening, using the man's heat to melt the oil, and pushed it inside with first one, then two fingers. Stephen was already relaxed and welcoming. The ring of muscle opened so sweetly for him that William had to take a moment and close his eyes as the feeling of Stephen's channel eagerly grasping at his fingers nearly made him spend.

William wasted no more time. When he had mastered himself enough, he withdrew his fingers from Stephen's body and slicked them with more oil, gingerly coating his already leaking cock in the cold salve. The sudden chill of the oil, coupled with that of the air, helped a bit, and William took a moment to let the somewhat unpleasant sensation calm his ardor. It would not do to release the moment he entered his lover's body. A man had to maintain a little pride in his prowess.

Gritting his teeth at the pleasure, William pressed against Stephen's opening and felt his swollen member welcomed inside with all the affability his fingers had been. He moaned at the pleasure of it and Stephen echoed him, throwing his head back against the pillows and arching his back. As William slid slowly into Stephen's body, feeling the slick heat wrap tightly around him, he had to fight down a sudden savage need to plunder that sweet cavern, so that he could go slowly and make their pleasure last.

Stephen had other ideas, however, for no sooner did William bottom out than Stephen wrapped his legs around William's waist, grabbed William's hips, and started fucking himself on William's cock. Not to be outdone, William grabbed one of Stephen's shoulders in one hand and the nearest poster of the bed in the other and began pounding away at his young lover. The sounds of their bodies slapping together and their combined grunts and moans drowned out everything else until it felt to William as if they were the only two people in the world and nothing else existed beyond the boundaries of their bed.

Stephen let go of his hips then, braced one hand against the head of the bed, and grabbed his cock with the other, pumping it furiously. Four strokes were all that it took before he yelled and streams of his spend erupted from his cock, coating his chest and belly. His channel clamped down on William hard, forcing a shout of his own, and he grabbed Stephen's hips in a grip that was sure to leave marks and buried himself as deeply as he could, flooding his lover's body with his seed.

When the last tremors left his body, William collapsed onto his side next to Stephen, panting. At least this time he had not fallen *on* his lover.

When he got his breath back, he managed a weak laugh. "I had forgotten lesson number three: to maintain one's health when one lies abed all day, one must engage in frequent exercise."

Stephen choked out a laugh of his own between gasping breaths and rolled to face William, his face mere inches away. His eyes were sparkling and his cheeks flushed with vitality. No longer did he look so tortured and confused, which William happily counted as a victory—a small one, but a victory just the same.

William reached out and ran the backs of his fingers over Stephen's cheek. "You need never feel too ashamed to ask anything of me. I take great pleasure in giving pleasure, whatever forms it takes." William's grin turned wicked then as he leaned forward and nuzzled

Stephen's jaw, whispering, "And should you ever wish me to play ewe to your ram, you need only ask. It would be my pleasure to oblige you."

Stephen pulled back from him then, his eyes wide and his mouth dropping open. "Truly?"

"Certainly. I am a great supporter of pleasures of all kinds, as you have witnessed. Libertine that my reputation brands me, it should not surprise you." William sobered again, putting as much sincerity into his voice as he could muster. "I meant what I said. Accepting the pleasures your body provides does not make you any less a man. Though it *has* been a long time since I have enjoyed that particular pleasure, so you will have to be gentle with me." William grinned at that and kissed Stephen firmly on the lips.

"I...." Stephen swallowed visibly, suddenly looking very nervous. "I would like that, very much. Just, not yet."

"You need only ask." William gave Stephen another peck before rolling to the edge of the bed and retrieving another flannel. As he tossed it to his young lover, he said, "But for now, I shall ring for our tea while you select our next reading."

The rest of the afternoon passed in pleasant companionship. Stephen selected *Captain Singleton* for his reading, and they spent a few hours fighting their way through the wilds of Africa and engaging in pirate adventures on the high seas. Maud brought them tea and sandwiches, and they enjoyed them in contented silence. William held his tongue, mostly out of a desire to keep Stephen relaxed and happy.

Before long, the sun dipped below the horizon and the gray light turned to black. The shadows deepened in the room, and William was forced to light the lamps so Stephen could continue reading. Maud returned after a time to see to the fire and remove their chamber pot and soiled flannels. She returned a little while later with their dinner: a steaming tray of cottage pies that William would choose over the finest of French pastries and two tankards of ale rather than the traditional wine. When Stephen's eyes lit up at the sights and smells coming from the tray, William could not help but smile at the woman in deepest gratitude. Maud seemed to have taken a liking to the young man, now that he was behaving himself, and had rightly guessed that he might prefer more wholesome fare than what William had originally planned for them.

"Thank you, Maud. That smells wonderful," Stephen said before William had the chance. The young man's gratitude was written all over his smiling face.

Maud smiled back at Stephen and winked at William on her way out of the room. Stephen tucked into his food with enthusiasm after his silent prayer, and neither of them stopped to talk until their plates were empty and their bellies full. Though the hour was not late, William could see Stephen's eyes drooping once they had finished, so he set the tray and their tankards aside and settled himself down onto the bed, pulling Stephen against his side again.

"Lesson four." William had to stifle his own yawn before he could continue. "An exhausting day abed should always end with a well-earned rest."

Stephen snorted but did not disagree, and soon William heard his breath slow in slumber. William kissed the top of Stephen's head and closed his eyes, falling asleep with a smile on his face.

Chapter *Ten*

THE next day dawned insufferably bright, and William was most displeased to learn that Stephen rose with the sun and was just as revoltingly cheerful. While William grumbled and attempted to pull the bedding over his head to block out the morning light, Stephen threw back the counterpane and walked cheerfully from the room. He returned only moments later in his trousers, shirt, and waistcoat and announced loudly that he would go and fetch a kettle so they both might bathe and make themselves ready for the day.

At William's growl, Stephen chuckled and said, "Do not be such a bear. We spent all of yesterday in that bed. Surely you are rested enough to make better use of today?"

William pounced on Stephen then and dragged him back to the bed, straddling his hips and pinning his arms to the mattress. "In my opinion, we made excellent use of yesterday. Perhaps you need a little reminder?"

Before Stephen could form a response, William swooped in and claimed his mouth. Stephen's lips yielded almost immediately, and they spent several long minutes exploring each other's mouths. When William's hands dropped to the placket of Stephen's trousers, the younger man gripped his wrists and held him still.

"You are sin personified. Do you never think of anything else?" he panted.

William shrugged off the mild rebuke. Stephen was hard beneath his hands, giving lie to his disapproving tone. "The lad doth protest too much, methinks," he said with a chuckle, attempting to go back to what he was doing.

Stephen's grasp held firm, keeping him from his goal, so William decided to take another tack. "I will make a bargain with you. Give me what I want now, and the rest of the day is yours. We will do whatever you wish."

Stephen stared at him dubiously for a time. "I have your word?" When William nodded, Stephen sighed and said, "Agreed."

William grinned and set to opening Stephen's trousers again. When he had relieved Stephen of all of his clothes, he bid the younger man lie on his side, then grabbed his ankles and dragged him partway down the bed. Ignoring Stephen's confused grunt, William drew his shirt over his head and crawled beneath the linens, lying on his side with his head pointed toward Stephen's feet. They now lay at opposites, and William was most pleased to discover that Stephen was no longer confused when he felt the man take the cock that was now positioned within inches of his face in hand and set to work on it with those wonderfully full lips. William did the same with the now fully engorged rod in front of him, and they worked one another in concert for a time.

Despite his earlier protestations, Stephen seemed to warm quickly to the activity and allowed William to set a slow and sensual pace for both of them. They sucked and licked tenderly at one another, pausing from time to time to nuzzle beneath at the soft, lightly furred skin of their bollocks or along the join of hip and groin. It was tender and decadent, just the way William wanted to begin every morning.

When Stephen seemed to be mirroring his every move, William decided to see how far the younger man was willing to go. He grasped Stephen's cock in hand so it would not feel the loss of his mouth too keenly and moved to nuzzle behind his bollocks again, sliding his arm between Stephen's thighs and encouraging him to lift his leg. When Stephen obliged him, William lifted his own leg in invitation, then set to teasing the sensitive strip of skin just behind Stephen's sac with his tongue, nuzzling at it gently and delivering tender, sucking kisses. Stephen's body shivered beneath his ministrations and he groaned in pleasure, but he still attempted to reciprocate, and William was momentarily distracted as a bolt of sheer pleasure shot through his body.

Forcing himself to concentrate, William licked a line up to Stephen's opening and was quite gratified when, after only a moment's pause, Stephen did the same to him. He wet the tender skin there liberally, before sliding his tongue back down to Stephen's sac, replacing his tongue with his finger at Stephen's opening and pressing the single digit inside. Stephen moaned and lifted his leg further, fully opening himself to William's penetration while struggling to remain in control enough to reciprocate. William lifted his leg further, and it was not long before he felt Stephen's finger push cautiously inside. At William's rumbling groan of approval against Stephen's bollocks, the younger man let out a strangled giggle. Intrigued, William ignored for the moment the wonderful sensations of Stephen's exploration of his channel and hummed against his bollocks again. When the younger man jerked and giggled again, William grinned.

"Ticklish?"

Stephen stopped tonguing his bollocks and said, "Perhaps a little. But if you wish for me to continue with what I am doing, you will not take advantage of the fact."

"Another time then." William grinned, and Stephen's abused sigh turned into a moan of pleasure as William renewed his exploration within his channel and stroked over just the right spot with his finger. William decided to quit teasing and took Stephen's cock back into his mouth, sucking on it with purpose and working his fingers with precision within the slick heat of Stephen's body. Stephen took several shuddering breaths interrupted by moans of pleasure before he could master himself enough to give William the same treatment, and soon they were both lost to anything else in the world. Every bit of William's concentration was taken up with the gift and receipt of pleasure, but it was not long before neither one of them seemed to be able to keep a steady rhythm.

When Stephen's hips began to buck, William dropped his hand away from his lover's cock and concentrated only on creating a tight cavern of his mouth for the man to fuck and keeping his fingers within Stephen's channel at just the right angle for his lover to ride. Stephen did the same, and William took over his own pleasure, fucking Stephen's plush mouth in turn and grinding his arse against Stephen's fingers. Stephen fell from the precipice first, his body jerking and his seed erupting in William's mouth, but William followed close on his heels, swallowing Stephen's spend along with his own cries of release. He was only brought back to himself at the sound and feel of Stephen choking and sputtering around his depleted organ, and William drew back immediately, climbing up the bed to see what was the matter.

Stephen gave him an apologetic smile as he wiped William's spend from his chin. "Forgive me." He let out an embarrassed cough. "I fear I was a little too distracted to manage that properly."

William grinned and took Stephen's mouth in a deep kiss, sucking the remnants of himself from Stephen's tongue. "Nothing to forgive. You were marvelous. Practice is all that is required. Though I must say I quite enjoy making you lose control of your wits."

Stephen's amused frown said plainly that William's words were not particularly comforting, and William only grinned the wider at it. In retaliation, Stephen threw back the counterpane and hopped from the bed. William hissed as the cold air hit his sweat-dampened body, but Stephen simply ignored him and began dressing.

"Now I shall go and fetch some hot water," Stephen announced firmly as he picked William's shirt up from the floor and threw it at him.

"We could simply ring for Maud," William grumbled, his good humor somewhat diminished. "The only reason she has not come already is because I am rarely awake this early in the morning."

"No need," Stephen said cheerfully, obviously enjoying William's discomfort. "I will go and fetch it and tell her you are awake, and we shall eat breakfast in the dining room, like civilized men."

Those last words were thrown over his shoulder as Stephen left the room. William grumbled peevishly to himself as he pulled the counterpane up to his neck, snuggling beneath the linens for warmth. He could not keep a small grin from curling his lips, however, as the scents of their coupling filled his nostrils and a pleasant ache in his arse reminded him that he had at least gotten his way for a little while.

Stephen returned a short time later with a steaming kettle and a small ewer and poured some from both into the basin on William's washstand before heading for the door.

"I would make use of that while it is still warm if I were you," the imp called out cheerfully.

The sounds of his footsteps in the hall and the opening and closing of a door told William that Stephen had decided to wash and dress in his own bedchamber. William sighed a little in disappointment. He had hoped the process of washing and dressing could have been made a bit more enjoyable, were they to share it, and perhaps he could have convinced Stephen to delay their plans a little longer in the process. But it was not to be. With a resigned sigh, William climbed from the bed and made his way to the washstand before the water did indeed become cold.

He did not know what Stephen had in mind for the day, so he dressed simply in a blue-gray wool coat and a dark blue damask waistcoat and gray trousers—nothing too extravagant. Despite the chill in the air, he had decided his hair needed a wash to fix the tangle it had become from his exertions. Seeing himself in the glass for the first time in nearly a day, he had noticed that some of the dark waves were jutting out from his head in a most alarming fashion, giving the slightest impression of horns on his head, and he could only imagine what he must have looked like to Stephen's eyes this morning.

William grinned at his reflection and set to work with his comb so he might at least *look* respectable. If showing a little proper reserve would get him what he wanted—that being *Stephen*, happy and content—then that was what he would do. His grin faltered a little as he remembered that he had only two more days to win the young man's trust and affection enough that he might convince him to prolong their

Stephen's expression softened, and the happy smile that caused William's chest to tighten appeared on his face. "Thank you, that would be wonderful."

"Excellent. Finish your breakfast, and I will go see to the arrangements."

Stephen must have been too pleased with William's plan to note the oddity of him going to seek out his servants instead of ringing for them to come to him, for he merely nodded happily and tucked into his food while William rose to find Stubbs.

William found his man in the kitchen with Maud and pulled him into the hall.

In low tones, so Maud would not overhear, William said, "Young Mr. Smith and I are going on a country ride this afternoon. I want you to watch the streets when we leave and see if anyone follows." At Stubbs's quirked eyebrow, William explained, "Perhaps I am being overly cautious, but I am not convinced my band of thieves from the other night did not follow me all the way from this house, and I would like to put that to the test. We will be going north to Islington and Wilcox's stables to collect Asmodeus. We will take a small circuit of the fields, and then follow the New River further north. We should stop to picnic on the river, somewhere near Newington Green, I think. Follow us when you can and keep your eyes open. If I am mistaken, then we will be left to enjoy our afternoon in peace. If not...." William shrugged. He would leave the rest to Stubbs's good judgment. "I will leave it to you to decide what you say to your wife, but please ask her to pack something for our repast. Something small that I can put in Asmodeus's saddle."

"Aye, sir. Ye think Graves has it in for ye?"

William smiled at the sharp gleam in Stubbs's eyes. It had been many years since they had participated in any kind of intrigue, and it seemed his old friend was looking forward to a little adventure. He chuckled and said, "I would rather err on the side of caution than be caught unawares again. Do not engage. If we are followed, simply note how many and their faces if you can. You may follow them back if you wish, but do not put yourself in danger. We can always contact your friends and Maud's in the stews to see if they can enlighten us further. Tomorrow is her day to visit, is it not?"

"Aye, 'tis. She 'as two young missus up t'stick that she's a'lookin' after. Time's a'comin soon fer both, and then there'll be two more poor childer in the world wot has no home."

William shook his head. No matter how many young women Maud tried to help find a better life, there were always dozens more in need. She and Stubbs had never had children of their own, so the young girls who got with child while plying their trade were particularly dear to the good woman's heart.

"Take the house money with you tomorrow, all of it. Give it to the girls and the children and see if anyone has come forward on your inquiries about Graves and Bradshaw. Talk to them about the other night. A band of four such as those who attacked us cannot have gone unseen by the girls, particularly so near St. Giles."

"Aye," Stubbs nodded, and William had to grin.

"Just like old times, eh?"

"Sure hoop not."

William grinned wider at his man's grumbled response, then turned down the hall to rejoin Stephen at breakfast. He ate a few pieces of toast and had another cup of coffee before Maud appeared with a covered basket—a very *large* covered basket.

"Maud, you should not have gone to such trouble," William said, wondering where on earth he was going to put all of that during their ride.

"'Tis no trouble, sir," she said as she set the basket down near the door. "I jus' want to thank ye, sir, for yer generous gift. Stubbs told me of the 'ouse money, sir, an' I'm sure the girls'll be mos' grateful."

"You are welcome, Maud. I shall endeavor to follow your example and do more with all that I have been given from this day forth. It has been selfish of me not to." He smiled kindly at the woman as she collected some of their empty dishes and left the room with a bobbed curtsy and a watery smile.

"The house money?" Stephen asked.

"Merely a trifle." William waved a dismissive hand. "Maud and her husband do what they can for those in need of charity. Over the years, they have seen many young women and children on to better lives than they might have had otherwise. I should have done more before now, but... perhaps I simply needed someone to show me the error of my wicked ways."

Stephen turned to look where Maud had gone with a contemplative frown on his face, not answering William's subtle suggestion and the not-so-subtle waggle of his eyebrows.

"Come. If you have had your fill, we can be on our way."

Stephen smiled and nodded. They both stood and William rang for Stubbs. Anticipating their needs, the man came carrying their coats, hats, and gloves. William opted to leave his cane behind so he would not be burdened with it during their ride, and simply took a moment to slide his knife into the sheath in his boot, out of sight of Stephen. They finished getting ready, and William lifted the basket, nodding to Stubbs as he let them out into the street.

He did not see anyone taking particular notice of the two of them as they made their way to the coach stand, but he would trust Stubbs to worry about that and simply concentrate his efforts of making the day as enjoyable as possible for Stephen and himself. The jarvey made good time, and they were at the quiet country yard where he stabled Asmodeus in under an hour. Heading away from town was always quicker than trying to get through it.

William had chosen this stable for his stallion because the stable master, Wilcox, had come highly recommended. Many gentlemen of William's acquaintance paid handsomely for the care and attention Wilcox lavished on their mounts, and the man seemed to have an uncanny way with the beasts. Even brutish, ill-tempered Asmodeus became gentle and docile as a lamb under the man's skillful hands, which had convinced William from the first that the man was well worth the investment.

As expected, Wilcox had a horse for Stephen, a sweet brown mare that Asmodeus seemed to take little interest in, and they were mounted and on their way in no time at all, their saddlebags stuffed to brimming with Maud's gratitude. William led them on the path he had discussed with Stubbs, a winding trek about the fields. The sun shone brightly, but the air was quite brisk, and their noses and cheeks were red after only a few minutes in the open.

As the cultivated gardens, cottages, and factories of Islington gave way to gold-and-brown fields, William urged them from their leisurely canter into a gallop. Asmodeus seemed to sense that they were not there to race, but that did not mean the beast did not wish to stretch his legs a little, and William had no wish to deny him. Nor would he deny himself the pleasure of Stephen's shining eyes and happy smile as the young man rose high in his saddle, urging his mount to keep pace. Watching his young lover move with the animal beneath him, William was forced to admit that Stephen had quite a good seat, actually—in more ways than one. That irreverent thought brought fond memories of the last two nights to the fore, and William could not help but wonder if the young man would not be a bit sore after all his *seat* had been put through.

William slowed as they approached the river, and Stephen steered his mount to walk abreast, eyeing William's guilty grin warily.

"Why the cat's grin, Mr. Carey?" he asked, still a little breathless from their ride.

"You may continue to use my given name now. We do not have to revert quite so far into formality. Particularly as we are quite alone here," William offered, and Stephen gave him a sheepish smile and nodded his agreement. "As for your question, 'twas nothing but a queer fancy that passed and is gone now."

Stephen did not look as if he believed William, but he shrugged and let his happy smile return regardless. "Where shall we go now?"

"I thought we might follow the river for a space, then find ourselves a pleasant spot to rest and eat?"

"Excellent," Stephen said merrily, and he set his horse to follow the track down to the riverbank. Being man-made, the New River lacked some of the character of its more natural brethren, but trees and shrubs still dotted its banks, and reeds sprang forth in happy abandon from the shallows. There were even a few waterfowl and other small creatures that could be seen in the distance, making quite the bucolic backdrop for their excursion.

They traveled in silence from then on, soaking in the sounds of the river, the soft clump of their horses' hooves on the muddy riverbank their only addition to the scene, and William watched Stephen's face as he took in the world around him. The young man seemed much more at peace out there than he did in town, and William basked in the knowledge that he had finally chosen well. Stephen was the one to finally break the silence when he turned to William and pointed toward a small copse of trees.

"What do you think?"

William smiled and nodded, and they both steered their mounts toward it. They tethered their horses to two small willows and set about preparing for their picnic. William threw down the blanket Maud had included in their basket and set to emptying Asmodeus's saddlebags. Stephen did the same, and soon they were settled comfortably on the blanket, tucking into the food Maud had prepared for them.

The woman had outdone herself yet again. This time she had made them pasties, or hobbin, as Stubbs and his men had always called them. Stubbs had taught her how to make them properly not long after they were married, so he would have a little taste of home from time to time, and the woman had perfected them in the decade that the two of them had been together. The pasties were so well-wrapped that they were even still warm, and as the onion and beef filled his mouth, William could not help but moan a little in pleasure. Judging by the speed with which Stephen finished his second and third, the younger man shared his delight, and soon enough, their bellies were full to bursting. Though the air was quite cool, William found himself relaxing in sleepy contentment. Basking in the sunlight, he leaned back against the tree they had picnicked under and closed his eyes.

The happiness Stephen had displayed on their ride was even more pronounced now that they sat quietly together in such an idyllic setting, and William began to consider that a move to the country would not be such a bad thing. Though he had not left London for more than a day or two in several years, it might just be time for a change. Suddenly he realized where his thoughts were going, and he had to chide himself. He was making plans for his and Stephen's life together as if it were a real possibility. He had known the young man for less than a week, and here he was picking out furniture and bed linens for their country home. He shook his head at his own romantic folly and opened his eyes again.

*Best not to put the cart before the horse.*

"What are you thinking?" Stephen asked, noting William's rueful smile.

"Merely that you seem so much more comfortable here."

"I suppose I am. I am not overly fond of London." Stephen's full lips twisted a little.

"What do you dream of for your life?" William found himself asking. Stephen seemed in such high spirits; perhaps he might let his guard down a little.

Stephen eyed him warily. "You promised you would not ask me such things."

*No. I promised I would not speak of it as long as you remained under my roof.* But William decided not to quibble. "I do not ask after your family or your home, only what dreams you have for your life. Surely my hearing such could not endanger your family."

Stephen seemed to consider his words carefully for a moment, then relaxed back against the tree and sighed. "I believe you might find my ambitions rather dull. As you may have guessed from my regrettable outburst the other night, I am a farmer, or I *was*. I am the son of a farmer, the grandson of a farmer, and so on. It is in my blood, and it is my passion. It is what I have always wanted. To manage the lands and the beasts my father managed. To spend my days on the sloping hills, to breathe the fresh air and watch the fog rolling into the

138

valleys like an ocean of clouds." Stephen had a faraway look in his eyes for a moment but quickly shook his head and blushed at himself.

"And what would you farm on those sloping hills and valleys?"

"Sheep," Stephen said somewhat defensively, as if expecting William to poke fun at him.

"Admirable profession," William replied, and Stephen gave him a sharp look as if to gauge whether he was being laughed at or not.

He seemed content with whatever he read on William's face, for he smiled in gratitude and asked, "And you, William? What do you dream of?"

*Someone to share my life with, someone to give me purpose.*

He did not say it aloud. Stephen was not ready to hear it, and William was not sure he was ready to say it, though he could feel that Stephen was fast becoming that someone. With every passing moment, the feeling of rightness grew stronger within him. Perhaps it would change or fade away in time, but he did not think so. He knew this feeling. He had known it only once before in his life, and as it cut its way through the fog of his gray and aimless existence, he knew he would not willingly let it go again.

Could he make this work? Would Stephen even let him? He knew he had damned well better be sure before he committed himself to that path. A life with another man would not be an easy one, even if Stephen were free and willing.

"I dream of days like this. Of good companions, good food and wine, and engaging conversation," he said instead, adopting a flippant tone he hoped would mask what was raging inside him.

Stephen gave him a sad and somewhat disapproving look that made William chuckle. "You do not approve of my answer, then?"

"I should think you capable of so much more," Stephen said, then shook his head and looked away. "But it is truly none of my business what you do with your life. It is not my place to say."

"It could be," William said very quietly, but Stephen heard him, if the confused and pained look he threw at William was any indication.

Before either of them could say anything more that might mar their lovely afternoon, William stood, brushed himself off, and bent to gather up the remains of their meal.

"Come. The sun has passed its zenith, and I believe I feel a sudden chill. We should perhaps make our way back."

Stephen looked up at him from his place on the ground, searching his face intently, but he simply shook his head and climbed to his feet. William waited while Stephen gathered up the blanket and shook it out, and they walked back to the horses together. While Stephen folded the blanket and packed it in his saddle, William fished out two apples for their mounts. After slicing them into wedges, he fed the first to Asmodeus, taking care that his fingers were left intact, and then walked to where Stephen was fastening the buckles on his saddlebag, offering the rest to him. When the younger man reached out for them, however, William drew back with a grin and shook his head, lifting one slice and running it over Stephen's full lips. Stephen's eyes widened a bit, and he looked about nervously. William merely grinned wider and stepped closer to the younger man, blocking his escape. He leaned in then and let his tongue follow the path the apple had taken. Stephen gasped in outrage, and William took advantage and deepened the kiss, plunging his tongue deep, before pulling back to suck on Stephen's lips again.

"Thank you for a marvelous afternoon," he whispered against his lover's lips before handing over the rest of the apple and turning to make his way back to his mount.

William knew he probably should not have done it, but he had not touched or kissed Stephen in hours, and despite the turn of their conversation, he was still giddy with delight at their day together. He had not been able to resist tasting the young man at least enough to tide him over until they were home. He *had* taken care to make sure they were alone and well shielded in their little copse, but he could tell Stephen was not happy with him. His lover urged his mare ahead of Asmodeus on the path and back the way they had come without a backward glance.

Asmodeus did not particularly like being left behind by the other horse, however, and was soon fighting William's attempts to hold him back. When he did let the beast pull abreast of Stephen's mare, his young lover's face was stony with disapproval, and William smiled apologetically. Perhaps it was the country air, or perhaps William still possessed as much charm as the gossips credited him with, for Stephen eventually threw him an indulgent smile and then burst into laughter.

"I believe you and your mount have a great deal in common, Mr. Carey. Perhaps your father should have given *you* that name so the world would have been forewarned." Stephen's smile had turned just a little wicked, and William was sorely tempted to drag the man into the underbrush and give him something to smile about.

Telling himself to behave, at least until they could be assured some privacy, William gasped in mock outrage and said, "You wound me, sir."

Stephen laughed aloud again and urged his mount into a canter and then into a run, throwing a challenging look over his shoulder, daring William to catch him up. Asmodeus was more than up for the challenge, but William found the view much more pleasant from where he was. He kept back as long as he could, but Asmodeus would have his way, and soon they were racing across the fields back toward Islington and home.

# Chapter *Eleven*

ASMODEUS won their little race. Of course he did. The big brute would rather break his wind or a leg than let a little filly like that best him. But Stephen's smiling lips and laughing eyes told William that his young lover did not mind the defeat overly much. The thrill of the ride was enough to leave the young man flushed and happy all the way back to the carriage, at which point William could no longer resist temptation. They had barely left Islington when William drew the curtains and, with a distinctly predatory smile, joined Stephen on his side of the compartment.

"Will? What are you—?"

Stephen did not get the chance to finish, for William grabbed his face in a firm grip and crushed their mouths together. Stephen resisted at first, but William was determined, and soon the younger man gave in and opened for him, returning his kiss with equal fervor. William pressed his advantage and bore his lover back against the padded bench. He made quick work of the placket of Stephen's trousers, opening the buttons by feel without breaking from their kiss, sliding his hand inside and wrapping it tightly around the younger man's stiff cock. Stephen moaned into his mouth, and William pulled away, giving his lover a wicked grin before diving down to swallow his erection.

"Ungh! God, Will!" was all Stephen could manage before William set to bobbing on his shaft and fondling his damp bollocks beneath. If Stephen had intended another protest, it went unsaid as the young man bit off a curse and curled over William's back, trembling and moaning through closed lips and scrabbling for purchase on William's back.

William took no time to savor the scents and flavors of his lover this time. He wanted all of Stephen, and he wanted it now. He worked his lover's swollen prick over and over, seeking to bring him the most pleasure as quickly as he could, desperate for Stephen's surrender. It was not long before Stephen's hips were thrusting in counterpoint to William's rhythm and his hand was gripping William's hair. A moment more and William felt Stephen's bollocks draw up tight in his palm and his cock swell as the jets of his spend coated William's throat. Stephen's hand left his hair as his body arched beneath William and he stifled his cry in his fist. William grinned and pulled back to admire his work, as a thoroughly debauched and disheveled Stephen stared back at him with glazed eyes.

"You should not have done that." Stephen's breathy rebuke lost some of its power when the young man drew his palm down William's cheek to cup his jaw and leaned in for a tender kiss.

"You will forgive me just this once," William said with a smile as they broke apart, pulling out his handkerchief to wipe his face, and then tucking it away in a pocket of his greatcoat.

Stephen gave him an embarrassed smile and a shake of his head as he quickly tucked himself back into his trousers and buttoned the placket.

"I do not understand why you gentlemen of privilege seem to feel such a need to tempt fate by flirting with discovery like this."

William did flinch a little at that rebuke, for he felt certain his behavior was being compared to Graves's, and he did not like it, not in the least.

"I did not do that to tempt discovery, Stephen," he replied rather sharply. "I was simply overcome with my passion for you. I am fully aware that I have little time left. I wished to make the most of every moment. That was all."

Stephen looked up at his sharp tone, and then looked away. Even the dim light of the carriage William could see the younger man's jaw clench. William waited for a sharp retort, but was surprised when Stephen simply let out a long breath and his jaw relaxed again. "Forgive me. I did not mean to insult you. I should not have said it."

What little flash of temper William had had vanished with Stephen's words, and he could not help the fond smile that crossed his lips. Perhaps his little hedgehog had lost some of his spines after all.

William ran his finger along Stephen's jaw and curled it under his chin, nudging it upwards so that he could see the young man's eyes. He smiled into those golden pools, luminous even in the dim light, and said, "All is forgiven, for both of us."

He leaned in for another kiss, just a brief, gentle meeting of lips, and rested his forehead against his lover's. William was still uncomfortably erect within his trousers, but his own needs could wait a little while longer, at least until they were safely home. He did not want to push his luck too far.

When they returned to Cecil Court, Stubbs opened the door and helped them off with their things. Stephen immediately headed for the stairs to get bathed and changed for dinner, and William waited only long enough to tell Stubbs that he would be down directly to hear his report, before climbing the stairs, two at a time, behind his lover. Stubbs would understand his urgency. Judging from the grin and raised eyebrow the man had given him after a brief look down at his trousers, his servant knew what a state he was in. William *did* want to hear what Stubbs had to say, but he had more urgent matters to attend to first.

Stephen stopped in the hall and cast a curious glance over his shoulder as William rushed to join him. William wasted no time in explanation; he simply grabbed Stephen's wrist and dragged him into his bedchamber, pulling the startled man into his arms for a passionate kiss. He ground his erection into Stephen's thigh to make sure the young man had no doubts as to his need, and Stephen answered by sliding his hand between them and fondling him through his trousers. After only a few glorious strokes, however, Stephen stepped back again and began shoving William back toward the bed. William went

144

willingly, backing up until his thighs connected with the mattress. Stephen quickly stripped off William's coat, waistcoat, and falls before yanking his trousers down to his knees and giving him another hard shove that dropped his bare arse to the bed.

Stephen dropped to his knees then and took William's aching prick into his mouth, lavishing attention on his crown while his hands gripped his shaft and cupped his bollocks. Once again William was treated to the wonderfully queer contrast of Stephen's soft lips and rough palms on his sensitive flesh, and he groaned his appreciation and relief. Stephen did not appear to need more prompting, so William simply leaned back on his elbows and surrendered to the younger man's skillful ministrations. This was the third time William had been treated to the pleasures of Stephen's mouth, but this time there was no anger or guilt, nor was he distracted with giving pleasure. He was being tenderly and skillfully taken care of by the man who was quickly becoming the center of his world, and it was heavenly.

William spread his legs as far apart as he could when he felt Stephen's hand move from fondling his bollocks to stroking the tender patch of skin behind. When Stephen drew his mouth off of William's cock only long enough to wet his fingers, William groaned in anticipation and tipped his hips, giving the young man as much room as he could and silently cursing the fact that his trousers were tangled around his thighs, preventing him from spreading them wider.

The feel of those wet fingers teasing about his opening as Stephen's mouth slid back down his prick set a fire at the base of William's spine that coiled in his belly and begged for release. Stephen must have sensed his need, for he set to with a vengeance, hollowing his cheeks and drawing upon William's flesh with a near-strangling tightness, working his fingers within William's body faster and faster. When Stephen's other hand dropped from the base of his cock, William looked down through passion-glazed eyes and saw Stephen's arm working furiously out of sight. When he realized that Stephen was working his own shaft desperately in response to what he was doing to William, that was all it took to send him over the edge. He felt his bollocks draw up and the fire in his belly erupt from his cock as a shout issued from his lips and stars danced before his eyes. Stephen drew off him then and buried his face in William's inner thigh, stiffening and letting out his own shout of completion before resting his heated cheek on William's leg.

Much too soon for William's liking, Stephen rose, wiped his face, smiled tenderly down at William's prone form, and buttoned his trousers. "Time to bathe and dress for dinner, I think."

When William only frowned at him, Stephen laughed. "You said we would do as I wished today. The day is not over yet. I would dearly love a clean set of clothes and some tea to finish warming me up after our wonderful, but *chilly*, excursion."

"I have a much better idea for warming you," William growled as he came up off the bed and advanced on Stephen. The younger man merely chuckled and danced away from him.

"You gave me your word, remember?" His eyes sparkled merrily as he held his palm out to stop William's pursuit. "A little tea and a pleasant sit by the fire while we wait for dinner, that is what I want."

At William's sour expression, Stephen dropped his hand and stepped into his arms. Looking up into William's eyes, he whispered, "We have all night to keep each other warm as you suggest. Will it not be worth a little wait?"

William smiled in surrender. Stephen was obviously enjoying their bargain, and truthfully, William had little to complain of, particularly after the pleasuring he had just received. "I suppose I can wait a little while longer."

"Good. Then I shall meet you in your study shortly," Stephen said firmly as he made his way out of the room.

William did not envy Stephen his choice of places to bathe and change. Maud was unlikely to have set a fire in his room. His young lover would need that warm sit in front of the fire by the time he bathed and changed in the icy air. William considered calling after him to tell him to wait until he could ring for warm water, but changed his mind. Stephen was a grown man. He could see to his own care.

He did, however, ring the bell himself, and when Stubbs answered the summons, he set to questioning the man quietly regarding his commission from earlier that day. Stubbs's report was brief but worrying: William and Stephen *had* been followed to the coach stand by two scruffy-looking men in soiled workman's clothes. Stubbs did not recognize either man as local to the borough, but with the number of people in the city growing exponentially every year, that should not have been surprising. Stubbs had kept himself hidden and followed the two men as they tried to keep pace with the carriage William had hired. The men were able to keep up within the crowded confines of the city, but as soon as the carriage hit the open road, they were forced to give up and turn back. Stubbs had then followed them back to St. Giles, but thought better of going any further. He and Maud were well known and beloved within certain circles in the rookeries, but no one was ever completely safe in those dark alleyways, and Stubbs had begun to feel his age by the time he neared home.

William praised him for his efforts and his decision to take the prudent path, then sent him off to rest up for the night. He had originally planned to send the man for hot water so that he might wash, but decided his man had done enough work for one day and washed in the chill water of his ewer instead. He bathed and dressed as quickly as he could but was still chilled to the bone by the time he had finished and hurriedly made his way to the study. Maud had put extra coals on the fire in preparation for him, and William basked in the warmth while he sat in the comfortably stuffed leather chair and considered all he had heard.

The men were not runners. That was fairly obvious. William supposed runners *could* have dressed in workman's clothes to disguise themselves, but it was unlikely that such men would have abandoned their pursuit without trying to hire horses or question the jarveys at the stand. From all he had heard and read of them, runners would not have given up so easily, so that left simply hired ruffians. Hired men meant it was a personal matter, not one for the magistrates, which was definitely a relief.

*But who hired them, and why?*

The most obvious answer would be Graves, of course, though William had not thought the man cared enough for *anyone*, apart from himself, to have paid men to guard their welfare. Of course there could be another, darker reason—perhaps blackmail, or some other scheme the blackguard was cooking up. William had relied on the fact that Graves could not blackmail him without implicating himself in the scandal from the first, and it seemed unlikely the man would take that risk, but perhaps he was wrong.

Could it be the man actually *did* care deeply for Stephen? Had he sent the rogues from the other night to take care of William so that Stephen could return to him all the sooner? Was Stephen even now plotting with Graves to swindle him or cause him harm?

William sat in his chair by the fire with these black thoughts running themselves around in his head until the clock on the mantel struck five, and he realized that Stephen had yet to join him. Something twisted in his stomach, and he was just about to rise and go searching for him when Stubbs opened the door to the study and Stephen walked through, carrying a tray with tea and biscuits. The dark turn of his thoughts must have affected him more than he had realized, for the surge of relief he felt at seeing Stephen's smiling face came as surprise. He was so happy to see Stephen was still there and had not run off that he did not even notice the incongruity of his lover playing the servant.

While William smiled in greeting to cover his chagrin, Stephen nodded and smiled at Stubbs as he passed the man. William was given another shock when his normally gruff servant smiled warmly back at his lover before closing the door and leaving the two of them alone. Stephen set the tray on a small table, sat in the second chair by the fire, and poured their tea while William simply sat and admired his young companion, all his doubts dispelled by the sweet, contented look on Stephen's face. His lover had changed his clothes, but had kept to day colors of green and brown, which better suited his coloring and made his eyes appear an even more brilliant shade of gold. The ride in the country had indeed done him good, for his cheeks still held a rosy hue, and his eyes were still lit from within.

"Thank you," William murmured as Stephen handed him his tea.

Stephen smiled warmly at him and picked up his own cup and saucer, relaxing back into his seat and extending his booted feet toward the fire. William decided that was an excellent idea and copied his companion's pose, letting all his earlier worries about plots and schemes melt away in the heat of the coals. Stubbs would continue his enquiries in the stews, and William would simply have to trust in Stephen and his servants.

William knew all too well that he only had a little more than a day left with Stephen, and he would not see it spoiled with worries and doubts, not for either of them. To Stephen he would say nothing of their being followed or the incident of the night before last. They would simply enjoy one another's company in the time they had left, and he would strive to keep his thoughts and feelings focused on how to convince the young man to extend their holiday.

His face must not have reflected his new resolve, for when he looked back up to Stephen, the younger man was studying him, concern written plain across his face. "Is there something troubling you?" Stephen asked when William met his gaze.

William forced a smile and replied, "No. I beg your pardon. I was merely lost in my thoughts for a moment, perhaps afraid of what my king of misrule has planned for the rest of his reign."

Stephen's face relaxed and his smile returned. "Nothing too strenuous, I assure you. Though I did notice a fiddle amongst your belongings yesterday. Do you play?"

"A little. I learned a few simple folk tunes when I lived in Cornwall. I have no great talent. I know only enough to amuse myself and friends who have a forgiving ear."

"Well then, as your king, I demand to be entertained." Stephen's smirk and loftily raised brows tempted William with thoughts of rebellion and delicious insurrection, but he decided to be good and keep his word.

Obediently, he stood and retrieved his fiddle case from the half-empty bookcase by the window, removed his fiddle, and took up position near the fire. He set bow to strings and checked to make sure it was still tuned properly. Then he bowed to his regal audience and asked, "Does his majesty have any requests?"

"I will leave it to the maestro's better judgment, I think," Stephen quipped with a negligent wave of his hand, obviously enjoying his role.

William bit back a snort and bowed again before beginning with "Searching for Lambs," in honor of his audience. Though he only played the tune without singing the words, Stephen appeared to know it, for his smile broadened and he laughed out loud moments after William had begun. William went on to play "The Grey Mare" and a few other comic songs until, over and above the enthusiastic foot-tapping of his "king," he heard a shuffling of feet in the hall. Aware now that his audience had increased by at least one, William switched his next choice to the "Cadgwith Anthem," a sweet little tune from Stubbs's home territory.

After only the first few notes of the refrain, William heard a snort from the other side of the door, and as Stephen turned toward the sound, William called out, "Come on, old man, do not hide in the hall. Our king of misrule has bid us entertain him, and your arrival, just at this moment, is most serendipitous. Will you oblige his majesty and sing for us?"

Stubbs opened the door, his usual scowl turned just a touch sheepish. The man's cheeks were too tanned and creased to ever show a blush, but William felt certain it was there just the same. Maud stood behind her husband in the hall, and though her cheeks were a little pink, her smile was merry. She was obviously pleased at the opportunity to hear her husband sing, rarity that it was.

William did not know if Stubbs agreed to sing out of guilt or because of the song, but when he began to play again, the older man's gravelly tenor joined him:

*"Cum fill up yer glasses an' let us be merry,*

*For t'rob an' t plunder it is our intent...."*

At the first words of the refrain, Stephen's eyes widened and his mouth fell open. He shot William a questioning look, but William merely smiled and continued to play. Stubbs was an excellent singer, and William was swept away on memories of long winter nights spent in taverns by the sea, in the company of rough but generous people who had as little love for the excise men as they had great love for one another. Little in the way of sea trade was possible during the winter months—the storms were too harsh to risk it—so he and his men were often idle during that long, dreary time and did what they could to make it pass more quickly.

It had been a long time since he had played with Stubbs, a long time since he had spent more than a few hours in the man's company. He had forgotten how close they had been in those long-ago days.

As he finished the last few notes of the song, William felt a small pang of remorse along with the pleasant warmth that had filled his chest with those memories. He had let too many important things fall by the wayside in the empty haze of the last several years. He should not have allowed it to happen, but he had.

In the brief silence that followed the song, William met Stubbs's eyes and gave the man a smile and a nod that he hoped conveyed some of what he was feeling. Stubbs quirked his lips in a half-smile of acknowledgement and turned to bow to his flushed and happy wife, who, along with Stephen, was clapping vigorously in praise of their performance.

William bowed to her and to his "king," then set his fiddle back in its case, flexing his fingers. It had been a long time since he had played at any length, and his fingers were beginning to cramp in protest. He was not even certain why he had chosen to have the instrument delivered along with his other belongings, but was glad now that he had. The smiling faces of Stephen and his friends were all the reward he could ask for, and in that moment, a sudden realization struck him: these three people, smiling and laughing together in that cramped and dingy little study, were the dearest to his heart in all the world. Even Stephen, whom he had only known a short time, was closer to him and knew him better than his own family. Perhaps he should have felt a little sadness at that, but he did not.

Some of his shock at the revelation, and the surge of tender emotion it caused, must have shown on his face, for Maud came to his side suddenly, stood on her toes, and kissed him on his cheek.

"Thank ye, sir. Tha' was bootiful. Dinner's almost ready. I'll 'ave it on the table direct." With that, she collected her husband and quickly left the room, closing the door behind them.

Stephen approached him slowly, his confusion and concern apparent as he hesitated only a few steps away, searching William's face. William closed the distance quickly and pulled the younger man into his arms, pressing his face into the golden-brown waves of his hair and breathing in his scent. Right then, in that moment, William knew he had everything he required to live the rest of his life as a happy man, if only he could find a way to keep it. He held Stephen for a long time in silence before pulling back and kissing the other man gently on the lips.

"William?"

Stephen's concern seemed to be mounting, so William smiled at him and said, "I am merely happy, Stephen. For perhaps the first time in years, I can say that I am truly happy. That is all."

His words did not appear to comfort his young companion, however, for Stephen broke away from him and strode over to the window, looking blankly out at the street. "I am glad the demands of your king could bring you such happiness," he said quietly, though his tone seemed anything but glad.

William sighed inwardly at the sadness in Stephen's voice and moved to stand behind him, wrapping his arms around Stephen's chest again and leaning in to kiss his cheek. "And what does my monarch require of me now?" he whispered against Stephen's ear, and the younger man shivered in his embrace.

Stephen was saved from answering by a knock on the door and Maud calling out, "Dinner is served, sir."

William lifted his head and called out, "Thank you, Maud. We shall be there directly." To Stephen, he said, "After you, my king," and dropped into his most courtly bow. Stephen merely snorted and made his way to the door, the gravity of their earlier exchange now past.

Maud had laid out a truly royal feast of braised mutton with mushrooms and potatoes for them, and both men tucked in with enthusiasm. This time William requested that Stephen say his prayer of thanks aloud, and Stephen complied with a small, embarrassed blush. William wanted to learn all he could of the younger man while he had the chance, in hopes of finding some way to get Stephen to trust him. But as the evening wore on, each time William probed too close, Stephen would close himself off and grow anxious again. In frustration, William gave up and steered their talk to lighter matters, and they managed to pass the rest of the meal companionably.

They spoke of their ride, the beauties of the countryside, music, and books. Stephen spoke of songs he had heard at school and books he had read and would like to read, and William told stories of where and from whom he had learned most of the songs he knew. Stephen seemed on the verge of asking him more about his activities in Cornwall several times, but apparently decided against it and left his questions unasked. William would have answered truthfully if Stephen had asked him. He trusted the man not to betray him, but his young lover seemed reluctant to broach the subject, so William did not volunteer the information.

After dinner, they returned to the study for another game of chess and a few glasses of port. Once again, William managed to win, but only by the skin of his teeth and perhaps only because Stephen appeared to have partaken of a little too much port. The younger man's cheeks were quite flushed and his eyes sleepy and glazed by the time they finished their game, and William decided he had best put Stephen to bed before he had to carry him there. This was the first time William had seen the man drink more than a glass or two, and he had to wonder at the cause. Overindulgence did not seem to be one of Stephen's weaknesses; that was more William's province than his lover's.

William rose from his seat and banked the coals before grabbing the lamp from the mantel in one hand and Stephen's hand in the other, leading the way upstairs. After setting his lamp on the night table, William set about relieving Stephen of his clothing. The younger man attempted to help but only ended up making things more difficult until William was forced to trap his lover's arms in the sleeves of his coat while he finished unbuttoning his waistcoat, falls, and trousers. Stephen began to actually giggle halfway through the process, and William found the sound so endearing he could not help but join in.

Soon they were laughing together so hard they could barely catch their breaths, and their clothes were in happy disarray, half on and half off their bodies. They sobered long enough to remove their boots and the rest of their clothes, climbed between the linens and wrapped around one another for warmth.

This time their lovemaking was lazy and unhurried. Stephen was completely relaxed and receptive in his arms. They kissed one another languidly, sliding warm, gentle hands over each other's bodies, neither one of them taking the lead, simply exploring, tasting, feeling. William could feel Stephen's erection pressed tightly against his own, but his young lover seemed content to simply touch and be touched for a time.

With only the occasional crackle of coal in the fire or muffled voice or odd thump from the neighboring houses to disturb them, William and Stephen spent the next hours feasting on one another as if they were the only two people in the world and the night would last forever. When they did finally come together, Stephen wrapping his legs tightly around William's waist and urging him to press inside, it was with a sweetness and a rightness that William had not experienced since the loss of his wife, and he knew, without doubt, that this was where he belonged.

Stephen's eyes were completely unguarded and held a strange intensity of their own when they locked with William's, and William was nearly overwhelmed at the hope and longing he read there. He leaned forward until he could hold Stephen's face in his palms and kiss his swollen lips as he slowly worked himself in and out, stroking his lover from within with all the tenderness he felt in that moment. Eventually, when he could hold out no longer, William broke from Stephen's gaze and buried his face in the crook of his lover's neck. He slid his hands under Stephen's shoulders and up into his hair, gripping it tightly and bracing his elbows on the bed as his thrusts became more frantic. He breathed in his lover's scent with every panting breath, and crushed him to his body as if he could meld them together so they might never be parted.

Stephen tightened his legs around William's waist and wrapped his arms around his back, holding him close as he lifted his hips into each stroke. There was nothing left then but to surrender to passion, their panting breaths and moans blending until they were indistinguishable from one another. When Stephen cried out and stiffened against him, William was lost. Stars danced behind his eyes, and he could not seem to get enough air to shout his pleasure.

It was not until blood finally returned to his head that William realized Stephen had reached paradise without either of them touching his cock. Even in the aftermath of such a flood of emotion and passion, William could not help the smug smile that played across his face at that realization. Whether it was his to claim or not, he would accept the praise for it, and he turned his grinning and expectant face to his panting lover. Stephen merely rolled his eyes at William's expression and climbed out of bed, and William's grin turned to a bewildered frown. His lover quickly scurried across the room to seize two flannels before diving back beneath the linens with a wicked gleam in his eye, shoving his feet beneath William's bare arse. Even in the brief seconds the man had spent out of bed, his feet had become icy, and William yelped and tried to squirm away.

"Lesson number one, remember?" Stephen laughed as he threw William one of the flannels and chased him across the bed.

"Think you are quite the comedian, don't you?" William muttered as he decided to counter-attack with a flurry of tickling fingers along Stephen's ribs. His lover squirmed and laughed so much under his assault that tears fell from his eyes, and William decided he should stop there. He smoothed his palms over Stephen's sensitive ribs and kissed his tears away before retrieving the forgotten flannels and cleaning them both. He tossed the flannels to the floor, doused the lamp, and pulled the younger man into his arms. When Stephen snuggled against him with a contented sigh, William curled around him like another skin and fell asleep.

# Chapter *Twelve*

WILLIAM woke to the sound of rain on the roof and weak, gray light peeking through a gap in the velvet curtains. He was alone in the bed, and for a panicked second he forgot what day it was. Thankfully, he heard footsteps in the hall, and Stephen walked in wearing William's red and gold brocade banyan a moment later. The ornate dressing gown was another item William had procured at the docks from a man who swore it had fallen off a passing ship. Stephen carried their morning tray of coffee and scones, and William smiled his welcome and gratitude, trying to hide his flush of embarrassment at his second bout of near-hysterics in as many days at the thought that Stephen had gone.

"That becomes you," William said in open admiration of Stephen's beauty in the high-necked robe. Though Stephen's day as the king of misrule was over, William thought his lover looked quite the raja in his borrowed finery.

Stephen smiled his pleasure at the compliment and set the tray on the bed. "I did not wish to get dressed for the day yet when I woke, and I found it in your wardrobe. I hope you do not mind."

"Not at all. As I said, it suits you quite well. So well, in fact, that I believe you should keep it," William replied as he poured the two of them coffee.

"Oh no. I could not possibly—it is very kind of you, but I cannot." Stephen shook his head and removed the garment, draping it over the foot of the bed before climbing beneath the counterpane.

156

William was disappointed to see that Stephen wore a shirt and trousers beneath.

"Why ever not? It is mine to give, and it is far more handsome on you than it ever was on me."

Stephen sighed and looked pained. "Please, Will. Let us not quarrel. It is a handsome gift, and do not think that I am not grateful, but I cannot accept it. You *know* why."

William bit back the bitter retort that sprang to his tongue and simply sipped his coffee. He would not ruin their last day together with quarreling, especially as bitter words would not encourage Stephen to be amenable to his plans to extend their acquaintance.

"As you wish. I will keep it for you," he said quietly, and Stephen gave him a sad but relieved smile. "So what say you to another day in bed? I could ring for Maud and have her bring us more books from the study?" William went on, changing the subject before they trod on dangerous ground again.

Stephen's smile brightened and turned a little mocking. "Only one day of open air and you have need of another full day in bed? Perhaps I should call a physician for you."

"There is a very great difference between need and want, I will have you know," William teased back, though he knew it was untrue. He did *need* to spend the day just relaxing in Stephen's company, savoring every moment and not wasting even the tiniest measure of it with anyone or anything else.

Stephen simply chuckled and sipped at his coffee, seemingly unaware of the gravity of William's thoughts. They were quiet for a time as they finished off Maud's wonderful scones and coffee, until Stephen surprised him by removing William's cup from his hands, placing it on the tray, and climbing into his lap, tracing some of William's scars with his fingers and saying, "I will make a bargain with you, Mr. Carey. I will bow to your desire to remain here in bed all afternoon if you will agree to follow my lead after the sun has set... without question or demur."

157

William raised his eyebrows at that. Stephen was learning his tricks far too quickly. Rationally he should not trust someone whom he had only known for so short a time and who had, at one time, plotted against him, but his heart had never been rational. Eros and Fortuna had smiled upon him most of his life; only once had they failed him. He would simply have to trust in them and in Stephen if he were to achieve all that he hoped for—all that he needed.

William leaned back on his pillows and slid his hands beneath Stephen's loose shirt, smoothing his palms over the muscles there, which quivered at his touch. "Your bargain sounds fair. I accept your terms."

Stephen, whose eyes had closed in pleasure at his caresses, smiled happily and arched into William's hands, rocking his hips and rubbing their groins together. This time William introduced Stephen to the pleasure and control to be found in riding astride one's partner. It was awkward and embarrassing for the younger man at first, but he soon seemed to warm to the idea, and they were both galloping toward paradise in no time at all.

Sated and replete, they settled themselves in for a lovely afternoon of reading. Though William tried every trick he could think of to force Stephen to reveal his plans for the evening, the young man remained infuriatingly silent on the subject, and William was near to bursting with curiosity by the time the sun dipped low on the horizon.

Stephen finished reading aloud the last pages of *Fanny Hill* soon after darkness fell. It had taken him longer to read that book than any of the others because William kept interrupting him to act out most of the scenes. Though Stephen had not appeared to mind being interrupted.

As soon as Stephen closed the book, he batted William's hands away and climbed out of bed. "Stay there" was all he said as he donned the *banyan* again and left the room. William did as he was told, though curiosity had him straining to hear every creak and muffled word he could through the walls of his house. Unfortunately, he could hear the conversations of his neighbors and the men and women out on the street far better than anything else, so he was left without a clue as to Stephen's plans.

When there was a knock at the door, William turned in anticipation, only to find Stubbs carrying a bundle of clothes and a steaming kettle.

"Ye're t' wash an' put these on but ney shave yer whiskers," he said as he poured the hot water into William's basin and laid the bundle of clothing on the chair. At William's raised eyebrows and questioning smile, the man simply grinned and walked from the room without another word.

Curious, William left the bed and walked to the bundle on the chair. The cloth was coarse and rough to the touch. The stack included a plain linen shirt; dark-brown coarse wool trousers, waistcoat, and coat; and a rather wrinkled cravat of the same dingy color as the shirt. Hidden underneath, there was a pair of scuffed and dirty boots of similar quality to the clothes. Strange choices for the evening, and William had to wonder where the lad had found them. He did as he was told, however, and washed and clothed himself. Looking in the glass, he was not at all impressed at what the color and quality of the cloth did for his appearance, but he supposed Stephen had his reasons for wanting him to look like a laborer.

When he had finished, William made his way down to the dining room. Wonderful smells were emanating from the kitchen, and William only hoped Stephen's plans included them partaking of whatever Maud had concocted. Stubbs was waiting for him at the door to the dining room, but simply ushered him inside and closed the door behind him. Stephen was waiting for him at the table, and when the younger man stood, William saw that he was wearing a set of clothes nearly identical to the ones he had sent to William, although William had to admit they were much more attractive on his lover.

William's appreciation must have shown in his eyes, for Stephen flushed and quirked an embarrassed smile before motioning William to the other seat at the table. After Stephen gave thanks, they ate the wonderful meal Maud had prepared and talked about books and chess, but no matter how William pressed, Stephen would not divulge the reason for their strange apparel or what they would be doing.

After dinner they retired to the library for a glass of port and another game of chess. William played exceptionally poorly, as he was distracted by his burning curiosity. At least he was saved the mortification of an embarrassingly quick defeat by Stubbs's knock and announcement that their carriage had arrived. William turned curious eyes to Stephen, but the young man merely smiled and rose to follow Stubbs toward the front of the house.

"Come," Stephen said.

William was very happy to leave before his imminent defeat, and to have his curiosity satisfied at last. He caught up with Stephen at the door, where Stubbs had produced two rough but serviceable caps fitting the style of their clothes.

"I fear Stubbs could not find us coats, so we will have to make do with what we have on," Stephen said with an apologetic grimace. "We will not be out in the weather long, though, so we should not catch a chill."

"I will be comfortable enough in these. No need to worry." William smiled encouragingly, and Stephen relaxed and gave him a happy smile in return before stepping out into the street. William followed but turned back and threw a concerned look at Stubbs, casting his gaze up and down the street to convey his meaning. Stubbs smiled and nodded his acknowledgement of William's concerns.

"Don' ye worry. Enjoy yersel'," was all he said, though he did hand William his cane before closing the door. Well, if Stubbs did not seem concerned about them being followed, then William would not concern himself either. He climbed into the carriage after Stephen and settled himself comfortably in the seat as the driver set off. They were silent in the coach. Stephen seemed happy and excited but not inclined to talk, so William contented himself with keeping track of the streets they traveled and sneaking proprietary and speculative glances at his companion in the passing streetlamps. He was on the verge of proposing they pass the time in the same pleasant manner as they had on their previous carriage ride when they slowed to a crawl amongst a crush of other carriages and people on foot.

Looking out the window, William recognized where Stephen had taken him. They were only a short distance away from the Aquatic Theatre and not at all far from where he and Stephen had gone riding only the day before. When he turned back to look at Stephen, the young man was regarding him nervously, chewing on his plump lower lip.

"I wished to do something for you, for all the trouble you went through for, and because of, me. I spoke with Stubbs yesterday, and he informed me that you greatly enjoyed the theater, plays and operas and that sort of thing. I fear I did not have enough money to get a box for us or anything more than seats in the gallery, but Stubbs recommended this place, so I...."

All of this came out in an embarrassed and apologetic jumble that nearly broke William's heart. It was obvious to William that Stephen was ashamed that his gift could not be a better one, and William hated to see it.

He moved quickly to Stephen's side of the compartment, drawing the curtains on the windows before pulling the man into his arms, kissing his mouth playfully and enthusiastically until Stephen was laughing into his kisses.

"It is a wonderful surprise. I could not think of a better way to spend an evening. Thank you," he said between kisses, and he meant every word of it from the bottom of his heart.

"I am glad. I was not completely certain that this would please you, and I did not know if you wished to be seen with me at the theaters you usually attend." Stephen looked away from him as he said that, but he continued before William had a chance to deny it, as if what he had said were nothing. "Stubbs said the plays here were quite a spectacle and that you would enjoy it. He also suggested we wear these clothes instead of our own, as we would be among the rougher crowd in the gallery, and I thought it good advice. You do not mind, do you?"

William smiled and kissed Stephen soundly again. He did not like this new and hesitant Stephen. He would take the hedgehog back in a heartbeat before this. "I do not mind in the least, and we could have gone to my brother's box at the King's Theatre for all I care about us

161

being seen together. But this is from you, and I will cherish it as such and enjoy myself more than I would anywhere else, I assure you."

William could feel Stephen's cheek heat beneath his palms, and he smiled. The carriage stopped then, and the coachman called to let them know they had arrived. He and Stephen stepped onto the street, but when Stephen tried to give his instructions and deposit to the coachman, the man simply shook his head and said, "Stubbs took care o' tha'. I'll be 'ere to take you 'ome, and ye need fear no trouble." The last statement was accentuated with a wave of a stout cudgel, and William had to smile. Stephen looked confused by what the man said but followed William into the Theatre without comment.

The play was a revival of the *Battle of Gibraltar*, complete with a spectacular naval battle using wooden ships in the massive tank of water that was the Theatre's claim to fame. Stubbs was correct, it was very entertaining, and it seemed to be quite the favorite amongst the crowd—at least, judging from the amount of raucous hollering and stomping that was going on around them. William had never attended a play in the footman's gallery. It was an experience, to be sure, but not one he would choose to repeat. The shouts and smells and general jostling about made it very difficult to enjoy what was happening on the stage, and William had felt questing fingers on his person more than once during the evening. Thankfully he did not have any valuables on him, and his purse was stashed where no one could get to it easily. He only hoped that Stephen had thought to do the same.

When a scuffle broke out at the back of the Theatre, William decided they should make their way home. The play was almost over, and they would miss the crush if they left before it ended. Pulling Stephen along by his wrist, William used his cane to help clear them a path to the exit, steering clear of the worst of the melee. They gained the doors and their freedom just as a group of stout-looking men made their way inside to quell the disturbance, and William was very glad he had chosen to leave when he did. There were more men outside the Theatre keeping their eyes on the streets, making William fairly certain that this was not at all an unusual occurrence.

Thankfully, they made it back to their carriage unmolested, and their trip back to the house was equally uneventful. Stephen was full of the excitement over all that he had seen, and William almost enjoyed his exuberance more than the play itself. He forgot any plans he had of making use of the privacy of the carriage and simply leaned back against the cushioned bench and let Stephen exclaim over his favorite parts of the performance. It felt like no time at all had passed when they drew to a stop in front of the house, and William was almost reluctant to get out of the carriage.

The night air was chill, however, and he was beginning to feel it without his greatcoat, so he decided it would be more comfortable to continue their discussion indoors. When Stubbs let them inside and took their hats, William was surprised to see that the man had an ugly bruise and a small cut above his left eye. He looked closer to assure himself that the weak lamplight in the hall was not deceiving him, and unfortunately drew Stephen's attention to the mark in the process.

"Mr. Stubbs? Are you injured?" Stephen asked in real concern from behind William.

Stubbs merely grimaced and said, "'Tis naught, young master. A bit o' clumsiness, tha's all."

William could see Stephen frown in disbelief out of the corner of his eye, but Stubbs gave William a look that said they would speak of it later, so William forced a chuckle. "You should show more care, man. Maud would skin me alive should anything happen to you." William kept his tone light, but he knew Stubbs would understand his meaning. When he turned back to Stephen, the younger man still looked concerned, but he did not protest when William urged him up the stairs.

William took the lamp Stubbs offered and followed Stephen to their bedchamber. It was not until he had set the lamp on his night table that William noticed Stephen's face had changed from concerned to downright maudlin. The younger man would not meet his gaze and merely stared off into the dark corners of the room, standing tense and still next to their bed. William knew the cause. This would be their last night together.

William approached his lover slowly, cupping his face gently and raising it so he could see Stephen's beautiful eyes. "This does not have to be the end."

"Yes, it does." The pained whisper made William's chest clench.

"Why? Tell me *why*." William allowed some of his frustration and hurt to color his tone.

"Will...." Stephen fisted his hands at his sides and pulled away.

He walked to the fireplace and stood staring into the coals, the orange glow casting his lovely face in harsh relief. As William stood in silence, fighting his mounting desire to grab the young man and shake his secrets out of him, Stephen took a deep breath and let it out slowly. William could see Stephen purposefully relaxing his shoulders as he exhaled, and William tried to do the same. It would do no good for them to quarrel. They both had hot tempers, and though William's had been banked for the past several years, Stephen had obviously brought it back to life, along with everything else. When Stephen turned back to face William, he had a sad smile on his face and a pleading look in his eyes that calmed William better than anything else could have. "Please, Will. We have so little time left. You gave me your word that you would not ask. I wish...." Stephen shook his head and closed his eyes, pain clear in his expression. "There are so many things I wish were different. But they are not. These past few days have been a wonderful dream. Do not force me to face the world again. Not yet."

Just like that, William's anger evaporated into nothing, and he rushed to pull Stephen into his arms. Soothing Stephen's hurt was all that mattered to him in that moment. He knew now that he wanted Stephen happy and in his arms forever, but if he could not even manage the first, then the second would become meaningless.

He *knew* direct confrontation did not work with his fiery young lover, but he could not seem to help himself. The thought of this vibrant and passionate young man leaving his arms to go back to a man like Graves set his gut to clenching and his mind on murder, but what price would Stephen pay to give William what he wanted?

He wished Stephen would trust him enough to confide in him. *God*, how he wished that, but he must remember to be patient. Stephen would not *disappear* after tomorrow. William still had time to win the man's trust. He had managed to win Stephen's affection and admiration in only a few days' time, had he not? He could manage the rest. He just needed to keep his own temper in check and use his energy for something other than fighting with the man he loved.

"Forgive me," he whispered against Stephen's neck before kissing and nuzzling him tenderly beneath his ear. Before Stephen could do more than moan in response, William claimed his mouth for a deep and desperate kiss. They would not talk again tonight. That was his new strategy. He would not allow either of them time to dwell on tomorrow, and he would put every ounce of his will and determination into keeping them both distracted until morning.

He pulled away from the kiss and grabbed Stephen's wrist as he stepped back to draw the man into the center of the room.

"Stay there," he ordered roughly as he moved back the fire to stir it up and add more coals. Stephen's eyes had narrowed a little at the command, but William quickly returned and kissed him tenderly until the man melted in his arms. Breaking into his most wicked smile and leering up at Stephen through his eyelashes, he said, "Please?"

Stephen's eyes heated at once, and his tongue peeked out to moisten his lips. He nodded without saying a word.

"Thank you. All you have to do for tonight is obey my commands and allow me to thank you properly for my present. Will you do that for me?" William made certain that he continued to smile softly as he spoke, so Stephen would know this was only a lover's game. He hoped to prove to Stephen that if he would just trust William, all would be well and a world of pleasure and happiness would be his.

"Yes," Stephen whispered as if there were more in his acceptance than an answer to William's question.

William's heart clenched at the word and the emotion in the man's eyes, and he counseled himself to move slowly.

"Good. Do not move," he instructed, moderating his tone a little but keeping it strong and commanding.

He stepped back a few paces from Stephen and surveyed his young lover, letting his eyes roam lazily over every inch of that lovely body. Even in the dim light, William could see a blush creep over the younger man's cheeks, but he decided he could not see it well *enough*, so he set about lighting the other two lamps in the room. The incense brazier had been cleaned and put away, so William had to rummage in his wardrobe to find it. He also drew out the oils again, as well as the *banyan* that had looked so enticing on his lover.

He could feel Stephen's eyes on him as he moved about the room, but Stephen remained silent and simply stood, watching him and licking his lips nervously. When the lamps were lit and placed to his satisfaction, William laid the *banyan* over the chair closest to Stephen and slipped out of his borrowed coat, dropping it on the floor.

The fire warmed the air and the lamps illuminated Stephen perfectly, flashing gold in his hair and causing his day's growth of whiskers to sparkle. The thick velvet curtains over the window were closed against the cold, and plumes of perfumed smoke filled the room, adding an almost dreamlike quality to the air. William smiled, quite pleased with his efforts.

*The real world will not exist for at least a few more hours, my love.*

He would not say the endearment aloud, not yet. Given Stephen's fears and secrets, William was fairly certain his hedgehog would not take the word or any other pet names well, but that did not mean he could not think them.

Now that the setting was to his liking, William had one more item he needed. Leaving Stephen again to stare curiously after him, William knelt by the bed and reached underneath to pull out a small wooden trunk. Stephen leaned forward a bit, trying to see what was inside, so William turned the trunk so that the lid hid its contents. This was his treasure chest, and he did not wish Stephen to know all of its contents, at least not yet. He was quite certain Stephen would balk at a good number of the items in the chest, and now was not the time to explain the leather-covered manacles or the *legba*, a sixteen-inch West African wooden phallus. He did, however, select a glass phallus of much more realistic proportions; then he closed the trunk and pushed it back beneath the bed. Stephen's eyes widened and he flushed a deeper shade of scarlet when he caught sight of what William carried, but he said nothing as William placed it on the bed.

William returned to Stephen then and pulled his lover into his arms. Stephen responded immediately, wrapping his arms around William and pulling him close, opening his mouth and surrendering to William's kiss until they were both breathless. Then William pulled back, putting a few paces between them.

"Remove your clothes," he ordered. His tone was again brusque, but he hoped his smirk and the heat of his gaze would temper Stephen's reaction.

Stephen licked his lips nervously and began removing his coat and cravat after only a moment's hesitation. His chest was still rising and falling rapidly from their kiss, and his hands shook as he hurriedly fumbled at the knot of his cravat.

"Slower, please," William said firmly, holding Stephen's gaze and hoping the tone of his voice would help calm his lover.

Stephen took a shaky breath and slowed his hands, pulling the cravat from his neck and letting it fall to the floor before beginning on the buttons of his waistcoat. William followed every move his lover made with hungry eyes. Stephen seemed quite discomfited at first, but as he could see the effect his efforts were having on William, he appeared to relax, and his movements became more assured. He even smiled—a little cocksure smile that William found nearly irresistible.

Stephen removed his waistcoat and falls and slowly drew his shirt over his head, the coarse linen pulled away to reveal his smooth skin turned golden in the lamplight. William's eyes hooded in appreciation as Stephen looked down to his boots and back up to William, a question in his eyes. William chuckled and moved to kneel, to help the man.

There truly was not a seductive manner in which to remove one's boots, at least not one William had encountered. From his position on the floor, William looked up into Stephen's eyes and smiled. Stephen reached down and slid his fingers through William's hair as his eyes softened and then saddened a little. The heat was still there, but William could see other emotions creeping to the fore, and he could not allow that to happen.

William stood and backed away again after tossing the boots aside. "Finish, please," he said with as much authority as he could muster around the tightening in his throat.

Stephen took a deep breath and let it out slowly before unfastening the placket of his trousers. He raised his eyes to William's then and deliberately held his gaze as he slid his hands beneath the waist of the trousers and pushed the rough wool slowly down his hips. He bent further to push them and his stockings completely off, giving William a brief glimpse of his glorious arse, the sight of which sent whatever blood remained in the rest of William's body directly to his cock. His love did indeed have the most beautiful high and round arse William had ever set eyes on. His prick twitched within the itchy confines of his coarse woolen trousers, reminding him that he would be much more comfortable if he were rid of them, but he wanted to finish preparing Stephen before he removed that barrier between them.

When Stephen stood completely unclothed before him, William picked up one of the vials of oil and moved behind him. He poured the scented oil into his palms and smoothed it over the softly defined muscles of Stephen's shoulders and down his arms. Taking first one hand and then the other, William bathed Stephen's skin with oil all the way to his fingertips, leaving behind a sheen that glowed in the lamplight. As he worked, he could feel Stephen's body tremble beneath his hands and his pulse quicken beneath his skin. The object of his attentions let out a quiet moan and dropped his head forward when William returned to his neck, working the oil into the corded muscles with his thumbs.

William poured more oil into his hands and slid them down Stephen's back, enjoying the smooth play of silken skin over muscle and bone. He dropped to his knees and could not help a small bite along the underside of Stephen's gorgeous arse before setting to work with more oil. Stephen gasped and jumped at the feel of William's teeth, but held still as he had been ordered. William did not dwell on the beautifully rounded arse in front of him for too long. He could become easily distracted in worshipping it if he tarried, so he simply moved on to the backs of Stephen's thighs, and then to his well-muscled calves.

He slid around to Stephen's front, trying his best to ignore the hard and leaking cock only inches from his face as he worked more oil over Stephen's calves and up his thighs. He slid his palms over Stephen's hips, and down between his legs, threading his oil-soaked fingers through the thatch of coarse brown hair surrounding his lover's prick. He looked up and met Stephen's eyes as he cupped his bollocks and his twitching cock, smoothing the oil lovingly over the soft skin there. He could not resist burying his face at the base of Stephen's cock and nuzzling just a moment before drawing away again and standing to spread more oil over Stephen's stomach and chest. His lover let out a disappointed whimper when William stood and let go of his cock, and William could not help but chuckle.

"You chuckle? You are driving me to distraction, and you chuckle?"

*Distraction is exactly what I am doing.*

Aloud, he said only, "Forgive me, my raja. You will get your way soon enough."

He kissed Stephen briefly on the lips and picked up the *banyan*, holding it as a valet would for his master. The younger man looked confused but slid his arms into the garment and allowed William to settle it on his shoulders. William then took Stephen by the hand and led him to the stuffed leather chair by the fire and pushed him down into it.

When Stephen was seated, William stepped back a little and ordered, "Lean back and spread your legs."

Stephen's eyes widened a bit, making him seem even younger and more vulnerable, and William wished that he had some skill with paints or charcoals, for he would dearly love to capture this moment on canvas. The robe lay open at the front, draping only Stephen's arms and sides with deep red and gold tones. The flickering light from the lamps made the pale tips of his hair sparkle like spun gold, and his oiled skin luminous. He looked more the Viking prince than the raja with his fair coloring, but he was breathtaking nonetheless.

William held Stephen's heated gaze as he slowly began removing his own clothes. He used the bootjack to remove his borrowed boots, for he did not wish Stephen to move from his throne, and by the time he had finished his performance, Stephen's cock was so hard it kissed his navel, leaving a trail of pearly fluid that glistened in the lamplight.

William's own cock throbbed betwixt his thighs and ached almost unbearably, but he needed their encounter to last. He needed to keep both of them distracted as long as he could. He knew Stephen, being younger, would recover much sooner than he, so his own pleasure would have to wait.

William gathered up the jar of coconut oil and the glass dildo and knelt on the thick Persian rug, between Stephen's knees. He spread Stephen's thighs further apart and leaned in, pressing their chests together and claiming Stephen's lips while he let his hands glide over his lover's oiled torso. Stephen took the opportunity to do a little exploring of his own, and soon William felt the younger man's hands cupping and squeezing his arse. His lover used his grip to pull William closer, arching his back and pressing their groins together. William knew he could not allow that, not yet, or he would spend much too soon, so he pulled himself out of Stephen's embrace and sat back on his heels.

"Not yet. Be patient." Stephen gave him a most endearing growl of frustration and frowned, looking for all the world like a spoiled prince who'd been denied his wishes. William smiled and wrapped his hand around Stephen's cock, gripping it tightly at the base, and gave it a few lazy tugs, watching his young prince's face as his mouth fell open on a moan and his eyes closed in appreciation. William leaned forward then and took the leaking rod in his mouth, lazily swirling the head with his tongue and savoring the flavor of Stephen's excitement.

Kneeling naked between his lover's thighs, William drew the length fully into his mouth until his lips met his hand. Then he drew back, suckling gently, creating enough suction to give pleasure but not enough to bring Stephen to the precipice too soon. He kept his grip firm on the base of Stephen's cock so his young prince could not spend too quickly and wreaked sweet torture with his lips and tongue. He was enjoying himself and the sweet moans and soft cries too much not to make it last just a little while longer.

"Oh God, Will, *please!*"

William could not help the surge of devilish satisfaction he felt at the strain in his lover's voice. Stephen's bollocks had drawn up full and tight against his body, and his hands were flexing fitfully in William's hair. When William drew off his cock and sat back to grin up at his lover, Stephen whimpered pitifully.

"Is this for me?" William asked, grinning evilly and rolling Stephen's sac gently in his palm. Stephen gave him a pained and pleading look as he nodded his head vigorously.

"Say it," William demanded

"It is for you. Only you," Stephen panted.

"Only me," William agreed, a slight growl the only hint of the depth of his feelings.

He dove back onto Stephen's shaft then and sucked hard, bobbing his head and releasing his grip on the base. He dropped his hand to Stephen's hips and encouraged his lover to thrust. He did not have to wait long. Stephen only managed a few thrusts before shouting out his release and curling himself over William's back. William drank every last drop his lover had to give as Stephen trembled and thrust his hips weakly a few more times.

When there was no more to be had, William pushed Stephen back into the chair and captured his lover's mouth in a punishing kiss, forcing his tongue inside and giving Stephen a taste of himself. Stephen gasped between kisses, out of breath from his release but equally unwilling to pull away from William's kiss. They remained locked tightly together, their mouths fused in passion, until William felt

Stephen reaching between them, seeking William's cock, and he knew he needed to stop him. One touch at this moment and he would spend.

He pulled out of his lover's embrace again and caught Stephen's wrist, stopping its progress. This time he only shook his head at Stephen's confused look and leaned back to search for the jar of oil and the dildo before returning to his earlier position. Stephen's eyes had been sleepy and half-closed in satiation, but when William lifted the glass rod and began oiling it, they widened considerably and seemed much more awake.

William took his time slicking the cool, amber-colored glass with oil and letting its smooth surface glide over his palms, paying particular attention to the ridged head, until he could see Stephen's cock begin to twitch and fill against his belly. Then he smiled and moved closer to his beautiful lover, sliding his hand beneath the other man's right knee and urging it upward. Stephen hesitated a moment, searching William's eyes, before smiling nervously and propping his foot on the edge of the seat.

William understood Stephen's trepidation. Though they had already exchanged many intimacies with one another, it was different to allow oneself to be pleasured while one's partner remained detached, to lay exposed and vulnerable to another man while he, in turn, was not. The very fact that Stephen felt comfortable enough with William to allow him free rein with his body sent another pang of intense emotion rushing through him that took him by surprise. He had not known, until that moment, how much he needed to see some sign of trust in the younger man's eyes. Even if that trust could not make it beyond the bedchamber as yet, the mere sight of it soothed his soul. He had begun this game as a means to distract both of them and to bind Stephen to him with physical pleasure, but yet again, Stephen's very nature, the depth of his heart and the passion in his eyes, had turned it into so much more.

William broke from Stephen's gaze and turned his attention to the jar of coconut oil and the dildo to distract himself. He smoothed oil-slick fingers beneath Stephen's bollocks and back to his exposed threshold, teasing his fingers about the puckered flesh as he ran the acquaintance. William sighed and pushed the disheartening thought from his mind. He would continue on, wooing as best he could, and hope that his newly awakened determination, and perhaps a little luck, would grant him what he desired.

Squaring his shoulders and giving his waistcoat a good tug, William turned and made his way down to the dining room. Maud had already served breakfast, and Stephen sat quietly at the table, sipping coffee and reading one of the copies of the *Times* that William had had delivered along with his books and other belongings. When William entered, Stephen looked up from the pages, smiled warmly, stood, and said, "Good morning to you, sir" as if they had not just shared a bed only an hour before. But William could play along.

"Good morning to *you,* sir. I trust you slept well," he said as he sat and poured himself some coffee.

"Quite well, thank you," Stephen replied, but William could see by the quirk of his lips and the blush of his cheeks that the man did acknowledge some of the absurdity of their conversation.

As Stephen made himself a plate of toast, ham, and poached eggs, William merely sipped at his coffee and asked, "So what *are* you going to do with me today, now that I am entirely at your disposal?"

Stephen choked a little on his mouthful of food and had to take a sip of his coffee before he could answer. Giving William a disgruntled frown, he said, "It appears that we are to have another marvelous day of sunshine. Perhaps we should go riding again? Though I insist we *hire* our horses this time."

"If that is your wish, then I agree it is an excellent idea. Though perhaps you might allow me to improve upon it?"

"What did you have in mind?" Stephen asked, a skeptical frown playing about the corners of his mouth.

"Merely that we go a little further afield and take a ride outside of the city," William explained innocently. "I have my stallion stabled only a short way out of town, and we could hire you a mount and spend the afternoon in the fresh air of the fields… get away from the crush?"

glass phallus up Stephen's length. Stephen moaned and his hands gripped the leather arms of the chair tightly as the cool, slick glass teased his cock. He canted his hips forward in a silent plea for more as he watched every move William made. William tried very hard to concentrate only on the beauty of the amber glass against the silken marble of Stephen's skin, blotting out the sweetness of his moans and the heady scent of his arousal mingled with the dark, woodsy aroma of the different oils coating his skin. If he did not, he would not be able to continue.

He rubbed Stephen's length with the dildo as he worked his fingers inside the sweet rosebud beneath. When Stephen's opening relaxed and welcomed him in, William removed his fingers and slid the glass further back, rubbing it beneath Stephen's bollocks and then down to his threshold. He slowly pressed the amber glass inside, watching the molded head disappear into the first ring of muscle, then drawing it back again. Stephen moaned and threw his head back against the chair, arching his neck until William could see the play of muscles and veins beneath the taut skin.

"Beautiful."

William did not realize he had said the word aloud until Stephen suddenly tipped his head forward again and met William's eyes. A world of emotion swam behind those eyes, too much for William to decipher, so he simply put as much sincerity and caring into his own gaze as he could while he worked the smooth glass in and out of Stephen's body, until the man was trembling and thrusting his hips in counterpoint, chasing his pleasure. William leaned in again and placed wet, open-mouthed kisses up Stephen's shaft before taking it in his mouth again. He sucked gently on Stephen's crown and watched his face contort in pleasure.

"God, Will, please. I need—oh!" Stephen arched his back off the chair and suddenly grabbed William's jaw, halting his movements. "I need *you*. I want *you* inside me. Please."

William did not need to be told twice. He had been struggling to maintain control over his body, teetering on the edge of what he could withstand, for what seemed like forever. Stephen asking for him, pleading with him to meld their bodies was more temptation than he could refuse.

He dropped the dildo to the floor immediately and pulled Stephen's legs over his shoulders, bending the other man nearly in half as he positioned his dripping crown at Stephen's opening. He pushed himself in, bollocks-deep, in one quick thrust. Stephen's channel welcomed him like a glove, surrounding him in exquisite heat, the slick walls gripping him tightly enough to force his seed from him without any further effort, if William allowed it. William had to close his eyes and bite his lower lip to keep from spending at once under such excruciating pleasure.

He had almost mastered himself when Stephen took matters into his own hands, gripping William's arms hard and flexing his hips such that William lost all restraint. He swore and thrust into Stephen's body hard and fast, over and over, without rhythm or finesse. Bent as he was, William could not reach Stephen's cock, but his lover apparently did not need any additional stimulation. Stephen dug his fingers into William's arms, cried out, and spent in thin ribbons over his belly and chest, and William followed him with a howl, straining to fill Stephen's body with all he had.

William collapsed against Stephen's chest, allowing his lover's legs to fall from his shoulders, but Stephen only wrapped his arms and legs around him again, pulling him close and holding him tightly. William burrowed his hands beneath Stephen's back and squeezed him just as tightly, pressing his forehead to his lover's shoulder while he attempted to catch his breath. They lay entwined like that for several long minutes until the clock on the mantel chimed one and William's knees began to protest their abuse.

He pulled away enough to look in Stephen's eyes as he brushed gentle fingers over his lover's stubbled cheek. Stephen brought his own hands to cup William's face and draw him in for a tender kiss. William sank into it gladly, ignoring the twinges in his lower extremities and seizing every tiny moment of tenderness he could. Only when Stephen pulled away again did he lever himself to his feet. Stephen took his offered hand and rose on unsteady legs, chuckling quietly at his condition. William could not help but chuckle himself, and draw Stephen into his arms again. Stephen's laugh was intoxicating, a headier elixir than any he had ever smuggled onto English soil, and William knew he would be quite content to remain drunk on it for the rest of his days.

*If only I could convince my hedgehog of that.*

The wistful thought made him tighten his grip on Stephen's shoulders for a moment before he stepped back and pushed his lover toward the bed.

"Get in there. I will see to the lamps."

He patted Stephen on the arse and moved to the washstand. After he tossed Stephen a flannel and used one to clean himself, he doused the lamps, banked the coals, and made his way to the bed. By the time William returned, Stephen was already snoring softly beneath the counterpane, and William realized that there was a distinct drawback to loving such an early riser. William supposed he would need to change his habits to suit, in the long-term.

*If he gives me the chance.*

That unhappy thought, and others, unfortunately left him quite awake long into the night as he lay curled around his sleeping lover, and it was only a little before dawn that he finally fell asleep.

# Chapter Thirteen

WHEN he finally woke, it was to find Stephen fully dressed and sitting at the foot of the bed, regarding him sadly. William's gut clenched at the sight, and he could not seem to get enough moisture in his mouth to speak. They stared at one another for several long minutes, and Stephen appeared to be at as much of a loss for words as he. Stephen was the first to break away. He bit his lip and looked down at his hands, which were nervously clenching and unclenching in his lap. The sight spurred William to find his voice at last.

"Stay. Whatever your secrets are, I do not care. I can help you if you will only allow it. You have been happy here with me. I know you have. Stay." As he spoke, William sat up in the bed and reached out to clasp Stephen's hands.

Pain flashed across Stephen's handsome face as he lifted his eyes to William's again. "You know I cannot."

"I do not know anything of the kind," he replied, anger coloring his tone for a second before he reined it in.

Stephen sighed and closed his eyes for a moment before he whispered, "I am sorry, Will. I cannot tell you how sorry I am, but I cannot stay with you."

"You *will* not. And you *will* not tell me why." William knew bitterness and anger would do no good, but he could not seem to stop the words.

"I *cannot*!" Stephen cried, pulling his hands from William's grasp and rising to pace the room. "I *told* you I have debts to repay and a family to care for. Would you have me abandon them? Abandon my duty and my honor?"

William remained seated in the bed and tried to fight his temper down. He was exhausted from too little sleep and he was handling this badly, but now that Stephen's departure was so near, he found it difficult to be rational. Taking a deep breath, he tried to moderate his tone. "If it is money you need, you know I can provide ten times more than Graves ever could. I can give you what you need."

It was the wrong thing to say. William knew it the minute the words left his mouth. Stephen stared at him a moment in silence, though his eyes proclaimed his injury louder than any shout ever could. But Stephen, being who he was, did not remain silent long. That fire in his eyes that William so admired roared into life, and his jaw clenched in fury.

"I do not need your money!" he spat. "I do not need either of you! You are all the same. The boys at school, Graves, you! Rich, titled, spoiled, all of you! I wish only to be left alone and to be given the chance to take care of myself and do my duty by my family. All of you can go to the devil for all I care!"

William leapt from the bed and caught Stephen by the arms before he could storm out of the room. "I am sorry, Stephen. Forgive me! Please forgive me! I know you do not need me, but...." William took a pained breath and let it out. "Did it ever occur to you that I might need *you*?"

Stephen flinched in his arms, turning his head away as if William had struck him. "We barely know one another, Will. How can you say such things?"

"Because I know they are the truth. Because I have felt this way only once before in my life, and I know it well. My heart knows."

Stephen took a shaky breath and lifted pleading eyes to William's. "I am sorry, Will. But one of us must be sensible. This... whatever is between us, it cannot be. *Everything* forbids it. Even if we *could* live together, out in the open, without fear of the hangman's noose, your home is here in London. I *hate* London. I do not belong here. I know my station and have spent enough time with my *betters* to know I would be miserable here. My father tried to improve my prospects. He sent me to school with the sons of title and wealth, and they never let me forget that I was not one of them. London has been no different. I would be miserable, and I would make you miserable. I would come to resent you and perhaps even hate you in time. I could not bear that. I could not bear hating you as I do Graves." The fury in his voice had dissolved into anguish that tore at William's heart. He would rather have the anger than this.

Stephen raised his palm to William's cheek as unshed tears welled in his eyes. "I want to go home, Will. I want to be with my family, to run my father's farm… to leave this cursed city and never come back again. Can you understand?"

"I would go with you, if you would only ask?"

"You know that is impossible."

"Nothing is impossible, Stephen. Not as long as you are willing to fight for it."

Stephen threw up his hands and stomped a few paces away, frustration and pain clearly stamped on his face. "For God's sake, Will, who would we be fighting!? My family? My village? The Church? God and Country? Even you cannot change the whole world!"

*I can, if you would ask me to.*

Only he could not say it aloud. He could not say anything. He hurt too much to continue fighting. Stephen refused to even try. He refused to trust William with his secrets. He refused to listen to his arguments. He was willing to give up and return to that blackguard Graves without even a whimper. The pain of that realization cut William to the bone, sucked the strength from his limbs and left him empty. Stephen must have sensed the change in him, for he stopped pacing the room and moved to stand close to William again. When William would not look at him, Stephen lifted his hand as if to touch him, then dropped it back to his side.

"I *am* sorry, Will. I am not free to do as I please. I have more than myself to think of. I only wish to go home to a quiet life. I feel certain that Graves will soon tire of me. I see it in his eyes at times. He tires of all of his playthings eventually." Stephen sighed. "It is the best that I can hope for, that he will set me free and allow me to return home, that he will allow me out from under his thumb long enough to rebuild the farm and free myself from him forever. I cannot give you what you seek. You deserve so much more, but I do not have it to give. You will forget me soon enough and find someone so much more worthy of your affections than I. A woman you can marry and live out in the open with and not have to hide and skulk about in the shadows, as you would with me."

William merely clenched his jaw and remained silent. Stephen sighed and leaned in to kiss him on the cheek, before turning and walking quietly from the room. From the doorway, William heard him whisper, "Thank you… for everything. You truly are a wonderful man." Then the door closed behind him, and the only sounds were his footsteps receding down the hall.

In the silence that followed, William stared blankly about the room. He was unclothed and chilled to the bone, but he could not seem to bring himself to do anything about it. The sound of a carriage pulling away from the front of his house sapped the last bit of strength from his limbs, and he simply dropped to the floor and leaned his back against the foot of the bed, closing his eyes.

Stubbs's disgusted sniff, followed by the *banyan* landing in his lap, finally roused him enough to open his eyes. The man himself stood a few feet away from William with his arms folded across his chest, scowling his most disapproving scowl. William might have chuckled if his heart were not bleeding out at that particular moment.

"So, what are we a'gonna do now?"

"Nothing," William said despondently.

Stubbs growled low in his throat. "Naught? Feh!" he spat. "Seems t' me, settin' on yer arse's not a'gonna get ye what yer after."

"I did not think you approved of my association with the young man," William shot back, knowing he sounded petty and childish but not being able to stop himself.

"Don' matter who 'tis, awnly tha' yer back among the livin'. We b'aant had this much fun in years."

William looked up to find the man grinning at him, and William could not stop the corners of his mouth from quirking. When Maud came in a moment later, carrying his tray, Stubbs sobered again but for the twinkle in his eye. When the good woman saw William on the floor, she fussed and fluttered at him until she had him wrapped in the *banyan* and ensconced in the leather chair, coffee in hand.

"Fool man. Catch yer death, ye will."

She continued to mutter on in a similar bent until he was settled to her satisfaction and the fire was built back up in the grate. Then she moved to stand next to her husband. Stubbs still stood with his arms across his chest, waiting for orders, his stance making it plain that he would not accept William's earlier despondence.

William closed his eyes and sipped at his coffee, allowing its heat to spread from his stomach to the rest of his body and keeping his mind blank. He began to feel much better after only a few sips, and by the time he had finished the cup, he was feeling almost himself again.

Stubbs simply watched him, his eyes expectant and challenging, while Maud glanced back and forth between the two of them until the good woman appeared to run out of patience. She was the first to break the silence, harrumphing and throwing her hands in the air as she flounced out of the room, muttering to herself about bloody fools.

William sighed and quirked an embarrassed grimace at Stubbs. The older man was right. William would not get anything he wanted by sitting on his arse and weeping. Stephen had hurt him with his refusal, but Stephen was so buried beneath his own mysterious troubles he could not see his way clear to anything at present. The young man did not know William well enough yet to trust him with his life and the welfare of his family. It would be a lot to ask of any man so soon. William would simply have to find a way to prove himself.

Stephen's happiness and his own were now intertwined. If William truly loved the young man, then he would not give up until he saw him happy, thereby ensuring his own happiness in the process. William was neither selfless nor a saint, but he *was* clever and determined. All he had to do was convince his little hedgehog of that, and the world would be a much brighter place. He had to make a plan. He could not wallow in misery all afternoon. Stephen's departure only made things more difficult, not impossible. *Nothing* was impossible for Gentleman Black, scourge of Cornwall and the Devon coast.

William's smile grew broad and just a little wicked, and Stubbs raised his brows and broke into a grin of his own. His man had seen this particular smile many times over the years, and was obviously delighted to see it again on his master's face. "'Bout damned time. Orders?"

"Find boys, young enough to be overlooked but old enough to be trusted to follow orders, and stay out of sight. Make sure they are washed and presentable enough that they will look like servants to any overzealous shopkeepers or watchmen. I want two watching Graves's house night and day. One is to come to you at once should they see anything of note, most particularly if there are any signs of the house packing up. Find enough of them so they can work in shifts and pay them whatever you think fair. I will make the rounds of my acquaintances and learn what more I can of Graves in society, and you continue to do the same in the stews."

"Aye, sir." Stubbs also had a familiar gleam in his eye, and William could not help chuckling at it.

"This is hardly high adventure, Stubbs."

"No. But 'tis good te 'ave ye back, sir."

"It is good to *be* back, old friend. I believe we are a little too old to repeat some of our more infamous exploits, but perhaps it is time for a new adventure. And while we are speaking of infamous exploits, you have yet to tell me of your adventure last night and where you got that bump on your head."

The story was a short one. Stubbs had noticed two men watching the house when he had gone to fetch the carriage. He went to confront the men after William and Stephen had driven away. The men were so caught up in their pursuit of the carriage that they never saw him coming. He had knocked the first man unconscious straight away, but the other had gotten in a lucky blow before Stubbs could take him down. He had tied the men up and waited for them to rouse. When they did, he questioned them thoroughly, but they had little of use to say. They had been hired by a "flash cove" who did not give his name. He was tall and skinny with a moustache. They had been instructed to watch the house and follow if the master left. They would receive the second half of their payment when the gentleman came to hear their report.

When he finished telling his tale, Stubbs offered to try to find the man, but William refused. He was fairly certain who had hired them. It did not matter who was actually sent to do the deed, and risking Stubbs's neck to be sure was not acceptable. Maud really would skin him alive.

William decided to continue with his plan as it was. The watcher would now become the watched, and William would force himself to be patient until he knew more. At present he knew almost nothing of the facts of his love's life. Stephen had told him very little, and though Graves was whispered about often, there was never anything useful said about the man.

William would go back to Mayfair and make the rounds as he had planned. He would play the dissolute gentleman of fortune as he always had, and behave as if nothing was amiss. He would do nothing to alarm Graves, and he would simply have to hope that the gossip mills would provide him with enough clues for him to plan his next move.

When he returned to his house in Mayfair, there was a letter from Horace waiting for him among the stack of cards and invitations Hume had left on his desk. William was not in any humor to deal with his brother, missing Stephen as he was already, but he supposed it would be better to get it over with, so he pulled the letter from the stack and broke the seal.

Coldly formal as ever, Horace had expressed his gratitude upon receiving the packet of letters William had retrieved for him from Mr. Bradshaw, then proceeded to express his regrets over the "unpleasantness" of their last interview. He encouraged William to provide contradictory information, if such existed, regarding the topic they had discussed so that they might meet under better circumstances in future. William had snorted at that and tossed the letter into the fire. He had no desire to waste his energy or his breath in setting his brother to rights at present. He had more important matters on his mind. In time, Horace would learn the truth on his own, or not. William did not particularly care one way or the other. Unless the girl herself came forward to accuse him, this gossip would fade into dust and be forgotten. William hoped to be living happily on a sheep farm somewhere in the country by that time, so it was of little matter.

William had his suspicions on the origins of that bit of gossip. Horace's "unknown source" was likely not *unknown* at all, but it was only a minor irritation, one among several that William would see redressed before he was done with Graves. In point of fact, he should probably thank the man for his aid. If William had not had that "unpleasantness" with his brother, he and Stephen would not have quarreled quite so fiercely, and they might never have come together so splendidly afterward. Graves had done him a favor.

# Chapter *Fourteen*

THE next few days seemed endless for William. He visited salons and called upon friends. He went to his club and to an evening assembly. He gently probed all to whom he spoke for information on Graves, but as he had feared, there was little of substance to be heard. The man was continuously whispered about, but no one would speak openly against him. The only information of value that he did manage to learn was that Graves spent much of his youth in the lake country, at a place called Greystoke Castle, one of his father's many extensive properties. The castle itself was said to be not much more than a derelict pile of rubble, but the family had built a small country house nearby, and Graves was said to be quite fond of it.

The information gave William some hope. There were hills, valleys, and sheep farms in the north, and Stephen and Graves had to have met *somewhere*, but the connection was tenuous at best.

William tried to show patience, but after only three days, what little he had was already wearing perilously thin. Though he filled his days with the hunt, his nights were spent alone and lonely. He found himself reaching for Stephen in the night, only to wake alone and aching, reminding him of the first terrible months after Cora had died. It surprised him how quickly he had become accustomed to having Stephen in his bed, but it was only more proof of the depth of his feelings. His heart and his body had decided on Stephen. It was left only for his mind to puzzle out how to give them what they wanted. Without sleep and someone to calm his restless soul, however, his mind was quickly losing the battle, and he was on the verge of forgetting all his good intentions and storming Graves's home to carry Stephen off when he finally heard from Stubbs.

On the fourth morning after he had left Cecil Court, Stubbs came calling at his door. William was at his desk, rereading all of his letters and cards, searching for anyone he had not already spoken to, when there was a quiet knock on his study door. Hume, his butler, entered, frowning most unpleasantly, and informed him that a *person* calling himself Stubbs had come to the *front* door, not the servant's entrance, and was most anxious to speak with him.

"He said to tell you it was urgent, sir. Though I may be mistaken, as I could barely understand the man," Hume sniffed.

"Send him in at once, please."

*Urgent?* William's mind spun with the possible implications of the word as his pulse quickened. By the time Hume returned with Stubbs, William was pacing the room in agitation.

"Thank you, Hume. You may go," William ordered brusquely. When the man had gone, closing the door behind him, William turned anxiously to Stubbs. "What is it? What has happened?"

"They left this morn, sir. Don' know where they've gone."

"What? How? The boys were to report immediately if there were any signs."

"Weren't none, sir. No sign a'tall. This morn, a'fore dawn, carriage cum wit' marks covered o'er. The trunks an' gents packed off quick as ye please. No 'ired coach, thisun, neither. Fam'ly coach, 'tis sure. Boys come soon as th' could."

"Damn!" William swore. "Did they have nothing else to say?"

"Awnly tha' they headed north and the gents was screechin' at one 'nother like fishwives a'fore they climbed in carriage."

William had to smile a little at that. A picture of Stephen, flushed with fury and giving Graves hell, filled his mind for a moment. He took a few deep breaths and rubbed his temples, trying to calm himself so he could think.

They went north. William had already deduced that Stephen must have come from the North. His speech, though educated, was colored from time to time with a Northern accent, a small lilt here or there. Graves's father had property in the lake country, and the man had spent much of his youth there. It was the only connection William had at the moment.

*I just want to go home.*

Stephen's pained words echoed in William's memory. Perhaps Stephen had convinced Graves to take him there.

"Sir?" Stubbs's gruff voice called him out of his thoughts for a moment, and he smiled apologetically.

"Pour us a drink, man, and take a seat. You look as if you ran all the way here."

"Hardly tha', sir," Stubbs snorted as he poured whiskey from the decanter on William's desk into two glasses and sat in one of the two chairs near the fireplace. William joined him, and they sat in companionable silence for a time. Stubbs waited patiently for William to decide what they would do, just as they had done in their early days together. William had always been the schemer, and Stubbs had always seen it done.

The only course William could see was to head north after Stephen. In this, his heart and mind were in perfect union. He had no idea if they were going to Stephen's home or not, but William could not sit idle in London any longer with no hint as to when or *if* the two men would return. He would go mad. The last few nights had been bad enough. The prospect of weeks, months, or even *years* of the same was simply unimaginable. His gut told him to go north. The answers he sought were there. They had to be.

"How would you fancy a holiday, Stubbs?" William asked, finally breaking the silence

Stubbs raised his thick eyebrows and pursed his lips. "Holiday?"

"I believe I have a strange desire to visit the lake country. I think the fresh air would greatly aid my constitution. Maud would join us, of course, and I would like you to find that young scamp Phillip as well."

"Missus won' leave town jus' now. Not wit' bairn a'comin'." Stubbs gave him an apologetic look.

William frowned. He had not thought of that. It was true that Maud would be unwilling to leave London when the young girls she was caring for were so near their time. Would she allow her husband to go without her? Could William leave her alone, unsure whether the men who had followed him and watched his house were truly hired by Graves?

William pondered this for a time until he thought of a possible solution.

"If I were to allow her to shelter the girls under my roof with her, do you think she would allow you to accompany me? If I were to pay for a doctor to check in on them often? You could hire anyone else you wish to see to her protection and well-being while we are gone."

Stubbs thought about it a moment, then grinned happily. "Aye, sir." It appeared the man would be quite happy for an excuse to leave the women's matters to the women, as long as his wife were to be looked after.

"Excellent. Then go home and tell her. We will be gone at least a month, perhaps two, so pack what you need. I will have the servants here pack some clothes for you to act the proper gentleman's servant, but you will need to pack the rest and return here by dawn. We will leave at first light."

Stubbs scowled at the mention of proper clothing but nodded and stood, throwing back the last of the whiskey in his glass before turning to leave.

"Two more things, Stubbs," William called after his retreating back. "First, keep someone checking on Graves's house while we are gone, in case they return. Maud can send word through the doctor. He will be writing to me to keep me informed. And second, I would still like Phillip to join us, if he can."

"Aye, he can. He's a'tween jobs at moment." Stubbs grimaced and rolled his eyes, but William could see the affection behind his friend's feigned disapproval.

Phillip, Pip, was another one of Maud's orphans. He was a bit of a scamp and a rogue, but he held a special place in her heart, not to mention the hearts of any other women he set his sights on. The lad had a rather sordid history and never seemed to hold a job for more than a month at a time, but he was young, handsome, and charming, and that was just what William needed for his plan.

"Good, then bring him with you. I will see to his clothes. You will both be traveling as my servants, so see that he looks respectable for our journey, and we will purchase whatever else he may need on the way."

Stubbs left with another "aye," and William was left alone with his thoughts. As most of them screamed for him to go chasing after Stephen immediately, he decided it would be best to distract himself before he did anything rash. He had no idea how long they might be gone, but there were business matters that should be attended to, and packing and closing down the house. He had to find a doctor for Maud and make provisions for his servants as well, so there were plenty of things to keep him from dwelling on the fact that Stephen was traveling further and further away from him with every minute that ticked past. William growled and rose to find Hume. He needed to be out and doing *something*, or he would drive himself mad.

Before dawn, the hired carriage was packed and ready for their journey. Granger, his valet, had William dressed and shaved shortly after six, and Hume came in only moments later to inform him of the arrival of his traveling companions. William was anxious to be on his way. He had not slept at all that night, and though the prospect of over a week's travel confined in the compartment of a coach did nothing to lighten his spirits, he knew the sooner his journey began, the sooner it would be over. He descended the stairs quickly, pulled on the coat Hume held for him, and donned his hat and gloves. Grabbing his cane, he stepped out into the cold dawn and made his way to the waiting carriage.

Stubbs, Maud, and a yawning Pip were waiting for him, and William felt some of his anxiety ease at the sight. Maud was smiling, though she carried a handkerchief and dabbed at her eyes from time to

188

time. Stubbs was scowling, as always, but he had his arm wrapped comfortingly around his wife and was murmuring in her ear. Pip did not appear to be awake, but he was dressed respectably, if a little rumpled, which was all that William needed of him for the moment. William let out a breath he hadn't known he was holding and smiled a welcome to his companions. All would be well. With people such as these to rely upon, how could it be otherwise?

"Good morning to you all. Maud, have you decided to join us?"

"No, sir. Only to see ye off and to thank ye for lettin' the girls come to stay in their time of need." Maud bobbed him a curtsey while watching Hume uncomfortably out of the corner of her eye.

"You are welcome, Maud. And you know you need only send word to this house if you have a need. Hume has been instructed to give you whatever you require in my absence."

Hume scowled, and Maud smiled a little brighter.

"Oh, thank ye, sir, thank ye." The woman's eyes had misted, and William thought it best to move on.

"Phillip. It is good to see you well, and I am grateful you will be able to join us."

"Aye," he said, sounding remarkably like Stubbs for a moment until Maud gave him a slap to the back of the head.

He grinned a little sheepishly and rubbed at his auburn curls while he ducked his head and said, "Forgive me, sir. Beggin' your pardon, sir. 'Tis a pleasure to accompany you, sir." Maud had raised her hand again to deliver another slap for Pip's cheeky response, but she halted when William laughed.

"You'll do, lad. You'll do. Now, we really must be off. There is precious little daylight this time of year, and we have a long journey ahead. Say your good-byes and let us depart."

Maud kissed Stubbs and Pip, giving the latter a tug on his ear and reminding him to be respectful. Then she turned to William and bit her lip.

"I will take care of them, Maud. You have my word," William assured her.

Her lip trembled a little, and she rushed to kiss William on the cheek before hurrying off to the carriage waiting to take her back to Cecil Court. William smiled after her, and turned to wave the other two men toward their carriage.

The journey north would take more than a week, even with changing horses at every stop, and Stephen and Graves had a day's lead on them already. They needed to make a start.

During the first few hours in the coach, William simply sat with his eyes closed and allowed himself to rest. Deprived of sleep and tense with worry, he was most assuredly not at his best. Stubbs and Pip were equally quiet across from him, and William decided it would be best to wait until later to talk to them of his plans. They had plenty of time to speak of such things in the coming days, and William's plan was not a complex one.

They traveled in sleepy silence for several hours before stopping for a rest and a meal at the first coaching inn. William allowed himself and his servants to eat their meal in peace, but when they returned to the carriage, he could wait no longer to speak to them of his plan. If he told them early, they might have time to think of questions or suggestions before they reached the end of their journey.

When he knew he had their attention, William leaned forward and gave his instructions as the carriage continued to bounce and rock over the rutted road. The plan was simple. From what little he knew of Graves and Stephen, Greystoke Castle seemed the best place to start their search. Penrith was the nearest town of any size, and would most likely prove the best place to learn what more he could about Stephen. They would set themselves up at an inn, and William would put out enquiries as to any houses to let in the neighborhood. They would introduce themselves as just who they were: a gentleman of wealth and noble family, looking to invest in the area, and his two manservants.

William would do what came naturally and charm himself into the local society, Stubbs would spend his days in the pubs and ale-houses, talking up the local men, and Pip would simply roam about being his handsome and charming self and allow the servant girls and young ladies of the village to flock to him like bees to clover. By this, they would have nearly all avenues of gossip well covered: widows for William; farmers, laborers, and old men for Stubbs; and swooning serving maids for Phillip. They should know all there was to know about Penrith within a week. Beyond that, William did not know what to expect, and they would have to wait and see what they could learn.

Stubbs was his usual self and simply grunted an "aye." Pip grinned broadly and clapped his hands together, rubbing them in apparent anticipation—a little too much anticipation for Stubbs's liking, for the man clapped him lightly on the back of the head and leaned in to growl, "Ye'll keep yer prick in yer trousers. We b'aint leaving no bastards behind us."

"I 'ear ye, cove. I'll be a saint. I promise." Pip gave Stubbs his most innocent, wide-eyed look, and Stubbs snorted in disbelief but still ruffled his hair affectionately. William merely smiled in amusement at the exchange, realizing how the lad managed so well with the ladies. He had the face of an angel with those wide brown eyes, auburn curls, and pouting lips. No one would believe that such a face could hide such a scamp.

"Just be careful, Pip," William felt it necessary to add. "I may wish to live in this town someday, and I will not have you cutting a swath through every willing chit in the village, understand? You will flatter them and woo them until they tell you what I need to know, nothing else. I have no wish to have to save you from jealous husbands or wrathful fathers."

Phillip nodded solemnly, and William ignored the twinkle in his eyes. The boy was truly a good lad, if a little misguided at times. William knew his angelic face and charming smile hid more than just a puckish disposition. There were things in the young man's past that he would not speak of, things that haunted his eyes sometimes when he thought no one was looking. William knew for a fact that the young man had spent a year in Bridewell Prison when he was barely thirteen, and the experience had changed him. William had done what he could to give the boy prospects, at Maud's urging at first and then of his own accord, because he saw the potential in the boy. Pip was a survivor and would turn out well, Maud would make sure of it, and William would help where he could.

The rest of their journey was as tedious as he had feared. Hours and hours on his arse in the bouncing carriage and sleepless nights at the inns, tortured by visions of Stephen and Graves together, did not make for a happy William. Stubbs remained blessedly silent for most of the trip, attuned to his master's ill-humor, but Pip could not seem to bear the silence and insisted on filling it with whatever popped into his head. When the lad finally ran out of words, he would begin whistling and humming until William was near to gagging him and strapping him to their trunks on top of the coach. Stubbs seemed to know when William was at a breaking point, however, and would put a hand on the lad's shoulder to silence him, which worked for a little while, at least. But by the fourth day of their journey, Pip had decided, in the interests of self-preservation, to spend much of his time up with the coachman and their trunks, away from the two grumbling older men, and William was able to rest in quiet.

They arrived in Penrith late, but despite feeling exhausted, William would not rest until he knew if Graves and Stephen were in the neighborhood. Pip volunteered to have a chat with the serving girl that brought William his dinner, and the lad was back within minutes, his face flushed and his lips kiss-swollen, to inform William that Graves had not been in the neighborhood in over a year. At least chasing the son of an earl did have a few advantages. Even in a town as large as this one, should Graves set foot in the valley, news of his arrival would be on everyone's lips within minutes.

William tried to quell his disappointment. Perhaps they had stopped somewhere on the way or simply taken a more leisurely journey. He need not panic just yet.

After the third day in town without word, however, William began to truly fear that he had chosen wrong. He hid his growing doubts behind his most winning smile and kept to his original plan, making himself charming and delightful to all he encountered in hopes that some word of his love would come to him, but it was hard.

He first made himself known to a Mr. Wilton, the local house agent, and after a brief interview and copious usage of his family name and references to his many investments, William was invited to a dinner party with the man's family and a few close friends. From there, it was only a matter of days before he was introduced to the local magistrate, a few solicitors, a vicar, one of the town doctors, and a bevy of other good people in the neighborhood. He was soon paying calls regularly and subtly probing all of Penrith society for information about Graves.

It was not until his second week in the town, however, that fortune finally smiled on him. At another dinner party held by Mr. Wilton, he was finally introduced to exactly the kind of treasure he had been seeking in the persons of Miss Imogen Harlowe and her widowed sister, Mrs. Grant, two elderly ladies with a weakness for flattery and a penchant for gossip. He charmed and flattered them until the good ladies could not help but invite him to tea the next day. When their talk inevitably turned to the earl, the ladies were proud to tell him that the earl and his family were quite fond of their little valley, and had indeed spent a great deal of time there over the years, the youngest son in particular.

With a little prodding from William, the ladies spoke of Graves in greater detail, and their words gave William the impression that they did not believe he behaved in a manner becoming in a young gentleman of his station, but when William attempted to get them to elaborate, the ladies quickly changed their tune, and William was forced to grit his teeth in frustration. It was his own fault—he had pushed too hard—but he was soon very grateful that he had. The sweet ladies were at such pains to convince him of their admiration of that great family that they ended up telling him exactly what he most wished to know.

Graves was a fine young gentleman. Perhaps a little wild, but what young man was not? He was handsome and dashing. He was kind and generous to his father's tenants and all the families in the valley. In fact, only a few years before, he had shown one family such kindness and generosity as would shock and amaze anyone who did not know what a kind soul he was.

That last garnered William's full attention, and though he felt ready to retch over the glowing praise they were heaping on the man he despised, William went out of his way to encourage them to continue, and the sisters were happy to oblige him.

Over hot tea and almond biscuits, William was given the tale of the Carruthers family. At one time, the family had had the largest sheep farm in the valley and was admired and respected throughout the neighborhood. They had been tenants of the earls for generations and had always been very successful, until three years ago, when a sudden outbreak of sheep scab among their flocks had ended it all. The flock had been decimated, and the family had been ruined trying to save it. John Carruthers, the father, had died soon after in an accident of some kind, leaving his wife and two children with nothing. If the earl had not allowed the family to stay in their house and defer payment of their rents for a time, the family would have been completely destitute. But the sainted Graves and his sainted father had shown generosity to the grieving family, allowing them to stay. In fact, the earl and his son had even paid to send the daughter off to a respectable school for young ladies, and the son, newly returned from university, was even now traveling with Graves. The good man had taken the lad under his wing so that he might return someday and take his father's place, restoring the family and the farm to their former glory.

William had had to work very hard not to roll his eyes, but the news of the Carruthers family was more than enough to distract him. His heartbeat quickened in his chest with every word of the tale, and he *knew*, for the first time since Stephen had left his house, that he was on the right path. It *had* to be Stephen they spoke of. It could not be anyone else. He knew it in his heart, and his gratitude and glowing smile were quite genuine when he thanked the ladies for a lovely afternoon and bid them good day.

He walked back to the inn with a much lighter step than he had left with only a few hours before. The air seemed fresher and the sun brighter as he made his way through the streets of the town. He had a name now, Stephen *Carruthers*. This was his love's home. These were his neighbors. The certainty of that cast the whole town in a different light for him. The ancient market town with its red sandstone buildings and narrow streets, resting in the shadow of St. Andrew's Church, looked warmer and more welcoming with every step he took. If all went as he hoped, this would be *his* home soon.

He tried not to get too far ahead of himself. Hope was nearly as fickle a mistress as luck, but he could not help the lightness in his chest or the grin upon his lips.

*Stephen has to come home sometime.*

Wherever he was, Stephen would not allow Graves to keep him away forever. All William had to do was wait, and they would be reunited. William would not dwell too long on the fact that Stephen would *not* be particularly happy to see him there, but now that he knew some of the history, he hoped to learn enough to devise a solution to that minor problem before they were reunited.

Stubbs and Pip were not back by the time he arrived at the inn, so he was forced to wait to share his news. He had called on the sisters in late morning and had planned to make another call afterward, so his servants would not be expecting him back so soon. William hoped they would not stay away too long, as he was near to bursting with what he had learned, and he wanted to make certain his servants concentrated their efforts on the Carruthers family from then on.

When Stubbs finally did return, William learned that his servant had already been given much the same tale that very afternoon from an old farmer who spent most of his days in the pubs. Penrith was unusually blessed in the number of pubs it could boast, and it had taken Stubbs several days to find one that catered to the type of men they were looking for. He had only met the old farmer a day or two earlier, and it had taken him some time to earn the man's trust. He was very glad that he had made the effort when the old man admitted to being close friends with a man who used to work for the Carruthers family, and Stubbs promised William that he would do what he could to find and talk to the man.

By the time Pip returned, William and Stubbs had learned all the other had to tell and were sharing a quiet drink by the fire in his room. The young man was quite flushed and disheveled, but he was grinning and seemed quite pleased with himself.

"What have you been up to, ye scamp?" Stubbs asked.

"I'll tell ye if ye give us a tipple," Pip replied before dancing out of the way of Stubbs's backhand.

"Ye'll get nawt but a knock to yer nobbin if ye don' show yer master proper respec'," Stubbs growled, but William could see the amused glint in his eyes.

Pip was still grinning even as he made William a courtly bow. "Your pardon, sirs."

"Are you going to tell us what has you so pleased with yourself, Phillip, or are we going to be forced to guess?" William prompted.

Pip lifted a finger to his chin and appeared to think about the question quite seriously until Stubbs reached for one of the irons by the fire, at which point he laughed and said, "Yes, sir, sorry, sir. I do 'ave news. I 'ave just spent a luvly afternoon with a young girl named Agnes, a plump but pretty wench. She's serving maid to a cove name of Barnes, watchmaker, but 'er *sister* is a lady's maid, an' she heard tell from her mistress that the earl hisself was in the neighborhood and his 'ousekeeper was in town lookin' to 'ire extra servants." Phillip finished with a flourish and made another courtly bow, then cast pitiful eyes at Stubbs's cup.

"Did she say anything about the earl's son joining him?" William asked hopefully, distracting the man for a moment. Pip's cocksure smile faded a little as he shook his head. William rose to his feet and handed the young man his own glass before pacing to the window to think. Pip took his place by the fire, but William barely noticed.

Did it mean anything that the earl was in the valley without his son? Should he risk a visit to the man when he still knew so little of what had really happened with the family and the earl's connection to them?

It was possible the earl was just as much a villain as his son, and William might do more harm than good in calling on him, but it was not in his nature to refuse an opportunity to learn more, and the earl *had* to know at least some of the truth. He would simply have to take the chance and hope his luck held.

Chapter *Fifteen*

IT HAD been three days since he had sent his card to the earl's house, and he had still received no answer. Rationally, William knew the man might still be settling in, but the waiting still grated on him. Stubbs had continued to make friends among the farmers and had finally been introduced to the man who used to be head shepherd for the Carruthers family, Mr. Myers, but the man was proving to be even more circumspect than Stubbs, so they had learned nothing new as yet.

Pip continued to woo the serving maids and was able to tell William that the whole town was buzzing with the news of the earl's arrival, but not much else. The widowed Mrs. Carruthers kept a staff of only one old woman and a man she hired occasionally from the village to do the heavy work, but that was all. Pip had no way of getting information from inside the house, as all of the other staff had been let go long ago. William's own calls and engagements had become tedious repetitions of the same conversations he had already had, and he was fast losing patience with the lot of them.

At least the following day was market day in Penrith, and they might be able to meet new people. The excitement of market day could be felt in stately dining rooms and inn common rooms alike, and William felt certain that, with so much going on in the town and everyone out and about, they were sure to learn something new, something that could help them.

William decided all three of them would spend the day at the market. They would all keep their eyes and ears open for anything or anyone new. In his heart, William knew he was hoping Stephen would be there somewhere among the crowds, and he could not help watching for him in every face he passed.

Late in the afternoon, when he did finally spy a riot of golden-brown waves out of the corner of his eye, he nearly tripped over an elderly woman in front of him in shock. After begging the woman's pardon, William rushed off in the direction that the vision had disappeared and was brought up short at the sight of a lovely woman in a soft green gown and green velvet spencer jacket standing next to a finely dressed older gentleman, whom William recognized as the town doctor. The lady's hat was cocked to the right, leaving her hair free to coil about her head on the left, and that was what had caught his eye. Now that he could see her face, he knew she *had* to be Stephen's mother. They had the same heart-shaped face and full lips, though her eyes were green, not amber like his love's.

William was disappointed, nervous, and excited all at once. Stephen was not there, but here was an opportunity to meet his love's mother and to learn more about him—as long as he did not make too much of a fool of himself angling for an introduction to the lady.

He took a deep breath to calm himself and gripped his cane tightly to still his shaking hands. He walked toward the couple with purpose and, when the gentleman met his gaze, bowed and tipped his hat to both of them.

"Good afternoon, Doctor Jardine. Lovely day for a stroll, don't you think?"

"Good afternoon, Mr. Carey. It is indeed. May I introduce you to my friend, Mrs. Carruthers?" The older man tipped his hat at William as he spoke, and the woman smiled and gave him a nod.

"A pleasure to meet you, madam. I do not wish to seem impertinent, but I believe we have a mutual acquaintance. Mr. Stephen Carruthers?" William held his breath as he waited for her response.

"You know my son?" Mrs. Carruthers's startled eyes met his for a moment before she bit her lip and looked at Dr. Jardine. "You have seen him? Is he well? He sends me letters, but I never know...."

The lady seemed quite flustered and anxious now, and William could see where Stephen acquired some of his passion. He was surprised to see Dr. Jardine take her hand in his and give it a comforting squeeze, and found it quite interesting that the lady only blushed and took her hand back when she noticed William watching.

"Yes, madam. I met your son in London only a few short weeks ago, and I must tell you what a fine young man he proved to be. He was in excellent health the last time I saw him. You need not fear. In truth, he is the reason I have traveled to your lovely town. He spoke so highly of it during our acquaintance that I could not wait to see it for myself."

Mrs. Carruthers smiled and blushed prettily for him. "Oh thank you, Mr. Carey. You must know how a mother worries. London is such a big place, and Mr. Graves...." She stopped there and cleared her throat. "We were just about to go for tea. Would you care to join us so I might hear more of your acquaintance with my son?"

William smiled and felt some of the tension leave his body. "Certainly, madam, if you do not feel I would be imposing. I would like that very much, thank you."

The teashop was only a block away, and they were barely seated before Mrs. Carruthers began peppering him with questions again. Where had they met? Was Mr. Graves well? What had they spoken of? What had Stephen been doing? Did he seem happy? Did he say he planned to return home soon?

William answered as best he could. He avoided outright falsehoods unless they were absolutely necessary, but he obviously could not reveal the details of their relationship. From her questions, William, in turn, learned that Stephen had not, as yet, informed his mother of his departure from London nor of his plans thereafter. It was disheartening news, but at least William was a little closer to unraveling his lover's secrets and perhaps learning how best to see him happy. Throughout their conversation, William observed the interaction of the two people in front of him with interest. It was obvious to

William that they were more than *friends*, and he had to wonder if Stephen knew of their attachment.

His purely internal question was answered only a few minutes later when Mrs. Carruthers took him aside as they were bidding each other good day and said, "Forgive me, Mr. Carey, but I would ask a favor of you, if I may?"

"Certainly, madam."

"Dr. Jardine and I… well, we are…." The woman blushed brightly. "We are engaged, sir, but I have not told my son as yet, nor have we made any sort of announcement in the neighborhood. I did not wish to put such important news in a letter, and I wished to speak to him before we announced it. It is perhaps inappropriate for me to say such things to you, but my son was very hurt by the death of his father, and I fear he may need a little time to get used to the idea of his mother marrying again. I do not know the level of your intimacy with my son, but I would be grateful if you would not mention any of this to him if you should correspond. I would like to be the one to tell him myself."

The pleading look she sent him, from a face so like Stephen's, melted his heart, and he found himself wanting to give this woman anything she asked for. "Of course." William had to swallow around the thickness in his throat. "Of course, madam. I will not breathe a word of it. You have my word."

Her grateful smile was dazzling. "Thank you, Mr. Carey. You are indeed a fine gentleman. I cannot tell you how happy I am to learn my son has met with such men in his travels. I will look forward to our next meeting."

William bowed over her extended hand and smiled up at her. "As will I, Mrs. Carruthers."

William chose to return to the inn then, as he felt he had learned enough for one day and he wanted to think. There were two messages waiting for him in his room. The first was from Mr. Wilton, informing him that there were two houses in the neighborhood that might suit his needs, and if he wished to see them, he was to send word to Wilton's office and arrangements would be made. The second was from the earl himself, inviting William to call at his earliest convenience. Stubbs and Pip were still out at the market, so William had no one with whom to share his happiness. In one day he had made more progress than in the last several days combined.

The next morning, he sent word to Mr. Wilton that he wished to visit the houses that afternoon. Then he hired a horse and rode out to call on the Earl of Arundel. The note William had sent to the earl had said only that he was an acquaintance of Graves and would dearly love the opportunity to call and pay his respects. As William was ushered into the man's parlor, however, he was fairly certain the earl knew of his son's dealings in London, for the man barely made it through the required pleasantries before he said, "How much does he owe you, Mr. Carey?"

It took William a moment to respond, startled as he was by the man's directness. When the older man merely continued to watch him through lowered gray brows, his lips pursed beneath a thick moustache, William quirked an apologetic smile and answered, "Five thousand pounds, my lord."

The earl's lips twisted in a grimace then, and he stood to pace the room, silent but for the heavy tread of his boots on the thick gold Aubusson carpet. When the silence stretched painfully and William could see a vein in the man's temple throbbing beneath his skin, he decided he had best play his advantage and make the man an offer that should prove of benefit to both of them. "My lord?"

When the man ceased his pacing and looked up, William took a deep breath and leapt in with both feet. "I believe I may have a solution that might prove beneficial to both of us, if you would oblige me?"

The man's dark brows rose and his moustache twitched, but he simply motioned imperiously for William to continue.

"In my brief acquaintance with your son, I met a young man named Stephen Carruthers. Do you know him?"

"Carruthers? Farmer, yes? From here in the valley?" The earl looked puzzled, but he nodded.

"Yes, that would be him. The young man much impressed me with his wit and his spirit, and I have come to the valley with the intentions of investing in his future. Sadly, I have no children of my own, and of course my brother's children are well provided for, so I have a mind to see my fortune invested in someone worthy. I believe young Mr. Carruthers may be that man." It twisted William's stomach a little to speak of Stephen in such a paternal manner, but he had to give the earl just cause for his interest in Stephen, and this was as believable a reason as any.

The earl gave him a disbelieving look but said nothing to contradict.

William forced a chuckle. "I know my reputation precedes me in this, my lord, but I think it is time for me to leave all of that nonsense behind and settle into the country for a while, perhaps find some peace. My proposition is this: I will forgive Graves his debt to me if you will, in turn, forgive the Carruthers family *their* debts and your son will agree to allow Mr. Carruthers to return home and take his place as head of his family. From then on, your rents will be paid in full and in a timely manner, and all will return to the way it was before the tragic death of Mr. Carruthers's father."

Arundel regarded him sharply for a long time, and William began to wonder just how much the man knew of his son's involvement with Stephen and what had happened three years ago.

"I believe that would be a fair bargain, sir," the earl finally replied, breaking into William's thoughts. "I will speak with my steward and my solicitor, and if all is in order, I will sign the notes over to you. Will that be satisfactory, Mr. Carey?"

"Certainly, my lord. Thank you, my lord. And you will speak to your son?" William knew that Graves would not go down quietly. He could only hope that the threat of his father's displeasure would override any foolish impulses the man might have.

Arundel's eyes narrowed dangerously in response to his question, and he growled, "My son in not your concern, Mr. Carey. We have made a bargain, and I am a man of my word."

William decided it would best for him to beat a hasty retreat and plastered on his most innocent and apologetic look. "Of course, my lord. That could never be doubted. Thank you, my lord, for agreeing to see me and aiding me in this most unfortunate matter. You are very generous."

The man twisted his lips beneath his moustache and merely nodded. "Good day to you, sir. You will hear from my man in a few days."

William bowed and strode quickly out of the room, hiding his smile. He had gotten what he wanted from the man. That was all that mattered. Graves would have to bring Stephen home soon. His deal with the earl would make sure of that. All William had to do now was wait and plan for his return.

With nothing to distract him, William feared he would go mad with worry.

When Stubbs found him an hour later, wearing a hole in their new cottage's polished wood floor, his servant ordered him to put on his coat and join him for a night at the pub. William was so overwrought by that point that he did not even comment on the appropriateness of a servant giving his master orders; he simply donned his coat, hat, and gloves and followed his man into town. Anything would be better than stewing in his own misery for the rest of the night.

They were only at the pub for a few minutes before Mr. Myers, the Carruthers's old head shepherd, walked in, and William was convinced once again that Fortuna loved him. Stubbs introduced William to Myers, and they all sat down to have a few drinks together. Several hours and several pints of ale later, Myers was in the mood to talk, and William and Stubbs were finally able to learn the truth of the Carruthers family's misfortunes.

According to Myers, John Carruthers, Stephen's father, had, unbeknownst to the rest of his family, gone in with Robert Graves on a scheme he had hoped would revolutionize sheep farming in England. He had invested a fortune in a breed of sheep from Spain that Graves had convinced him would be a perfect blend with his own Rough Fell. The result would have been a hardy sheep that could survive the fells but would also produce a wool so fine and meat so savory that every farmer in the county would have been begging for their tups—or at least that was what Graves had claimed.

Myers had been skeptical, but it was not his place to argue with his master, so the sheep were purchased and transported to the farm. Myers had begged Carruthers to keep the sheep separate until they could be sure of their health, but they had all *looked* quite healthy when they arrived, and both Graves and Carruthers were impatient, so they had folded in the entire stock for the breeding not long after their arrival.

What happened next, William already knew: the sheep scab had spread through the flock in no time at all. It had also spread to some of the neighboring farms before it was discovered, and John Carruthers was left not only to try to save his own flock, but to make restitution for his neighbors' losses.

Ruined and shunned by his fellow farmers, the man had taken his own life, something William had *not* known and apparently no one else in the village would admit to knowing either. At that point in his story, Myers had paled as he realized what he had revealed in his drunken state, and Stubbs and William had had to spend almost an hour convincing the man that they would not tell a soul before Myers would continue his story. When he had calmed, Myers went on to relate what was common knowledge: Stephen had come home from university to find the farm ruined and his father dead, and Graves and the earl had swooped in to play the saints, taking Stephen away to London in hopes of repairing the family fortune.

By the time Myers finished his story, the poor man could barely string two words together and he was beginning to weep into his tankard, so William and Stubbs decided they had heard enough and helped him home before walking back to the cottage.

Pip was not there when they returned, but neither of them was particularly worried. The lad knew how to take care of himself, and wherever he was, it was unlikely he would welcome their interference.

Stubbs stirred up the fire and lit the lamps while William poured them each a glass of whiskey and they settled in to discuss what they had learned. For once, Stubbs actually made so bold as to share his opinions of Mr. Myers, and William couldn't help but think that his servant admired the man. They both agreed that Myers was a loyal man and could possibly be an ally for them. His love for the boy Stephen had been was as plain as his hatred for Graves, both of which made Myers a man to be trusted, in William's opinion. William encouraged Stubbs to continue to seek Myers out and thanked him for his help before bidding him good night and heading for his bedchamber. What he had learned did nothing to ease his fears about Graves and Stephen, but Stubbs didn't need to coddle and hold his hand while William fretted. The man deserved a good night's sleep, even if his master was unlikely to have one.

William settled himself in his empty bed, hoping that the combination of ale and whiskey would help him sleep, but he gave up trying after he tossed and turned for several hours. He spent the remainder of the night with questions chasing themselves around in his head.

Did Stephen know Graves had had a part in the scheme that had ruined his family? Did he know his father had killed himself? Did his mother know? Mrs. Carruthers did not appear to be a grieving widow any longer, so perhaps she already knew. Perhaps the knowledge of her husband's abandonment had allowed her to move on all the sooner?

William sighed and finally climbed from the bed as dawn cast its orange glow through the frosted panes of his window. He rose from the bed and donned Stephen's *banyan* before going to the fireplace to stir the coals. After the fire had perked up a little, he settled into one of the chairs in front of it and donned his slippers. Stubbs would probably sleep in this morning, and Pip still had not come home, so he would probably have to make his own coffee.

William had almost worked up the energy to make his way down to the kitchen when the quiet of his morning was rent by the clatter of boots on the stairs. A moment later, there was an enthusiastic knock at his door and Pip pushed his way in, all smiles and youthful exuberance.

"Sir, I 'ave news!" The young man was breathless, as if he had run from somewhere, and William sat forward in his chair at the excitement in his tone. "Your gents are comin' 'ome. I 'eard just this mornin'."

William's stomach flipped over, and he stood to pace the room. "Tell me."

Pip took a moment to catch his breath, and William poured the lad a bit of whiskey to help warm him up. His nose and his cheeks were red with cold, and he had to wipe his nose on his sleeve before he could continue. "Thank ye, sir. I'm a bit chilled." Pip took a few mouthfuls of the whiskey and moved closer to the fire. "Susan's an upstairs maid in the earl's 'ouse. I was wit' Mary when I met Susan, so I 'ad to break free of '*er* firs' a'fore I could talk to the girl. Las' night I met Susan at a dance they 'ad on the green. We got to talkin' and—*other things*—an' then we found a nice quiet place to spend the night... a bit cold but comf'table. Wasn't 'til this morn' tha' she told me she'd been run off 'er feet for two days straight, preparin' for the earl's youngest son t' visit. He's s'posed to be 'ere today, sir. I ran back soon as I could. Lucky for me she 'ad to be at the 'ouse afore dawn, else the 'ousekeeper'd know she didn't come 'ome las' night."

Pip's grin was broad and very self-satisfied, and William was so happy to hear his news that he did not even bother with reminding the lad that he was supposed to be keeping himself out of trouble. He clapped the young man on the shoulder and poured him another glass of whiskey.

"Thank you, Phillip. I cannot tell you how pleased I am to hear your news. You have done well. Now go and get some rest, you look as if you have not slept a wink."

Pip's grin, if anything, grew broader as the young man nodded and downed the last of the whiskey in his glass and left the room. William did not even hear the door close, he was so wrapped up in his own thoughts and feelings. Stephen would be home today. His wait was over. William was giddy with happiness and filled with anxiety all at once. He needed to plan his words and his actions carefully. The next several hours could very well determine the rest of his life.

He fussed and fretted over what he should do for almost an hour before deciding on a plan and dressing to go find Stubbs. By mid-morning he had shared Pip's news and his plan with his oldest friend and had sent the man off to the Carruthers's farm with a letter for Stephen. When Stubbs returned, he confirmed that Mrs. Carruthers was indeed expecting her son, but that he had yet to arrive, and William let out a sigh of relief that everything was going according to plan.

It was important that Stephen receive the letter before he could be allowed to leave his mother's house. In it, William had promised to explain himself and begged Stephen not to meet with Graves again until they had had a chance to speak. William did not know what the earl had told his son, and he did not trust Graves not to do something mad or stupid when he realized that Stephen was finally free of him.

William also wrote that, though he longed to see him as soon as possible, Stephen should stay at home with his mother that night, for the good woman had something she needed to speak to him about. William knew Mrs. Carruthers would not thank him for his interference, but he needed Stephen to know that his responsibilities and burdens were not as great as he might have thought *before* they had their talk. He would need all the help he could get, and he was willing to bear the brunt of Mrs. Carruthers's displeasure to get it. Now all William could do was wait for dark and hope Stephen would do as he asked.

The waiting was interminable, and William had tied himself in knots by the time the sun finally set. Stubbs and Pip had taken turns trying to keep him calm while they saw to the rest of the preparations, but it was a losing battle, and they soon gave up. Luckily for all of them, darkness fell early this time of year, and William had devised a plan to distract himself for at least a few hours that night. They were going to go have some fun.

As soon as full dark was upon them, four men dressed all in black mounted their horses and rode away from the little cottage toward the Carruthers's farm. They rode in silence but for the jingling of their bridles and the soft clump of their horses' hooves. The newest member of their party led the way, as he was the most familiar with the country, and William and his servants followed close behind. When they saw the lights from the grand farmhouse ahead, they pulled their mounts off the road and tied them in a small copse, traveling the rest of the distance on foot. In the shadow of the barn, they waited in silence until the sound of hooves could be heard on the drive leading up to the house.

William smiled as he saw a single rider dismount his horse and lead it off the road a short distance from the house before reappearing and creeping up to peek in the windows. As William had predicted, Graves's face was illuminated in the lamplight from inside the house. William had hoped the man would do something foolish like this and had planned accordingly. If Graves had not shown that night, William would have had his companions watch the house in shifts while he rode to the earl's house in search of him. He had had too many dealings with the blackguard to think Graves would simply walk away. William did not really care what the man had planned; he would not allow Graves anywhere near Stephen ever again.

As a group, they crept up on Graves and arranged themselves in a half-circle around him in the dark. They were so quiet that the idiot did not even know they were there until William spoke.

"I do not know what you intend, but I suggest you reconsider, Graves."

The man let out a startled yelp and swung around. "Who is there? Who are you?"

"You know who I am, and you know why I am here."

"Carey? How dare you!? You have no right to be here." Graves attempted to sound indignant, but the quaver in his voice revealed his fear.

"I have more of a right than you. Your father and I have an agreement, and I am here to make sure you keep to the terms. I will not leave until I am assured you will cause no more trouble for this family."

"And what will you do if I refuse?" Graves was showing a little backbone now, standing straighter and glaring about him.

William laughed. "I will not have to do anything. I believe your father will oblige me by taking care of your punishment."

"My father will not side against me, Carey. You made a fool's bargain. Stephen, this house, they are both mine. I will not lose him to some dirty...."

Graves's bluster was cut short by the feel of cold steel against his throat as William drew his sword and placed the tip under his chin. He could not allow Graves to continue with his speech, as the fourth member of their party was not fully aware of the nature of his relationship with Stephen.

"You cannot lose what you never had, Graves. Even a fool like you must know that. If the threat of your father's displeasure and your own dishonor are not enough to keep you from causing any more harm to this family, then there are more permanent means by which I can assure their safety and happiness."

"You would not dare!" William could see the whites of his eyes now, but the man still clung to his bravado.

"Again, I would not have to. Since the end of the war, the countryside is rife with highwaymen and cutthroats, men driven to desperation by lack of employment and poverty. Should you meet with an unfortunate accident, I assure you I will be warm and comfortable at a dinner party or some other engagement with plenty of witnesses when it occurs. The good farmers of this valley know what you did to this poor family. I would not have to search far for men to volunteer for the job." William grinned as he watched the man's face pale and his eyes dart around him to the shadowed shapes of his companions.

"Go. Take your reprieve and go back to London, take a tour of the continent, or go to the Americas, I care not, but do not show your face in the valley again. I will not give a second warning." William's voice was dripping with menace by the time he had finished, and none of it was feigned. He would love to see this blight wiped from the face of the earth, but he would not do it himself for fear that the backlash might touch Stephen in some way.

William stepped away from Graves and lowered his sword enough for the man to squeeze past him and run for his horse. As the man passed him, William thought he detected the faint smell of urine in the air, but it was too dark to verify his suspicions. The man took to the road at a gallop, and William and his men were forced to duck out of the way when Stephen appeared at the window to investigate the noise. As they quickly made their way back to the barn, William heard the front door to the house open and turned to find Stephen standing on the front steps. The lamp in his hands illuminated his handsome face and reflected off his hair, and William felt his heart clench in his chest.

Stubbs had to grab his arm to make him turn away, for William could not bring himself to do it alone. His man all but dragged him back to the horses and pushed him up into the saddle. It hurt to have to wait even one more minute, let alone the entire night, to be able to see and to touch his lover again. The only reason he could bring himself to

211

leave was that he knew his first meeting with Stephen would not be a pleasant one, and they would need plenty of privacy for his hedgehog to vent his displeasure before William could even begin the process of explaining himself.

By the time they reached the cottage, William was much calmer, and he was able to show proper gratitude to his servants and their newest co-conspirator, Mr. Myers. When they had all dismounted, the man came over to William, grinning from ear to ear. "Thank ye, sir."

"Thank *you*, Myers. You are a good and honorable man. I meant what I said to you and to Graves. I intend to see the Carruthers family out of their troubles and the farm back as it was. Young Master Carruthers will need men like you to make that happen. If you like, I will tell him to seek you out when we speak next."

"Aye, sir, thank ye, sir." The man ducked his head and went to collect his horse. As he mounted, he turned concerned eyes to William. "We frate his lairdship proper? Won't coom back? Still water runs deep wit' that'un."

William smiled to reassure the man. "I believe we frightened the man enough for now. Graves may be a sly villain, but he knows I meant what I said, and he knows I am not alone. All we can do is keep our eyes and our ears open and look out for the young master. All will be well, Myers. You shall see. There are happy tidings coming soon, and when all is revealed, we will all have much to celebrate, I assure you."

The man smiled happily and rode off while William tried his best to believe his own assurances. As he walked into the cottage and sat down by the fireplace, his anxiety over his next encounter with Stephen mounted. Doubts warred with hope and anticipation within him, and he knew he would not get a wink of sleep that night.

He had planned and planned for the moment when they would be reunited, but would it be enough? They had had so little time together. William knew his own heart, but could Stephen feel the same? He had reviewed every objection and argument Stephen had made until he had an answer for every one, but all of it would mean nothing if Stephen could not love him. It was the one part of his plan that he could not control, and it was the part that could cause all the rest to crumble to pieces.

William could not sit still. He paced in his parlor and fretted for what seemed like hours. Stubbs and Pip took turns checking on him, offering him food and drink and company, but he sent them away again every time. He could not bear the thought of food or polite conversation while he was in such a state. In fact, the next time Stubbs knocked and poked his head around the door, William nearly bit it off before the man's twinkling eyes and happy grin brought him up short.

"Some'un t' see ye, sir."

William stood staring, unable to believe his eyes as Stubbs stepped to the side to reveal Stephen. William could only stand and stare as Stephen stepped into the room and Stubbs closed the door behind him. After nodding to Stubbs, Stephen turned back to him, and they simply stared at one another for several moments.

"I did not expect you until tomorrow," William finally managed to say after swallowing past the sudden dryness in his throat.

"Those were the instructions in your letter, I know, but I decided the gravity of the situation warranted earlier attention. My mother gave me her news at dinner, and I had no intentions of seeing Graves again until the man forced me to, so there was no reason to delay."

William could not read Stephen's expression, and his stomach twisted a little. He had counted on Stephen's expressive face and passionate nature to tell him how best to proceed. He hated when Stephen's face closed off, for it gave him nothing to work with.

William took a deep breath and prepared to launch into the speech he had been practicing and refining for weeks.

*No time like the present.*

"Stephen—" was all he managed to say before the younger man took two strides across the room, grabbed his face roughly, and smashed their lips together in a desperate kiss. Stephen held William in place while he plundered his mouth as if he were starving and William were a feast set for a king.

William tasted blood, but he did not care. Stephen's warm body was pressed hard against his, and their mouths were melded together as if they would never be separated again. Their tongues battled and their panting breaths mingled as the kiss went on and on, and William's body positively hummed with joy. He had almost forgotten how delicious and soft his lover's lips were. While William relearned every inch of Stephen's lips, the young man panted out desperate confessions in between kisses.

"God, I missed you... so much.... It has been so awful without you.... I cannot say.... I did not realize... and then I left and... I could not bear it...."

William said nothing, he simply kissed and licked and sucked with all the emotion and need he had stored up over the past few weeks. This was not at all what he had expected from their first meeting, but he was overjoyed that he had been wrong.

After several more kisses, Stephen pulled away from him and gazed deeply into his eyes. "I do want to know all that has happened and how you came to be here—how you knew about my mother, everything, but not tonight. I do not care about any of it right now. Just take me to bed. I have missed you so. I need you. I need to lie with you, to feel you inside me. Please?"

William grinned and grabbed Stephen's hand and a lamp, then headed for the stairs at a near-run. He pulled them into his bedchamber and they began tearing at each other's clothes almost before he could manage to close the door. It was desperate and comical, but they managed to disrobe one another in seconds, and soon they were falling into bed, heedless of the icy bed linens.

They rolled about until Stephen lay beneath him with his legs spread to cradle William between his thighs, and they pulled each other close again and devoured each other's mouths. Stephen's hands were everywhere at once, clutching, squeezing, and stroking William until he had to pull away for a moment to catch his breath and master himself. When he spotted Stephen's dusky cock, stiff and leaking between their bodies, William could not resist diving down and taking the beautiful flesh into his mouth. Stephen moaned and arched beneath him but was soon tugging desperately at his arms and panting, "Stop. Please stop."

At William's reluctant withdrawal, his hedgehog smiled and chuckled. "Please. I will not last long. It has been too long. I want you inside me first."

William grinned and lunged for the drawer of his bedside table. He had stashed oil there in a moment of wishful thinking, and now he was very glad that he had. He quickly slicked his fingers and slid them back to Stephen's opening as he reclaimed Stephen's mouth for more passionate kissing. When his fingers penetrated the outer ring, Stephen moaned into his mouth and rocked his hips, and William felt an answering surge in his cock and let out a groan of his own. It had been too long for him as well.

Weeks of unaccustomed celibacy made the likelihood that William would embarrass himself quite high. He gritted his teeth against the throbbing in his cock and began moving his fingers again, stretching and preparing his lover. Stephen was impatient, however, and William suddenly found himself on his back with Stephen straddling his hips. His lover did not give William even a moment to accustom himself to his new position before he grabbed William's prick, placed it at his opening, and slowly lowered himself onto it. William swore and gritted his teeth, gripping Stephen's hips hard to keep his lover still for a moment.

"God! You will be the death of me," William panted.

Stephen laughed, which sent all sorts of interesting sensations through William's cock, and he could not hold back any more. He lunged forward and forced Stephen back onto the mattress, his lover's head hanging off the foot of the bed, then dug his toes into the linens and thrust hard into his lover's body.

Stephen wrapped his legs around William's waist, lifted his hips into every thrust, and soon they were both lost to the world. Thankfully, Stephen began stroking his own cock as soon as William pushed back into him, for William did not think he was capable of anything other than losing himself in his lover's body at that moment.

William spent first. He could not help it. All the loneliness, the tension, and the worry from the past several days and weeks blended with the joy at having Stephen warm and willing in his arms again and erupted from his body in an almost painful release. The moment was sublime and cathartic and utterly draining, to the point that William barely even felt Stephen's climax before he collapsed to the bed in exhausted slumber.

He woke sometime in the night to the feel of Stephen's warm body cuddled against his back and his rough hands smoothing over the planes of his chest. Somehow his lover had gotten them both moved to the head of the bed and beneath the counterpane without William waking. He must have been more tired than he thought, and he hoped he had not made too poor a showing.

When Stephen's rough palms grazed William's nipples, he hummed in sleepy pleasure, and his lover chuckled and bit the back of his neck. In that moment, William was so happy and warm and content, Stephen could have done anything to him and he would not have objected. His lover must have read his thoughts, for it was not long at all before the younger man's hands strayed between William's legs, one hand firmly gripping his cock while the other slid around and explored the valley of his arse. Stephen kissed his way down William's back while his hands did wonderful things between his legs, until William was spreading himself wide and begging for more.

"Oil." The command came from over his shoulder, and it took a moment for William to get enough blood to his brain to understand.

When he did, he moaned in anticipation and fumbled for the vial of oil he had discarded earlier. Stephen took it from his shaking hands, and soon he felt oiled fingers playing about his opening. He gasped a little as one thick finger pushed inside, but he forced himself to relax and enjoy. It had been a very long time since William had allowed anyone to play ram to his ewe, but he was more than ready for Stephen to change that.

His lover worked his thick fingers inside William's body for so long William was beginning to wonder if his hedgehog had lost his nerve. The fingers felt wonderful, but William wanted more. When

216

Stephen's ragged breaths could be heard over his own, William decided to help matters along. He grabbed his upper leg under the knee, drew it as far up his chest as he could, and looked over his shoulder, smiling at Stephen in invitation. Stephen's passion-dark eyes met his in the lamplight, and the younger man smiled nervously at him.

"You cannot hurt or disappoint me, my sweet. Please. I need you inside of me."

Using his lover's own words had the desired effect, as Stephen swallowed and climbed back up to kiss William while he placed the head of his prick at William's throbbing opening. At the first pressure and stretch, William groaned and reached back to grab Stephen's hip in encouragement. The younger man hissed in pleasure and continued to push forward after only a moment's hesitation. They worked in concert until Stephen was fully seated inside his body. Then his young lover simply wrapped his arms around William's chest and held him for several long moments. William felt so full and cherished in that moment, he hated for it to end, but his cock was aching for release, and he needed Stephen to move. William was the first to break the tableau, flexing his hips until Stephen took over. His young lover drew back and thrust into him slowly, moaning and trembling with the intensity of their connection.

William could tell Stephen tried to hold back, to make it good for him, but it was not long before he heard the younger man swear under his breath, and he soon began thrusting faster and harder. William grabbed his own cock and stroked frantically to follow his lover into heaven. Pleasure spiraled within him until he was overwhelmed with sensation, and the hot burst of Stephen's release inside him pushed him over the edge. He filled his hand with his own release as his vision went white, and Stephen collapsed to the bed behind him, resting his forehead against William's shoulder and panting. Afterward, they lay murmuring tender nonsense to one another until they fell asleep again.

In the morning, William woke with a start, frantically searching the room for Stephen. William found him curled on his side only a few inches away and breathed a sigh of relief. For a moment, William was afraid he would find that it had all been a dream or that Stephen had left without a word. When his young lover rolled toward him and greeted him with a sleepy smile, all the remaining tension left his body, and William smiled happily back, reaching out and drawing Stephen into the circle of his arms. He kissed Stephen on the forehead and simply held him close for a long time until the younger man broke the silence.

"Will you tell me how it is that you are here?"

"I followed the trail of breadcrumbs you left and prayed for luck to smile on me."

"You prayed?" Stephen's chuckle rumbled through William's chest, and he could not help but echo it.

"I did not say to whom I prayed. I know you asked me not to, but I could not allow you to disappear from my life. I would have prayed to the devil himself if it meant I could have you."

"Do not say such things. It is bad luck."

"I have you in my arms again. Luck is smiling on me."

"How did you know about my mother? Does she know who you are?" Stephen had propped his chin on the hand that rested on William's chest and was now staring intently at him.

William realized the time had come for explanations. Stephen did not appear angry, so that was a definite improvement over what he had feared. Perhaps this would be easier than he had thought.

After a deep breath, William launched into his tale of the last few weeks, from the day Stephen left him to the present. He left out a few details about how and where he had gained the information he had, and he downplayed his conversation with the earl, but Stephen's eyes still became wider and wider with each word, and William started to become nervous again. William ended his speech with as many assurances as he could think of that he would not interfere in Stephen's life any further unless asked, and then fell silent, waiting for his hedgehog's reaction.

He watched carefully as emotions played across Stephen's face one by one. There was anger and disapproval, fear and relief, hope and concern, but none seemed to hold court over the others, for which

218

William was grateful. When Stephen finally did speak, William's anxieties were eased, and he felt the first stirrings of hope.

"You have done all of this for me?"

"Yes."

"Why?" Stephen looked truly confused, and William realized he had not told his lover the most important part of his story.

"Because I love you."

Stephen's eyes turned liquid then as he searched William's face. "You love me?"

"Yes."

Stephen shook his head and closed his eyes for a moment. He let out a shaky breath and opened them again to stare at William, and he bit his lip. "I am free from Graves? You own my debts?" his young lover asked, as if he could not quite believe any of what he was hearing

William smiled cautiously. "Yes."

"You want to help me rebuild the farm? To live here in the valley?"

"Yes. I told you in London that I would go with you if you would only ask. You must know by now you may have nearly anything you want from me."

"Nearly?" Stephen's lush mouth quirked at the corners and he lifted one eyebrow, but William could not find it in himself to laugh just then.

"*Nearly*. If you ask me to leave, I do not believe that I will be able to honor that request," William admitted soberly, allowing his vulnerability and hope show.

Stephen also sobered and stared at him for a time, searching his face. "I would not ask that of you, Will. I... I missed you terribly from the moment I drove away from you. I did not realize I could feel so strongly after so short a time, and I did not think I had a choice. I did not think I could trust in your affection. Now, here you are, offering me freedom from the burdens and the fears that have weighed upon me for so long… offering me your love, and I hardly know what to do with myself."

William did smile then and pulled Stephen tight against his chest. "Live the life you told me you wanted. All I want is to be allowed to be a part of it. There are still people in this valley who would like to see the Carruthers farm restored to its former glory, and I will help you wherever and however I can, if you will only let me."

"I do not want you to support me, Will. I *will* repay my father's debts. Just because you hold them now instead of the earl does not mean I will not see them repaid." Stephen's brow had drawn down and his tone had hardened, telling William it would be pointless to argue, at least not *now*, so he simply smiled and nodded.

Stephen did not look as if he believed him, but he did not argue the point further. Instead, he sighed and relaxed against William's body. "I…. This has all happened so fast. One moment I am in misery, and the next I am home and the world is laid at my feet. I am afraid I will wake at any moment and it will have been a dream."

Stephen's words echoed his own thoughts from only a short time ago, and William could not help but pull the young man closer. His hedgehog needed time. William could understand that. He would do his best to give it, and hope it got him what he wanted in return.

"Do you know how my father died?" Stephen's whispered question cut into his reverie.

"Yes," William replied cautiously.

"Does my mother know?"

"I do not know. We have only spoken a few times. Our intimacy is not such that she would confide in me."

"Yet she told you that she was to be married?"

"I met her in the market with her betrothed, and she was concerned that I would mention it to you in correspondence before she could talk to you herself."

"Oh. Graves is the one who told me of my father's death. He swore that no one else knew, but I never quite believed him. Even in

220

*Chapter* $Sixteen$

ON THE third day after his meeting with the earl, the packet from the solicitor arrived, and William was relieved to find that all the notes were there. William was now the holder of all of Stephen's debts, and his love no longer owed Graves a single penny. At least the earl was a more honorable man than his son.

As he sat in the parlor of his newly rented cottage on the western edge of Penrith, William seriously considered tossing the lot into the fire, but soon thought better of it. He did not trust the earl *or* his son, and he might need proof someday that the debts had been discharged. It would be better for Stephen if William kept the documents, even though he never intended to collect on the debts.

William set the packet aside, leaned back in his chair, and stared out the window into the small garden behind the cottage. The shrubs and flowers were all brown and withered now, but he wasn't really looking at them anyway. His mind was far away, wondering where Stephen could be, and if he was well. The more time that passed, the more concerned he became that Graves had done something to his fiery young lover, but until William knew where they were, there was nothing he could do about it. All he could do was wait and hope, two activities that did little to calm his spirit.

William growled in frustration and stood to pace the room. He had used the excuse of getting situated in his new home to turn down several invitations, but now he was beginning to regret that decision.

the beginning, when he was gentle and kind to me, I never quite trusted him. I was lost and grieving when he first came to me, and I ignored the things about him that I did not like. I thought relations between two men *had* to be that way. When we went to London, he changed—or perhaps he did not change, he simply showed his true colors, and the few things I did admire about him disappeared. But by then, I was so indebted to him and his father that I could not break free. I could not risk him telling my mother or my sister of our father's shame, or *my* shame. We would have been penniless and homeless, and I might have lost the only two people whom I truly loved."

Stephen seemed to feel the need to explain, so William held him close and listened to him until his lover seemed to run out of words. When Stephen fell silent, William wished he could see his lover's face, to know what he was thinking. William was still not quite ready to trust his luck. Did Stephen fear William would betray him as Graves had? Things had gone unbelievably well so far, and he feared that Stephen would change his mind any moment now and refuse to see him again. William was already planning an alternate strategy in case of such an event when Stephen finally broke the silence.

His lover raised his head, looked deeply into William's eyes, and said, "I did not believe you when you told me I could trust you. I did not believe that respect *and* tenderness could coexist between two men as lovers. I did not believe I could feel self-respect as the partner of another man, particularly a man as strong and intelligent as you... but you changed that for me."

Stephen took a deep breath and gave William a watery smile. "I still do not believe that two men can live happily and safely together as lovers in England, but I *am* willing to believe that if anyone on this earth can accomplish it, it would be you. I love you, Will. I trust you. If you tell me you truly believe you can do it, then I will trust that you are right and do everything in my power to see it done."

William could not contain his happiness. He let out a whoop of joy and tackled Stephen onto his back, kissing his lover senseless.

When they finally broke for air, he said, "You will not be sorry. I will keep you safe and happy the rest of our days. You have my word."

# *Epilogue*

*Eden Valley, October 30, 1821*

WILLIAM sat astride Asmodeus and looked down with pride on the valley that was now his home. The hills around him, which had been empty only a year before, were now dotted with sheep, and though there were not as many as there had been in the years gone by, it would only be a few more years before they reached those numbers again, and beyond.

As he felt the cool wind kiss his cheeks and whip his stallion's mane across the backs of his gloved hands, William could not contain his happy grin. Today was an anniversary, after all, and he was looking forward to celebrating it, whether his little hedgehog wanted to or not.

William scanned the fells until he found what he was looking for: the distant shapes of two men, surrounded by dogs and sheep, and he urged Asmodeus toward them. His love was down there, talking with Myers as always, but William had another plan for the afternoon, and he had every intention of getting his way. This was *their* anniversary. A year ago today, he had raced Robert Graves for the right to claim Stephen, and he had won.

When William woke that morning, Stephen had already dressed and headed out for the day. His love had no intentions of celebrating such a "scandalous and embarrassing" anniversary and had told him so quite firmly the night before, but William would not be put off. He rejoiced in the day, for it was the best wager he had ever made, and he fully intended to celebrate it every year for the rest of his life.

William knew he would be able to find Stephen with little effort, so he had let his lover leave as always and had taken his time bathing and dressing for the day. Since taking over the farm, Stephen had spent nearly every day, from dawn until dusk, out with the men, caring for the sheep or seeing to the planting and harvesting of the silage. Stephen's father had always run the farm from a remove, rarely dirtying his hands, but Stephen loved to be out with his stock and had great plans for the future of his farm. This year he was even trying to grow turnips to supplement his flock's diet. Why? William had not the faintest idea, but it was not his job to know, so he left Stephen to it.

*William's* job was to make sure they remained safe and happy on their little farm, and he had to admit he was proud of his success so far. He had moved into the farmhouse not long after Stephen's mother had married and moved in with the doctor. As Stephen's benefactor and business partner, it was perfectly natural for him to share the farmhouse with him. The house was large and could certainly hold two intimate friends who worked with one another, after all.

Every week, William played the grieving widower and doting benefactor in town. He made calls and attended dinner parties and assemblies. He charmed the old ladies and went shooting with the men. He donated to worthy causes and supported the local vicar in any new project the man came up with. A well-fed vicar was a happy vicar, and more likely to turn a blind eye to any gossip he might hear, so William was happy to oblige him.

They would have to address Stephen's marital situation at some point. William had the excuse of grief and a grand passion for his first wife, but Stephen was a young bachelor, and William knew there were many mothers in the valley who had their sights set on him. William was fairly certain he could put them off for a few years at least. Stephen needed to put the farm back to rights and pay off his debts before he could even think about marrying, and by the time that excuse wore thin, William hoped he would have thought of a solution.

Stephen's successes with the farm helped them as well. The more successful the farm became, the more jobs they could provide for the community and the happier that community was to have them. In fact, they had quite a little family growing in and around the farm, and it only promised to get bigger.

William looked back toward the farmhouse, and he could see little shapes moving about the garden in the sunshine and larger shapes chasing them as they hung clothing on the lines. Maud and Stubbs had only agreed to move to the valley if William would allow her to bring some of her orphans and the two new mothers she was looking after. As William would have agreed to anything to ensure that the good woman came to take care of him and his lover, their home was now filled with the patter of little feet. Maud was even looking to find a school for the little things, and would soon have them on their way to better lives than the ones they had left behind—whether they liked it or not. While William had never been overly fond of children, Maud kept them well-behaved, and the young mothers, in turn, kept their masters' secrets, so he considered it a fair trade.

Pip had come and gone twice in that year, returning to the farm whenever he lost his most recent position or when he was hiding from a jilted lover or angry husband or father. The lad could never seem to keep still, and Maud despaired of him ever settling down, but the woman always kept a bed ready for him, and William was certain Pip would settle eventually. It had taken William many years and the love of a good woman to tame *him* when *he* was that age, so he could not fault Pip for his wild ways.

And it had taken William another six years and the love of a good *man* to gain him the happiness and the home he now possessed.

On that note, William grinned and rode the rest of the distance to join his love. As William neared the two men, sunlight glinted off of Stephen's hair and the wind blew his coat back to give a glimpse of his love's high, round arse, and William felt his trousers tighten a little in anticipation. His lover would be taking the day off whether he liked it or not.

"Good afternoon, gentlemen. How goes the farming?"

Stephen only shook his head and gave William an aggrieved smile. "All is well, Carey, thank you for asking."

"Excellent. Myers, I wonder if you would mind giving me a moment with the good master here."

"Aye, sir. Good day, masters," the man said with a nod of his head as he whistled for his dogs and headed away from them. The man had settled back onto the farm as if he had never left, and if he suspected anything about William's relationship with Stephen, he never let on.

William dismounted and tied Asmodeus to a fencepost not far from Gabriel, the gelding he had bought for Stephen as a half-anniversary present, and led the way into the small shed nearby.

"William, what on earth—" Stephen began, but William silenced him with a kiss and another and another.

When William's kisses moved to Stephen's jaw, the man panted, "We cannot do this here! What are you thinking? Myers is only a few feet away."

"Relax, my love. We are in the shed, and Myers cannot see a damned thing." William slid his hands down to cup Stephen's arse and press their cocks together through the soft wool of their trousers. "Come along now, my sweet. You know you want to come back to the house and spend the day with me," William whispered hotly into Stephen's ear before nibbling and sucking on his earlobe and grinding their bodies together again.

The only response he received was a moan, so William doubled his efforts until his young lover was panting in his ear and melting in his arms. William pulled back then and grinned into his lover's glazed eyes, sparking an embarrassed flush and grin in response.

"You are a devil, William Carey," Stephen said even as he licked his lips and dropped his eyes to the bulge in William's trousers.

William swooped in for another deep kiss, licking and sucking at those wonderfully plush lips. "Mm-hmm," he agreed. Turning his attentions to Stephen's ear again, he whispered, "But I am *your* devil."

William stepped back suddenly, and Stephen stumbled at his sudden withdrawal. William smirked and headed for the door at a jog. "I will race you home," he called out as he untied Asmodeus and mounted.

Stephen chased after him and quickly mounted Gabriel as William turned Asmodeus around and urged him into a gallop.

"What is my prize if I win?" Stephen called after him.

"You will have to win to find out!"

They both raced off toward the farmhouse, their horses' hooves thundering through the damp earth and their laughter echoing through the hills.

ROWAN MCALLISTER quit her day job in 2007 and moved to her dream home in the woods of Virginia to follow her muses and explore her creative side full time. She's a firm believer in practical romanticism, requires a strong cup of coffee every morning to be even remotely human, and has a healthy obsession with romance and fantasy fiction, small (and not so small) furry creatures, and anything to do with working with her hands. She can be found most days either hunched over her sewing machine or hunched over her laptop. Though she has spent a lifetime making up stories in her head when whatever task she was occupied with failed to keep her full attention, she only recently discovered the challenge and reward to be found in committing those stories to paper. Now that she has, there's no going back.

Contact Rowan at rowanmcallister10@gmail.com.

Also from ROWAN MCALLISTER

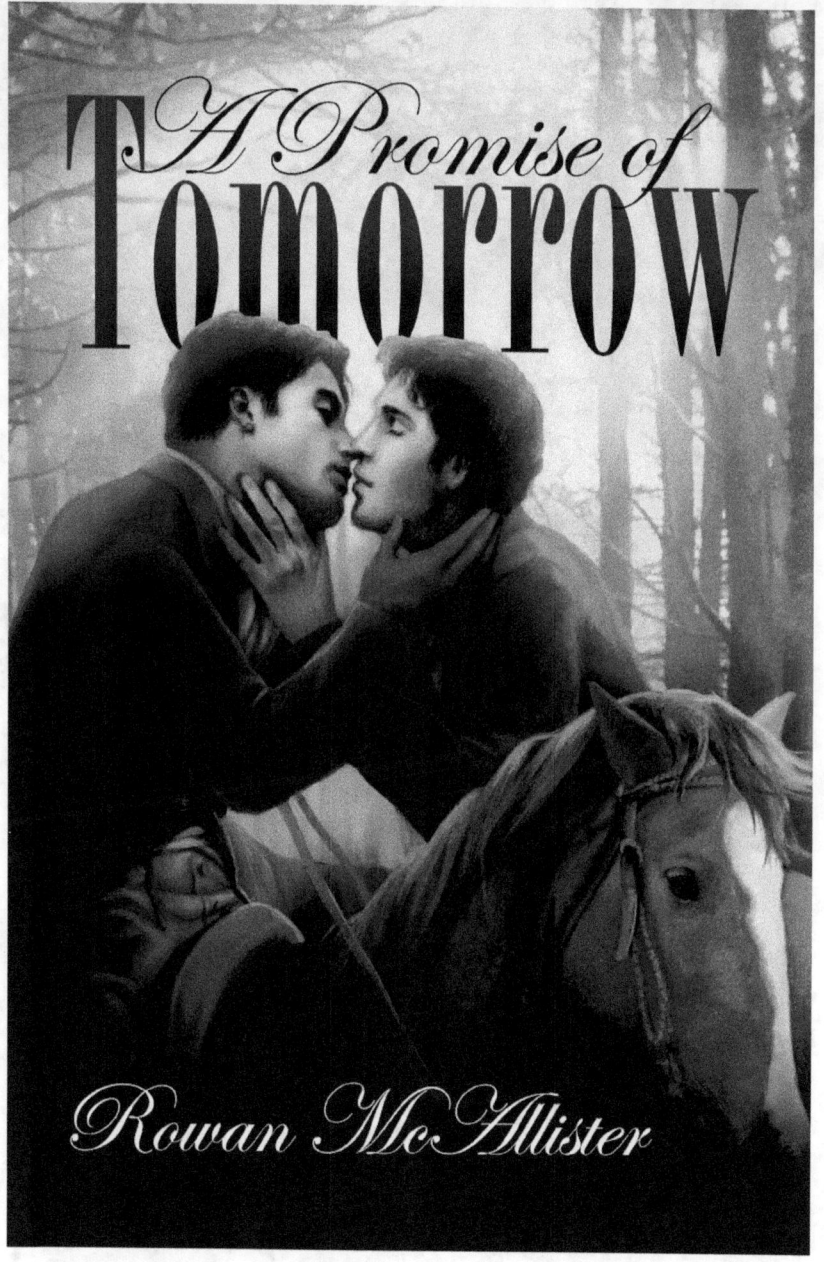

# Historical Romance from DREAMSPINNER PRESS